HOW THE OTHER HALF
DIE

HOW THE OTHER HALF DIE

P. C. ROSCOE

HODDER CHILDREN'S BOOKS

First published in Great Britain in 2025 by Hodder & Stoughton

1 3 5 7 9 10 8 6 4 2

Text copyright © Pippa Roscoe, 2025

The moral right of the author has been asserted.

*All characters and events in this publication, other than those clearly
in the public domain, are fictitious and any resemblance to
real persons, living or dead, is purely coincidental.*

All rights reserved.
No part of this publication may be reproduced, stored in
a retrieval system, or transmitted, in any form or by any means, without
the prior permission in writing of the publisher, nor be otherwise circulated
in any form of binding or cover other than that in which it is published
and without a similar condition including this condition being
imposed on the subsequent purchaser.

A CIP catalogue record for this book
is available from the British Library.

ISBN 978 1 444 90810 7

Typeset by Jouve (UK), Milton Keynes
Printed and bound in Great Britain by Clays Ltd, Elcograf S.p.A.

The paper and board used in this book
are made from wood from responsible sources.

Hodder Children's Books
An imprint of
Hachette Children's Group
Part of Hodder & Stoughton Limited
Carmelite House
50 Victoria Embankment
London EC4Y 0DZ

The authorised representative in the EEA is Hachette Ireland,
8 Castlecourt Centre, Dublin 15,
D15 XTP3, Ireland (email: info@hbgi.ie)

An Hachette UK Company
www.hachette.co.uk

www.hachettechildrens.co.uk

I'd say it takes a village to write a book, but actually all it takes is two really good editors, three excellent friends and a very understanding family. So a huge thank you to Anne Marie Ryan, Katie Lawrence, Stella Giatrakou, Julie Chivers, Laurie Johnson and the Roscoe/Bloom/Liu clan, whom I love enormously.

Content warning:
Strong language, violence, sexual assault,
alcohol addiction, suicide references.

Mokani Island Guestlist

Avery Finch
Annalise Finch
Jonathan Finch
Nora Miller

Sydney Devereux
Archie Devereux
Dennis Devereux
Carol Devereux

Hugo Vandenburg
Mark Vandenburg
Darian Vandenburg

Leo Walker
Mitchel Walker

PROLOGUE

From where I stand, the moon hangs so low it's in my direct eyeline. It's bold in a sky spattered with stars. The shadows in its face are so clear. Makes me wonder what it thinks of us, down here, playing the games we play.

The breeze on my face coming in from the sea is almost warm, despite the late hour. Salt, and something sweet – frangipani maybe. I inhale, deep, to fill my lungs with it and remember why they call this island paradise.

A groan behind me cuts through the moment and I ignore it, distracted by a burst of colour that shoots into the sky and explodes shards of candy-pink light.

Ohhhs *and* ahhhs *come in from the main beach further down, brought here on the wind. The gentle clink of glasses, the titter of indistinguishable conversation and laughter, and I can just imagine them all there down by the water, dressed in gold and white – the theme of the evening. Drinking champagne, gorging on caviar and gold leaf. Wearing their secrets and lies like diamonds and pearls, hidden in plain sight for the world not to see.*

There's a cough from behind me and a gurgled, 'Please.'

I turn back from the open window to see a pair of cloudy eyes staring up at the ceiling. One hand reaches up to press against the back of their head, hair matted and thick with blood. Red fingertips come away glistening in the dark room, illuminated only by another firework soaring into the night sky, visible through the huge open floor-to-ceiling windows.

A trail of red slips down their forearm.

They're shivering. Or dying.

Whatever.

'I think I need . . .' Their voice, groggy and broken, much like the rest of them, trails off.

'What?' I demand, rousing them one last time.

'Help.' The whispered word cracks through the silence, louder than any firework.

'I'm afraid it's a bit late for that,' I tell them with absolutely no sympathy.

This is all their fault, after all.

Breath is a rasp in their throat and I turn back to the view, bored now.

'Stop moving around so much,' I tell them as I look out at the rippling sea. 'You're getting blood all over the carpet.'

'Sorry.' The groggy response almost makes me laugh.

The waves roll back and forth over a crescent shore framed with palm trees so perfect, it could be a painting. The moon spreads silver on all it touches, until there is an explosion of gold in the sky. White dances into the spaces of the night, in between the gold shards that scatter like a dandelion. And suddenly the sky is filled with them; a thousand dandelions exploding with booms so loud, I can feel them pulse in my chest. It's unstoppable, relentless. Until it's not.

In the sudden silence, after my ears stop ringing, I realise that there are no more breaths to take. It's done.

I turn back and stare down at the piece of meat on the carpet. I bend to undo the now meaningless friendship bracelet around their wrist, struggling with the knot. It's twisted with another one but I'm able to pull it off.

I fist the friendship bracelet in my hand and I begin to lift the body up. My exertion is the only sound in the room until the villa's door swings open and a jagged question cuts through the silence.

'What did you do?'

CHAPTER ONE

AVERY

Avery thrust her hand out to grab the rail of the speedboat, bracing against the violent waves crashing against them.

'*Ohmygodohmygod!*' Nora cried in delight beside her, hands clutched to her chest, as if she wasn't the one with a fear of water, just as another powerful jolt rocked Avery on her feet.

'How can you be fine on a boat and still be afraid of the water?' Avery grumbled, feeling groggy from the flight to Nassau. Nothing *at all* to do with the number of drinks she and Nora had shared on the private jet.

'I don't make the rules, Aves. I just break them,' Nora grinned.

Sun prickled the haze of sea spray as the boat shot forward and Avery adjusted her sunglasses, hoping to dull the slight ache at the base of her skull.

Nora held her straw hat down against the wind as she collapsed into the seating on the speedboat, her legs folding beneath her. She held out a hand and pumped it open and closed, demanding Avery join her.

Unable to help herself, Avery smiled and went to sit beside the girl who had been a stranger only eleven months ago.

Nora turned the power of her full attention on her and Avery felt it like a beacon. She placed her hands either side of Avery's face, the slash of silver rings, cool little lines against her heated cheeks.

'This is going to be the *best* summer,' Nora invoked like a spell. 'It's going to be everything you need and more.'

After all Avery had been through in the last year – breaking up with her boyfriend, nearly failing her first year, her *exams* – Nora had been there for her, without judgement. And her support had meant everything. Especially when it had filled the deafening silence left by everyone else significant in her life.

Avery looked over to where her parents sat at the back of the boat, pretending like they weren't ignoring each other, until Nora tugged repeatedly on Avery's hand, making them both laugh, until Avery collapsed against her.

'OK, once more, just so I have this absolutely right,' Nora said, adjusting the hat, a strand of long bleach-blonde hair getting caught in her soft-pink lip gloss.

Avery didn't know why Nora had got it into her head that she needed to know everything about everyone. Avery had spent the entire year talking about her friends and the island, which was partly why she'd felt that she couldn't *not* invite Nora this summer.

'So, Sydney and Archie Devereux are twins,' Nora began. 'But not identical, right?'

'Not identical,' Avery confirmed. 'Basically opposites. Archie's, like totally laid back, and Syd? Well, she's . . .'

She's what? Sydney Devereux had been her best friend for the last ten years, even though they only saw each other several times through the year. Living in different states, it had been tricky, but they'd made it work.

Until last year, when, for absolutely no reason Avery could think of, Sydney had ghosted her.

She'd known Syd hadn't been happy when Avery had got together with Hugo the year before. Sydney had never liked to share. But Avery and Hugo had broken up months ago. And *still* nothing.

'Rich, popular, intelligent and a badass,' Nora ticked off the fingers of her upheld hand.

Avery side-eyed her.

'What? I checked her out on Insta,' Nora explained with a shrug.

'OK,' Avery said with a laugh. 'But yeah. Accurate.'

Nora's head dropped, the wind whipping her long blonde hair into a frenzy. Her pale skin was already flushed pink, despite her hat, and her arms glistening with the factor fifty she'd complained about wearing. 'She's gonna *hate* me,' Nora groaned.

'She's going to *love* you!' Avery cried, laughing when Nora shewed her away with her hand. It was Syd's feelings about *her* she wasn't sure about.

'I know her father, of course,' Nora said, her head coming back up.

'*Everyone* knows Dennis Devereux,' Avery replied.

'Tech tycoon extraordinaire, billionaire several times over and household name,' she reeled off. 'Husband to Carol

Devereux, queen of the charity circuit and setter of all New Hampshire trends.'

'Yep, yep and yep,' Avery confirmed. She had always found Carol intimidating, instinctively shying away from a coldness about the woman. But thankfully she'd drawn neither Carol's interest or disdain.

'Next!' Avery commanded, playing along with the game.

'Hugo Vandenburg,' Nora said, unable to keep the scowl out of her voice.

They had met once when Hugo had come to visit her at college and it had been . . .

Nora snarled.

Disastrous.

'Adopted son of Mark and Darian Vandenburg, the gazillionaire owners of the Caribbean island we are about to spend twelve a-maz-ing days on,' Nora announced. 'Captain of the lacrosse team, model good looks, studying government at Harvard and voted most likely to be President. *And*,' Nora stressed, 'a really shit ex-boyfriend to one Avery Finch.'

Avery nodded in agreement.

It was true. Hugo had been a *really* shit boyfriend. But even thinking that felt like a betrayal. It hadn't been his fault that she'd never felt the way she should have about him. And she still felt guilty for not being able to feel more. As if she'd failed somehow.

Avery had been so surprised when, a year and a half ago, her and Hugo's New Year's Eve kiss turned from friendly into something *more*. It had been . . . *nice*, flattering, fun – her head turning from the power of his attention. And while they'd been together – with the gang all around them – on the island or at various seasonal parties, it was wonderful. But when they weren't ... When it was just the two of them, it hadn't been *right*. It was as if they didn't work when the rest of the group wasn't there.

'Avery Finch, Avery Finch, Avery Finch,' Nora mused. 'Now, what can I say about Avery Finch?'

Avery groaned, half fearful of what she might say.

'Avery Finch, daughter of financial investment powerhouse duo Annalise and Jonathan Finch, loyal to a fault, absolute softie, lover of animals and friend to all, but *most* importantly ... college roommate to one Nora Miller: journalism major, future Pulitzer Prize winner and charming AF!'

Avery laughed, the sound eaten by the wind. 'And Leo, of course. Don't forget Leo,' she reminded Nora.

'Ahh, yes. Leo Walker, son of the island's private chef who was rumoured to have once turned down a Michelin star on principle. Gotta love a man with a strong moral code!'

'It's all true,' Avery confirmed, looking towards the island, surprised by how much she was looking forward to seeing him. Even though he wasn't from one of the families, he was their age and had always been on the island at the same time as them, so naturally they'd all come together. And while the others were often loud and brash, there was a steadiness to Leo that she'd really missed over the last year.

Throughout the last six months, she'd been thinking of him more and more. Wondering what he'd been doing, how he'd been getting on with his degree.

Nora's gasp cut into her thoughts.

'Is that it? Is that the island?'

Avery shaded her gaze from the sun's glare and looked to where Nora pointed. And there it was.

Mokani Island.

For two weeks before the summer started properly, and before the island's paying guests would arrive, the Finches, the Devereuxs and the Vandenburgs – friends since their own college days – would come together to celebrate Mark and Darian Vandenburg's wedding anniversary on their private island. It was and always had been nothing short of paradise.

Two jagged cliffs faced each other from opposite ends of the horseshoe-shaped island. Lush green foliage hid the dangerous rock beneath it, but the sight was nothing short of spectacular. White sand ringed the entire island.

'This is going to be so amazing!' Nora squealed jumping up and down, grabbing on to Avery's arm and pulling her into Nora's infectious excitement.

Nora was right. This *was* going to be amazing. Twelve days on an island so beautiful, so luxurious, only a few of the world's wealthiest people had ever set foot on it. And *this* year, it was going to be the best. It *had* to be, she thought a little desperately, after everything that had happened over the last year.

The boat lurched as it hit the wake of another speedboat making its way towards Mokani Island. A *bigger* boat. Her mother wouldn't like that.

The sun bounced off tinted windows and made her blink. She could just make out all four Devereuxs standing at the prow of the boat, laughing and joking together.

Avery looked back at where her mother perched, grim-faced

and thin-lipped on the white canvas seating, as if jealousy wasn't driving her out of her mind.

'Are you OK?' Nora asked, concerned, as if she'd noted the change in Avery's body language. 'Worried about college finding out?'

The boat swerved again and so did Avery's stomach as she reached for the rail and missed, banging her fingers painfully against the metal.

'Nora!' Avery hissed, a furious blush stinging her cheeks, adrenaline pricking her skin. *Fear.*

'No one heard,' Nora dismissed, turning back to look at the island.

Avery rubbed her hand and looked around to make sure her mother hadn't heard.

'Aves. Don't worry. I'm your emotional support guest, remember?' she teased, pulling Avery into her side with a strong firm hug.

Avery swallowed.

If anyone found out . . .

Avery shook her head, wishing for the hundredth time that Nora had never discovered her passed out on the exam paper for a test that no one had taken yet. An exam paper she'd paid an exorbitant amount for.

She'd be kicked out. Her parents would never forgive her. And if the press found out . . . they'd have a field day. She'd be yet another rich girl trying to game the system.

And could she say she wasn't?

'Your secret is safe with me. Pinkie promise,' Nora said, holding out her little finger for Avery to take in hers.

Letting Nora's promise soothe the unease at the casual way she'd mentioned her cheating, Avery slipped her finger around Nora's, feeling the press of her silver rings. They were all shapes and sizes, beautiful and different and not in the least bit expensive, but everything that Avery wanted to be. Carelessly, beautifully, chaotically wonderful. That was Nora. That's what she was envious of.

They hit another bump and this time Nora whooped and screamed, the sound encouraging the captain to steer them into another oncoming wave. The boat flipped up, salt spray in the air, glistening in the sun. Avery laughed while her parents scowled, and maybe, Avery thought, just maybe, if she pretended, she could be careless too.

LEO

Leo pulled at the collar of his white polo shirt, feeling like a complete idiot. He might have visited his dad here every summer for the last ten years, but this was the first time he was wearing a staff uniform.

Sweat trickled down his back as he shifted uncomfortably at the end of the line of staff, all present and correct, positioned on the grassy lookout just above the marina, ready to greet the guests as they arrived by speedboat from Nassau. He clenched his jaw, feeling Sven's piercing glare. His dad's boss, *his* boss too, managed the staff with a ruthlessness that bordered on brutal.

It wasn't what Leo had expected when his dad had messaged

to ask him to come out a week earlier than he usually did. He'd been surprised. Hopeful even. Maybe his dad was finally making time for him, instead of only giving him the brief snippets of his day between shifts. And maybe, he'd thought, just maybe he could tell his dad about switching uni courses.

But no. Instead of any of that, he'd been handed a uniform and put on the training rotation in order to get to grips with what he'd be doing for the next six weeks: porter, KP, waiter, cleaner, whatever was needed.

You're not a kid any more. You want to come? You work. Just like the rest of us.

And just like that, embarrassment heated his cheeks. Not because he was angry, or afraid of hard work. But because he'd been foolish enough to think that perhaps this time, this summer, things with his dad would be different. And that was when he knew he could *never* tell his dad about changing his degree.

Sven inspected the staff line, looking for the single hair that was out of place. Leo was half surprised he didn't have a magnifying glass. On any other occasion than this, *any*, the staff were to be neither seen nor heard. Because after 'the greet', this first moment where they were lined up to impress, the sole purpose of the staff was to be the invisible hand behind the luxury and indulgence. The guests were to feel as if they were waited upon by magical fairies and were to know absolutely nothing of the sheer volume of work that went into creating *paradise*.

Oh, Leo would be paid for his work. An eye-watering amount in exchange for servitude and an NDA. Enough to have made him bite his tongue instead of telling his father to go to hell. That, and the way his mother looked at him every time she'd sent him off halfway around the world to spend the summer with his father, was why he was here.

His mother was proud of herself for fostering what she thought was a positive relationship for him. Pleased that Mitchel Walker would, at the very least, provide Leo with a much-needed link to a part of his heritage that she couldn't.

She did so much for him; making their South London flat a home, raising him – despite financial challenges – to be part of an artistic and supportive community, was what gave her life. His mother had risen to every challenge that his father had failed to meet, and Leo wouldn't let Mitchel Walker take that away from her too.

'Eyes front, Walker,' Sven snapped. One of the staff further down the line sniggered. Leo had walked a fine line over the last ten years, not only as the son of the island's chef, but also because of his friendship with the children of the Vandenburgs, the Finches and the Devereuxs. The fact that they'd all been the same age had allowed their association to be tolerated by the adults for the two weeks they were on the island. And after they left, Leo had been on his own, often spending more time than not trying to stay out of the way of the island's other guests and staff.

But now he was walking an even finer line as an employee, especially since many of his 'new colleagues' had seen him in the past hanging out with the kids so rich they could topple a small country.

He'd received the piss-taking and the not-so-subtle digs

about him being on the wrong side of the island with as much good humour as possible. But every time they teased him, he wrestled with it more and more.

But one thing Leo knew for sure was that whatever the staff threw at him was nothing compared to what Archie and Hugo would do when they found out he was working here this year.

The piercing midday sun glinted off the two sleek speedboats cutting white lines into a crystal-blue sea as they neared the island's marina – a single wooden jetty reaching out from the highest point of the crescent, purposefully placed so as not to mar the beautiful white curve of the island's sandy bay.

It was the only way on and off the island. By *sea*. There were, of course, two helicopter pads. One for guests and one up at what everyone on the island *un*affectionately called the Big House.

A sprawling mansion, which far outstripped the four guest villas dotted around the island, the Big House had nine en suite bedrooms, three living areas each with different names, three separate kitchens, four terraces, one eighty-foot pool, two saunas, two plunge pools, three different steam rooms, one massage parlour, a hot tub the size of half a tennis court, an *actual* tennis court, a chapel, laundry services and private staff quarters.

In between the Big House and the rest of the island was the annex, which was essentially a tricked out media centre with a private cinema, games room with billiards, even a bowling lane and several table tennis tables. It also had a private pool that started in the building and continued outside into an infinity pool surrounded by a lawn, manicured to within an inch of its life, that peaked at the lower part of the island.

Leo knew all this because the staff were made to memorise the entire property brochure in case any of the guests ever needed reminding of how much the Vandenburgs' wealth outstripped their own.

'We're on, ladies and gents,' Sven warned in a sotto voice that still managed to travel down the length of the twenty-person line, all gleaming in their brilliant-white uniforms. The amount of money spent on bleach was – no pun intended – eye-watering.

But perfection was what Darian and Mark Vandenburg expected, and perfection was what they'd get. Working on Mokani, as had been drummed into him time and time again over the last week, was a once-in-a-lifetime opportunity. Having it on your résumé meant trust, discretion and unwavering loyalty. A glowing reference from Mokani meant you could work anywhere, no questions asked.

And if you messed up? They wouldn't find your body.

Probably because of the bleach.

The whirring of a high-speed golf cart came down the track, bringing Mark, Darian and Hugo Vandenburg to the jetty. They did this for every single guest. A near aggressive display of personal 'service' that started as it meant to go on.

Someone new to the island might be surprised by the petals in the pools in their villa, the champagne on ice, the caviar, the gifts of exquisite jewellery, fruit and chocolates in their bedrooms and on their terrace. They were certainly unlikely to expect the unobtrusive staff member on hand in their villa twenty-four hours a day.

But the Finches and the Devereuxs weren't new to the island, and they knew exactly what they were coming to the island for.

'Is the tennis guy not here?' Corrine whispered to Leo from the side of her mouth, her French accent tart in comparison to the lyrical lilt of the majority of the staff, most of whom had come from the mainland or nearby islands.

'He's part of the big reveal at dinner tonight,' Leo whispered back, having heard his father and Sven talking about the special guest, an Australian tennis star, earlier.

Leo watched the Vandenburgs exit their golf cart, unsurprised that Hugo hadn't noticed him standing amongst the uniformed staff lined up behind them. The wind ruffled the thick blond waves of Hugo's hair, the pink of his shirt pitched like an advert for the Hamptons or Martha's Vineyard. Not that Leo had ever visited those places. Outside of his trips here, Leo rarely got further from South London than the Watford Gap.

Darian slapped a hand across Hugo's back just as the deckhands finished tying off the speedboats, allowing the Finches and Devereuxs to disembark. They greeted each other on the jetty with smiles and cries of delight that sounded strained to Leo's ears.

His gaze quickly catalogued the people that he would be on hand to serve for the next twelve days.

Even from here, he could see the awkwardness between Hugo and Avery and he ruthlessly pushed down the relief he felt at not having to see them together like last year.

After a moment, Hugo shook hands with Dennis and Carol Devereux and then Annalise and Jonathan Finch. Behind him

Archie laughed at something and his sister, Sydney, glared at everyone around her.

Annalise and Jonathan were greeted by Mark, but Leo was distracted by the sight of Avery, arm-in-arm with a blonde in a straw hat who looked like she'd just won the lottery. Pretty, without a doubt, but his gaze locked on to Avery.

Long dark-brown hair reached towards her waist in soft layers. A pair of cut-off jean shorts hit mid-thigh, showing off toned legs. And once again he was slammed with a knockout jolt of wanting that had punched him, hard and fast, for the first time two years ago. Something he'd thought he could just shake off. Until he'd realised it hadn't been that easy.

The group was nearing the golf carts, lined up in front of the staff.

A laugh cut through the air as Avery's friend's hat was blown from her head and she chased after it, distracting Annalise, who looked irritated as she tried to speak to Darian. And that was when Avery looked up.

He saw the moment she realised he was there, lined up with the others. The blink. The beginning of a smile. Her hand rising as if she were going to wave . . .

She'd seen him. She'd been happy to see him.

And then her hand dropped, and one of the staff laughed again.

He clenched his jaw.

'But why?' Annalise's question pierced the moment, her objection clear.

'Oh, didn't Mark tell you?' Darian explained. 'We're having

some work done on Luna, so we've had to put you in Coastal. I hope that's OK.'

Before she could reply, Darian had turned to the Devereuxs. 'We've made some changes to Solar since you were last here, and I cannot *wait* for you to see them,' he said ushering Carol Devereux towards the golf cart as Dennis and the twins followed.

Annalise was left open-mouthed staring after them.

It was a snub. All the staff that had heard it knew it. And *she* knew it too.

Annalise closed her mouth and went to the golf cart Sven directed her towards, while Jonathan and Avery Finch tried to ignore the awkwardness.

He felt the brush of Avery's gaze on his as he forced his attention straight ahead, ignoring how it felt to be on the other side of the island. Things were going to be different this year, that was for sure.

CHAPTER TWO

AVERY

Avery winced at yet another squeal of delight from Nora, knowing it would grate on her mother's already frayed nerves. Annalise Finch was intolerant at the best of times, and this was *not* the best of times.

'Nora,' Avery whined as she heard her mother pacing around the living room.

'Sorry. It's just that this place is so good I could *die*!' Nora said, hanging off the doorframe of the en suite of the room they were sharing, before going to finish topping up her make-up.

Tapping her finger against her thigh, Avery crept out into the hallway.

'They know,' her mother whisper-hissed.

'They don't know,' her father insisted.

'Why else would we have been downgraded like this, huh?' her mother demanded. 'Coastal is *much* smaller than Tidal. *That's* empty. So why we can't stay there? And my daughter, forced to share a room?'

'This is a downgrade?' Nora whispered from beside her, nearly giving Avery a heart attack.

'Jesus, Jonathan, this is a disaster,' her mother pressed on. 'How are we going to get them to give us what we need, when they're already not taking us seriously?'

Nora left her side and bounced on to the bed, eyebrow raised.

'Are the 'rents gonna be OK?'

'If they can keep it together,' Avery replied, throwing herself on to the bed beside Nora. She stared up at the ceiling where a rattan fan spun in circles that made her dizzy. Nora's hand slipped into hers and the sounds of her parents' argument grew quieter as they retreated to their room on the opposite side of the villa.

Avery turned her head to look out of the large floor-to-ceiling windows, separating them from a deck with a sunken hot tub that looked out on to one half of the curved island and the large rocky cliff at the tip, reaching into the sky.

AI couldn't have produced a better image of paradise.

Dark wood floors, cream walls, the four posts cornering the handmade bed with draped netting made the villa romantic, *historic*. Gold, not brass, finished the fixtures and the sofa and armchair looked as if they'd never even been sat on. Rich-green plants dotted around the room dragged the gaze from the interior to the exterior, cleverly and purposely.

Outside of these two weeks, the villas were rented for amounts Avery couldn't even imagine. She'd tried to Google the island once, but it wasn't online. Nothing. No pictures, no website. If you didn't know about it, you'd never find it.

'Is that real?' Nora asked, squinting at the painting on the wall.

Avery nodded.

'Huh. Just a Rothko. On the wall. *Fancy*,' Nora teased.

Avery actually preferred this villa to Luna, the villa they'd spent the last few years in. It was slightly further away from the Big House and from the central areas where the guests could gather. At this point, anything that added distance between her and Hugo was a gift.

Her stomach had knotted the moment she'd seen him. Just like that, the last six months had disappeared and she was right back to the last time they'd seen each other – the day she'd broken up with him.

Why? I just don't understand. What we have, it's perfect.

But it hadn't been. And that he'd not seen it was warning enough. But she'd not been able to tell him that, so she'd tried her best with, '*Things have changed, Hugo.*'

And then *it* had been there. A flash of barely suppressed anger, covered so quickly that if she hadn't been looking for it, she wouldn't have seen it. She pressed her teeth together, bracing against a wave of emotion she tried to keep locked down. Guilt, regret – she *had* wanted it to work with Hugo, but she just hadn't seemed to be what he wanted. It was as if she'd always been having to pretend.

Beside her, the bed dipped as Nora got up and went to the wardrobe where all their things had been put away.

'It's kind of creepy.'

'What is?' Avery asked, pulling herself out of her thoughts.

'Someone touching your underwear.'

Avery looked over to where Nora had opened a drawer and was looking through Avery's clothes.

'They weren't *touching* it, they were putting it away.'

'Yeah, but you don't know *who*, do you?' Nora teased.

The thought made Avery squirm. She'd never considered it before. It was just something that happened. Clothes were put away, petals in pools were made to disappear before they wilted and bruised. Candles were snuffed and replaced.

But someone did all that.

A person.

Leo, maybe?

She hadn't realised that he'd be *working* here this year.

When she'd first seen him, she'd been surprised – *happy*. And then, breathless. He looked *good*. It was his height that had drawn her gaze because for at least the last three years, Leo had been nearly a foot taller than her. The sun had already deepened his light-brown complexion, which was perfectly balanced between the lightness of his mother's and the richness of his father's. And the muscles on his arm filled out the white shirt, the belt around the waist of the khaki chinos showed a leaner physique than last year. But it was his eyes she'd sought. The way that honey had poured into hazel to make those molten amber eyes that were almost always startling at first. Not that she'd been able to see them from where she stood.

It had been instinct to raise her hand and wave, before realising that he was working. That he might *not* appreciate her calling attention to him when he was on duty. And it made her feel . . . frustrated because the fact that he *was* working meant she wouldn't get to see him as much. And she'd been looking forward to seeing him. It was something she hadn't mentioned to Nora, because she thought Nora might—

'Can I borrow this?'

Avery raised her head from the bed to look at the dress Nora was holding.

'Not tonight,' she replied, eyeing the high-cut black tight-fitting dress that she'd bought on a defiant whim shortly after breaking up with Hugo. He hadn't really liked to see her in things like that. 'Think less *risky* and more *graduation*.'

'Sunday school. Got it. I mean . . . *I* don't got it, but *you* do,' Nora said with a laugh, fingering the clothes hangers until she reached something more suitable. 'What about this?'

Avery had planned to wear the dress tonight, but she knew better than to argue with Nora, who would pout, charm and cajole her way into eventually getting what she wanted. Deciding to save them both some time, Avery told Nora it was perfect, before disappearing into the bathroom to have a shower while Nora got dressed.

Avery still hadn't got used to Nora's complete lack of self-consciousness when it came to her body, not even after ten months of sharing a room with her at college. Nora would strip down to nothing at the drop of a hat and borrow clothes and make-up like someone who had long ago decided that what was Avery's was Nora's. And while thankfully she'd stopped teasing Avery for 'being such a prude', it was still there, the smallest of digs, every time it came up.

Avery got into the shower, letting the spray wash away the sea salt and funk from the journey here, wishing she could wash away the knots in her stomach just as easily.

She was nervous about dinner.

Normally it was one of her favourite nights of the whole

holiday. Mark and Darian liked to bookend the twelve days with a first-night welcome feast and then the final night with fireworks celebrating their anniversary.

But tonight felt as if it would be different.

Sydney had spent the whole time on the jetty ignoring her, which had twisted her stomach into knots. She hated not knowing what she'd done wrong and knew that she'd have to speak to her at some point. They couldn't ignore each other for the next twelve days. The island was big, but not that big.

Archie didn't seem to have a problem, though, and had slung his arm around her as if nothing had changed, as careless as he always was. Things with Hugo had been as awkward as she'd expected.

There was no point hoping that Nora would be able to rein herself in for the dinner either. Nora would never be the quiet, picture-perfect, seen-and-not-heard person her mother would have wanted as a best friend slash college roommate for her daughter. She'd been apoplectic when Avery had told her that she'd invited Nora – only marginally less furious than when she'd found out that Avery had broken up with Hugo.

Avery flinched remembering the howl of anger her mother had made when she'd heard the news.

'What have you done?! You've ruined *everything*.'

Her mother had planned an entire future around Avery and Hugo.

'It's perfect. When you're married, they'll be family and it will be amazing. We'll be invited everywhere. Jonathan – just think of the clients we'll attract with a daughter as a Vandenburg.'

And for that brief period, Avery could do no wrong. It had

been a blessed reprieve from the constant nitpicking and fault-finding that, to her mother, was as unconscious as breathing. But when she'd broken up with Hugo all of that had gone. As well as the access her mother had wanted so badly.

Access they sorely needed right now.

A bang on the bathroom door made her jump.

'Aves. Come on.'

'Coming,' she called back, unsurprised when Nora continued to bang on the door until she opened it, wrapped in a towel.

And there Nora was, hanging off the frame with an infectious smile, before she stuck her tongue out and snapped a pic of Avery on her phone. Avery squealed, reaching for it, desperate to delete it but Nora danced back out of her way.

Avery frowned when she realised what Nora was wearing – the smallest bikini she'd ever seen.

'We've got dinner in half an hour.'

'No, Aves, what we have is a hot tub on a balcony, with a bottle of champagne!'

'We *do* have that don't we,' Avery said, feeling excitement fill her veins for the first time since she'd got off the plane.

HUGO

Hugo had been on edge from the moment he'd known that Avery had stepped off the plane. He'd heard Sven tell his dads that they'd been picked up by the car service. But seeing her? For the first time since they'd broken up? It was like a punch to the gut.

It hurt. Like really hurt. He'd felt like everyone was staring at him as they'd met down on the jetty. Mark's attention, tentative; Syd's gaze a little too narrow; Avery's gaze a little too short; Archie's lazy one-armed hug held just a little too long, an extra thump on his back as if he was someone to be pitied.

But he wasn't.

Tension clenched his jaw. Half of him wished he could have stayed back in Boston. The other half didn't. He couldn't have *not* come this year – even if his parents would have let him stay behind. He needed to see her. Things still felt unsettled.

When they'd broken up, Avery had said it was because he'd changed. But everyone changes, right? Like, *she* had. Especially around her roommate Nora. The one who had come with her to the island. And, yeah, there had been other things. Things that he could have worked on, things that would have come with time.

But Hugo *knew* that if Nora hadn't interfered, he'd still be with Avery. Because *before* Nora, things had been perfect. They'd had fun. And everyone they'd met had told him how lucky he was, how great she was. It had been a dream.

Until Avery had started college, and roomed with *her*. She'd been there non-stop, whispering in Avery's ear, messing things up. But he had a plan. All he had to do was just speak to Avery. Get her alone. And then she'd see. She'd remember how great they were. And then they'd get back together and it would all be OK.

He grabbed the shirt Darian had left out for him to wear – apparently not trusting him to pick out his own clothes for dinner. He hated the welcome dinner. It was always such a nightmare. It was the one night that his parents had him on a leash.

Because welcoming guests, whether they paid or not, was *part of the experience*. Of course, his dads shied away from using words like service. No way would Darian Vandenburg ever serve *anyone*. Scorn burned through Hugo's veins. Darian was the biggest hypocrite of them all.

There was a knock on the door.

He didn't answer but Mark gently pushed the door open anyway. Sympathy in his gaze.

'You doing OK, kid?' his dad asked.

No.

'Yeah,' Hugo replied, doing up his shirt in front of the mirror. He flicked a gaze to his dad in the reflection. Mark edged his way into the room, nodding as if he understood. But he didn't. He didn't even know *half* the things he'd need to understand him.

And then Hugo felt guilty. And sick.

'After tonight, I could get the helicopter back and you could go home? You just have to say the word,' Mark offered.

Could he? Should he?

'That's OK,' he said with a shrug. 'I wanna be here.'

'Was it hard? Seeing Avery? I know you liked her.'

I loved her and she left.

'S'fine.'

'I'm serious about you going home if you need to. I know what Darian said, but if you want—'

'I said I was fine.' Hugo's words filled the room with impatience and anger, pushing Mark out of the room with his hands raised in surrender.

'I'll join you on the beach. Soon,' Hugo conceded, hating

that he'd done that to Mark. Mark who was good and kind. Mark who had no idea.

'If you change your mind at any time, the offer is there. I love you, you know,' Mark said, as a statement rather than a question.

He *did* know. But would Mark still love him if he knew the secret he was keeping from him?

His dad closed the door and Hugo wanted to punch something. Because if Mark ever *did* find out about the secrets he was keeping, it would ruin everything. He'd lose everything that he had. Because how could Mark *not* blame him?

No. Hugo knew what Mark would do. He'd come to the same conclusion as his birth parents. That he was more trouble than he was worth. That they were better off without him.

Hugo glared at the tie he was supposed to wear that night and, instead, threw it across the room. It was a small act of defiance, and one that wouldn't go unnoticed. Darian liked everything to be perfect. And if it wasn't? There would be hell to pay.

He checked himself in the mirror. Dark trousers, blond hair perfectly styled, white shirt showing off the tan he'd already picked up, the perfect pearl-white smile of a successful rich young man. Everything his dads wanted him to be. And the lies continued to claw at his stomach.

He left his room and jogged down the wide central staircase heading for the door. Dusk had taken away the edge of the day's heat and a cool breeze skittered over his skin as he stalked over to the electric golf cart. He slipped behind the wheel, pressed the ignition and headed down towards the main beach.

There were seven different beaches on the island and with

only four villas plus the Big House, it was feasible that every single group visiting the island could have one to themselves. Darian had refused to add more villas – even though it would bring in an obscene amount of revenue.

The harder to get, the more they want.

Hugo's mind turned back to Avery. And he hated that his dad was right.

The golf cart sped over specialised smooth-set stone pathways that connected each villa to the public areas on the island like the tennis courts and the spa centre – a deceptively simple name for a space dedicated to every conceivable beauty treatment and wellness therapy including, but not limited to, Botox, laser therapy, cryogenic therapy, touch therapy, full microbiome assessment, colonic irrigation and anything else your little heart could imagine. For a very high price.

Always for a price.

He'd loved it here once. He'd been truly, magically, totally in love with it. It was Neverland. It was the impossible for a baby who had been born to drug-addicted parents out in the Ozarks. His life could have been so damn different, a future seen only in his nightmares. He'd read his file; he knew the neglect that the social worker had noted, the malnutrition, the abuse.

And despite that, Mark and Darian had apparently fallen in love with him at first sight and moved heaven and earth to take him home with them. They'd even tried to keep in touch with his birth mother. But she had taken the money they had given her and disappeared.

The golf cart jiggled as it met the wooden slatted path towards the island's main beach where dinner would take place.

He stopped the cart and sat for a moment, the engine ticking, looking out at a scene so luxurious it was ludicrous.

A large banquet-style table sat on ornate silk carpets imported from Turkey. Tall wooden stakes had been driven into the sand at all four corners of the area, with netting hanging in swathes. Firepits had been dug further out but closer to the table were nearly three hundred individual candles plugged into the sand, protected from the winds by wax-paper cylinders, and some poor bastard had to light every single one of them.

He looked over to where his dads stood and caught Darian's glare.

He'd noticed the tie.

'Get over here,' Darian mouthed, as the golf carts bringing the Devereuxs and the Finches arrived from the opposite direction, the painful warning in his voice clear.

Yeah. Hugo wanted to rebel, but he wasn't stupid.

CHAPTER THREE

AVERY

Avery fell against the frame of the golf cart as it turned the corner, tipsy from the champagne she'd shared with Nora in the hot tub. Nora laughed at her and Avery giggled until she felt the burn of her mother's glare.

'I don't know what's got into you two, but it stops right now,' Annalise ordered.

'Chill, Mom, it's all good,' Avery replied.

'It is *not* all good,' she hissed, glaring at her husband as if it were his fault somehow.

Avery rolled her eyes, something she would never have done had she been sober. The golf cart turned towards the beach and Nora inhaled a gasp. Avery reached out and slapped her hand across Nora's mouth.

'I swear, if you say "oh my god" one more time,' she threatened, but Nora pulled her hand away.

'Tell me that isn't worthy of an OMG, Aves. Tell me!'

Avery looked out to the beach and gave up.

Oh.

It was definitely worthy. It looked as if a thousand stars had fallen on to the beach.

And for a moment she forgot. She forgot Hugo, she forgot her parents' bickering. She forgot college and the mid-terms. She forgot the unrelenting pressure to be more than she could be . . . and just *sank* into being in paradise with her best friends with nothing but twelve days of all the sun, sea, sand and cocktails she could imagine.

From the corner of her eye, she saw the Devereuxs come from the direction of their villa and Avery would bet money that the growl she heard wasn't from the golf cart's engine.

She watched her mother's glare morph into the fakest smile that anyone had ever seen, just for Carol and Dennis Devereux, waving as the carts pulled to a stop.

Once everyone had arrived, they were offered glasses of champagne. Avery and Nora hung back while the adults went ahead.

'Avery!' Archie exclaimed, his fists pumping into the air, as if they hadn't just seen each other barely an hour before.

'Hey, Archie,' she replied, smiling at his enthusiastic welcome. The only one of all of them who was dressed in jeans and a T-shirt, acceptable solely because combined, his outfit probably cost more than all the jewellery her mother wore that night. He ran a hand through thick, carelessly grown-out sandy brown waves, flopping them from one side to the other as he shot her and Nora a bashful grin. Ink-blue eyes that matched his sister's twinkled in the twilight from a face so near perfect, it looked airbrushed.

Used to him by now, Avery laughed off his flirting and

looked up to find Sydney gesturing her to the side with a nod. Stomach tightening, Avery followed, the brush of Nora's hand on her arm a reassurance she needed, but something that wasn't missed by Sydney either.

After an awkward beat of silence as Sydney looked everywhere but at her, Avery couldn't take it any more.

'Where have you been, Syd?' she asked, trying to keep her voice down around the others, and the hurt out of her tone.

Sydney shook her head. For just a second, Avery thought she might have got something sincere. But the mask went up, and Sydney said, 'Sooooo busy. Look, I'm sorry about being a flake this year. My bad. Friends?'

Avery wanted to say no. She wanted to say that wasn't good enough. But, instead, she smiled and said, 'Of course!'

Satisfied, Sydney returned to the group, greeting Nora with a couple of air kisses and a 'Nice to meet you, babes', before strutting down on to the beach, slinky gold cowl-neck dress glittering in the dusk and long blonde hair swaying to reveal the sharp blades of her shoulders.

Nora raised an eyebrow. 'Babes?' she mouthed, and Avery shrugged and smiled, as Nora pulled her into her side.

Hugo loped over to them and Avery pushed away a spike of discomfort. Forcing a smile, she greeted him.

'Come on, guys. You broke up. It's not like someone *died*,' Archie whined. 'Just kiss and make up,' he said, receiving a hard glare from Hugo. 'Or don't. Whatever.' Archie stalked off towards the waiter holding a tray of cocktails.

'It's fine. It's cool. Hey, Avery,' Hugo said, leaning in to kiss her cheek.

His aftershave, the feel of his lips ... and nothing. Which had been the problem. As much as she wanted it to be different, she just felt numb. And she didn't want to feel numb, she wanted to feel *everything*.

'Hey,' she said back, wishing it could have been different.

A gong sounded.

Hugo half bowed and gestured them towards the table. Nora half curtsied back and skipped down the path. Archie grinned to follow, his eyes on her ass. When it was just her and Hugo, he held out his arm for her to take.

'Just as friends,' he said.

'Just as friends,' she repeated.

Hors d'oeuvres were served on platters, while an entire side table was given over to a frozen ice sculpture of the island with half-shelled oysters nestled into crevices and Denia red prawns glistening in the firelight.

But it was hard to ignore the suckling pig being spit-roasted over the open fire barely ten feet away.

Avery hid the shiver that ran across her skin from the sight of the metal protruding violently through the pig's mouth, and she turned away from the dark spaces where its eyes had once been. The juices dropping from the meat hit the fire and sizzled and snapped. Nora's eyes nearly popped out of her head, and Avery sent her a warning glare. If she was impressed by this, she'd probably pass out by the end of the evening.

They came together around the table for the eight-course menu, while gentle live music surrounded them, played by invisible performers. The first course was sea bass ceviche with diced mango, baby tomatoes, red onion slivers and avocado mousse, served with a Guizhou cactus pear reduction, over which the adults caught up with the rundown of investment exchanges that had happened since last New Year's Eve.

'No, we decided to sell early April,' Carol explained, her voice carrying in the breeze. While the adults jumped right back into the swing of things, it seemed harder for Avery and her friends.

'Lucky you got out when you did. I got stung for five and a half mil on that,' Darian said, tipping his glass in Carol's direction.

Nora choked beside her, the noise loud and awkward. Sydney inhaled her disdain, while Avery squirmed. Avery had not really been conscious of the money around this table before. But rooming with Nora in college had made her see things a little differently. And while all Avery had thought of was how much Nora would love being on the island, she hadn't thought about how people might feel about having her there.

'Actually,' her father said, clearing his throat, 'we might be looking for investors.'

Tension whipped through Avery's body like a parachute cord, every sense on alert, cringing at how desperate he sounded when he pressed on, saying, 'There are some exciting opportunities ahead for—'

'But then I decided to dump Exkil and buy, oh, what's it called. You know,' Carol said, clicking her fingers at Darian completely cutting Jonathan off. She tutted and turned to her husband. 'Donaldson's company, what's it called again?'

Dennis narrowed his gaze in thought. 'Fenright.'

'Fenright. That's it,' Carol confirmed.

'How much?' Darian asked over his champagne glass.

'Ten,' Carol said. *Million*. 'Testing the waters.'

Avery cringed deep down inside, knowing that her mother had noticed Carol's cut. She looked up to find Sydney watching her, curiosity a glint in her eye.

Avery pushed the food around her plate. The last thing she needed was for Sydney to find out about the trouble her parents were in.

In some ways, Sydney was a little like Nora, Avery realised for the first time. Amazing when she was in a good mood, and unpredictable when she wasn't. And usually Sydney would be half a bottle of wine down by now, but she wasn't. So perhaps she'd changed. Like they had *all* changed. Hugo, Sydney. *Her*.

Archie hadn't, but Archie was Archie.

Sydney snapped up her glass, all but one of her bracelets glinting in the flickering candlelight. The one that didn't glint was made up of a series of small white cubes, each with letters on them that read: BEST FRIENDS. They'd bought them four years ago on a trip to the mainland. Silly little friendship bracelets that had cost less than a dollar each. And Sydney was still wearing hers.

Avery frowned and looked up, caught by Sydney, who pointedly held her gaze.

Where's yours?

Guilt twisted her stomach, chasing away any traces of hunger, and her earlier, deliberate choice not to wear her friendship bracelet suddenly felt petty and mean.

The dull conversation droned on between the adults at the

other end, filling the slightly awkward silence that had fallen over their end of the table, until Archie cleared his throat.

'So, what's the plan for the next couple of weeks? Sun, sea, sand?' he asked, pushing his empty plate forward and leaning back in his chair.

Sydney brightened up. 'Oh, I was thinking that we could take the boat out and go snorkelling out by the reefs?'

'That would be cool,' Hugo said, Archie chiming in with a 'Yeah, dude'.

Nora looked down at her plate and Avery winced.

'You know, I think we'll probably just hang back here?' Avery hedged.

'Why?' Sydney demanded, as if that was the most stupid thing she'd ever heard.

'Because—' Avery began to find an excuse.

'I have a fear of the water.' Nora's statement was met with shocked silence.

'You're on an *island*,' Hugo pointed out.

Nora shrugged.

'No, but seriously,' he pressed. 'What are you going to *do*? We're literally surrounded by water.'

'It's more like being *in* the water,' Nora explained, and Avery hated the way it felt as if her friends were turning on Nora. 'Like, I'm fine on a speedboat, but snorkelling, or swimming or being in the sea . . .' She scrunched her nose and shook her head. 'It's just a hangover from some childhood thing.'

'That's weird,' Hugo said dismissively.

'We don't mock the afflicted, Hugo,' Sydney scolded.

'Jesus, Syd,' Avery exclaimed, shocked by the way everyone was behaving.

'What?' Sydney asked, all innocent. 'Fear is an affliction,' she said with a shrug, while Archie tried to hide his laugh by dropping his head to his arms and Hugo smirked. 'Nice dress, though,' Sydney added, as if it were the only nice thing that she could find to say.

'Thank you,' Nora beamed, as if Syd hadn't just been a complete bitch. 'It's Avery's, she let me borrow it. I don't have anything nice enough to fit in here with you.'

On the back foot, Sydney was left speechless, undecided as to whether Nora had been making a dig of her own.

'You look well, Hugo,' Avery's mum said, cutting through the conversations on both ends of the table. Avery wanted the ground to swallow her up.

'Thank you, Mrs Finch,' he said, putting his cutlery down.

'How are you enjoying your degree? Politics, isn't it?' Annalise asked, oblivious to the way that everyone's attention was now on them.

'Government,' he nodded. 'But, yes, pretty much politics. It's excellent, Mrs Finch. It's an incredible amount of information to take in, but it's everything I'd hoped,' Hugo said, the poster-boy for ex-boyfriends, Avery thought miserably. 'Boston is an amazing place to study.'

'*And* he's head of the lacrosse team,' Mark chimed in proudly.

Avery frowned, sure that she remembered Hugo being dropped from the team just before they'd broken up. She looked at him, but he ignored her – for perhaps the first time that evening.

'Go, Crimson!' Jonathan Finch cheered, but Hugo's responding smile was a little dull.

'You went to Harvard too, didn't you, Mr Devereux?' Nora asked up the table towards the adults' end.

Avery caught Syd pulling a face at Archie, who shrugged off the question aimed at their father.

'Yes, dear. And it was a great place to be and to learn,' he replied, before turning his attention back to his plate.

Avery was about to nudge Nora under the table, when she heard, 'Have you finished?' and her head snapped up.

'Oh my god, are you serious, dude?' Archie demanded, so loud it cut along the entire table. 'Leo?' Archie slapped the table and burst into hysterics. 'What are you wearing?'

'Archibald,' Dennis's voice lashed out.

'Dad, come on, it's *Leo*,' he said, pointing up at Leo, who was doing his best to ignore Archie.

But the glare Mr Devereux sent his son was so chilling that Avery looked away.

Hugo peered around Sydney. 'Bro! If you needed money—'

Sydney slapped his chest, cutting off his laughter with an 'ouch' just as Darian called Hugo's name in a warning tone, causing Hugo to scowl.

'Ignore them, Leo,' Sydney said. 'Thank you, I *have* finished.'

Leo nodded, a small smile curving his lips as he took her plate and reached for Hugo's.

But as he did, Hugo grabbed for his drink, knocking it over, the champagne splashing down Leo and his uniform.

'Oh god. Jeez, Leo, I'm sorry,' Hugo replied, genuinely

shocked, leaning back in his chair to avoid the liquid splashing off the table.

Avery's gaze flew to Leo, whose face was unreadable in the low light of the night.

LEO

Leo inhaled, grabbing for oxygen and patience.

'That's OK, *sir*,' he said, standing back from the table, grimacing from having to call Hugo 'sir' as much as from the way his trousers were now soaking wet. He caught the eye of another staff member, who jerked his head away from the table.

'Hugo,' he heard Avery complain as he walked away, and he wanted to tell her not to. That he could fight his own battles. But apparently he couldn't, he thought with disgust. Because he'd just had to stand there and take it. And call Hugo *sir*.

He headed to the truck tucked out of sight of the guests that served as storage for everything that was needed to ensure that dinner on a beach was still a five-star dining experience.

Including spare uniforms.

'The hell was that?' Domingo asked as he returned to the truck with more empty plates.

'Just an accident,' Leo dismissed.

'Was it? You're on *this* side of the island now, dude. And they're not going to like having you there to remind them of that,' he warned.

Leo shrugged as he took off the dirty trousers and put on a clean pair. 'No harm, no foul,' he insisted.

Domingo dropped a 'whatever' and went back to clear the rest of the table.

Sven arrived. 'Stay down the adults' end for the rest of the dinner.'

'It's fine,' Leo insisted.

'Did I stutter? Did you hear a question?' Sven's voice lashed out.

'No, sir. I'll stay at the adults' end,' Leo said, swallowing his objection to the sudden reprimand, but before he'd even finished speaking Sven had walked off. There was no point complaining about things not being fair.

There was only one rule when it came to working on the island.

Staff were to be neither seen nor heard.

And he was too visible. He clenched his jaw, even more pissed at his dad. Was this the lesson that he wanted to teach his son? To learn his place in this world, forgetting that this wasn't Leo's world at all?

The money you will earn here . . .

Yes, the money would be enough to cover a year's worth of student debt. and accommodation. Money he could *really* do with. But at what cost?

Leo returned to the beach and moved towards the far end of the table. By that time, conversation had resumed and he'd been all but forgotten.

The second course was now being served and he picked up the bottle of wine that perfectly matched the sous vide duck breast. He topped up the adults' glasses, only Mark turning a smile on him, the rest working hard to ignore him, all the while Domingo's words ringing in his ears.

Leo knew that it was part of the fantasy, that unseen hands provided limitless luxury and wish fulfilment without having to ask. That it was important – even vital – that staff remain inconspicuous. Leo had thought that meant unobtrusive. But only Avery had seen him standing there at the end of the staff line earlier that day. Not that she'd been willing to acknowledge that, remembering her hand dropping away, her expression unreadable.

To everyone else, he'd literally been invisible.

Until now.

He risked a glance down at their end of the table and saw Avery watching him with those large brown eyes of hers, before she looked away again. And it reminded him of a night two years ago, on this very beach, when she *hadn't* looked away.

The night he'd let her slip through his fingers.

Staff began to serve the next course – Sven shaking his head at Leo, glaring at him until he understood the telepathic order for him to remain on the drinks station and as far away from the guests as possible.

Sven pressed a finger to the earpiece he wore discreetly that allowed him to control the evening with god-like precision, and Leo figured that it was time for the arrival of Nick Dawson – the Aussie tennis player who crashed out of Wimbledon hard after a knee injury that he'd spent the last twelve months recovering from.

In direct contrast to all the others, Nick's golf cart was intended to draw attention and come down the central pathway lit up like a Christmas tree.

'Ah, our special guest,' Darian announced, not fooling anyone.

'Guest' in this instance meant 'celebrity visitor', a person who had been hired to provide specialist services for the *actual* guests. Last year it had been an actress-turned-wellbeing-life-coach.

Cutlery was put down and glasses picked up as the dark-haired Australian exited the cart dressed in tennis whites, as if that was a normal thing to be wearing at night. Annalise drooled over him, and Carol coolly glanced over. Even Avery's roommate seemed to give him an appreciative once-over.

Nick waved – Leo was half surprised that he didn't have his tennis racket with him – soaking in the attention, clearly used to being appreciated for his physique and appearance.

'Ladies, gentlemen,' he said, leaning into his Australian twang. 'What can I say? Thank you so much for welcoming me to paradise!'

'Nick has kindly agreed to be on hand for lessons, one-to-one or couples, or even to have a few games with anyone confident enough in their backhand,' Mark explained.

Nick winked at Annalise, and Leo rolled his eyes.

'I'll be here for any of your tennis wishes or desires, whenever and wherever,' he said with a mock bow worthy of a grand-final win. 'But it really is my honour to meet you all. It's going to be a cracker of a summer!' he exclaimed.

'Would you care for a drink?' Annalise asked.

Leo knew that Darian had strictly forbidden any staff member to drink with the guests, but Nick gracefully raised his hands in surrender, apologising and claiming jet lag, as if he too hadn't been here the full week that Leo had.

'Maybe another time,' he said as Dennis Devereux finished his wine.

Leo was by his side in a second.

'Whiskey,' he insisted, with no other words to cushion the command, a hooded gaze watching one of the female staff serving at the other end of the table.

Leo was back at the table with Dennis's favourite whiskey and a separate glass of ice and a small jug of water.

The man didn't even say thank you.

Leo stifled the irritation and felt someone's gaze on him as he retreated into the shadows at the edges of the beach. Casting a quick glance at the other end of the table, he noticed Nora looking his way.

Nick made his way round the table, a word or two for each guest, while conversation at the adult end of the table resumed.

'This really is paradise, Darian,' Carol observed, leaning back in her chair to take it all in.

'We do our bit, but really the island speaks for itself,' Darian said graciously with a smile. 'Did you decide to pass on Ekanau?'

Leo frowned. The smaller island was about twenty minutes by boat in the opposite direction of the mainland and home to several of the staff employed here. He wondered if they knew it was up for sale.

Dennis huffed a laugh, around his mouthful of lobster tail. 'Why would we buy an island when we can use yours?'

Carol's face didn't move an inch, but Leo knew she hadn't liked that one bit.

'We wouldn't let you go anywhere else anyway,' Mark said, leaning forward a little and trying to ease whatever had ruffled the air. 'We love having you here. We love having you *all* here,' he said loud enough to carry around the table. 'There aren't any other people that we could imagine celebrating our anniversary with,' he added, taking Darian's hand in his.

Darian sent a smile to his husband, the visual equivalent of 'yes dear', and Leo went to top up his glass before he could finish it.

Archie's laugh wedged into the night air, the squabble he was having with Sydney a familiar backdrop as the evening settled a little.

'You didn't!'

'How was I to know it wasn't real?' Archie defended.

'Oh my god,' Avery said, descending into giggles. Nora joined in and even Sydney seemed to have relaxed a little.

If Leo had been aware of the differences between him and his friends in the past, it was now glaringly obvious. The uniform . . . The money . . .

Nora asked a question that Leo didn't hear and Sydney made a great show of trying to hide her laughter. She turned to her brother and mouthed, 'Who is she?' – which was missed by absolutely no one at the table.

Leo felt the sting of it all the way from here. Nora showed no sign of having seen, but Avery had. And he wondered if she could see them, the lines that were being drawn across the island, between the haves and the have-nots. Between him and them.

CHAPTER FOUR

AVERY

Sun soaked into Avery's skin. She could actually feel it warming her muscles and heating her bones. It was *delicious*.

Three days into the holiday and she and Nora had fully indulged at the spa centre. Deep-tissue massages, facials, mani-pedis, waxes, scrubs – *not in that order* – wraps for water retention, steam rooms to sweat it out, saunas to dry it out and frigid plunge pools to reduce inflammation. Avery had been so shocked that she'd squealed, causing Nora to burst into hysterics, until Avery splashed ice-cold water at her, and her laugh had turned into a scream.

A yoga teacher had been flown in, and they'd even joined a class until their giggles had drawn glares from her mother and Carol Devereux, so she and Nora had scuttled off to the spa's sunloungers and, feeling hungry, ordered whatever they'd fancied.

Nora hadn't believed that they could order anything and had jokingly placed an order for a hamburger from Shake Shack and a side order of sushi from Nobu. The look on her face was priceless when, less than thirty minutes later, a helicopter whirred overhead.

'No!' she'd exclaimed.

Avery had smirked, secretly delighting in impressing Nora.

'I want it on a T-shirt,' Nora declared as she'd bitten into the juicy burger.

'What?'

'A helicopter delivered my burger.' She'd not been able to stop giggling for the rest of the day.

When they hadn't been eating or at the spa or the hot tub on the deck outside their room, they'd come out to the pool where Avery could cool off, and Nora could sit in the shade.

Now, with Nora back at the villa on the phone to her mother, Avery looked out at the view from the comfort of her sunlounger.

Nora had declared it 'straight out of a James Bond villain's lair'. Avery eyed the cliff warily. Once, years ago, they'd tried to climb it, despite the warnings. Hugo and Leo had scratched their hands so badly they'd had to visit the island's infirmary. Leo still had a scar across the palm of his hand.

Avery frowned, surprised that she'd remembered that.

'Avery?'

She turned to find Corrine offering her a fruit cocktail.

'Again?' Avery groaned.

'Did you want something else?' Corrine asked.

'Absolutely not!' Avery cried with laughter. 'You make the *best* cocktails; they're just lethal!'

'Doesn't she? I want her to come with me wherever I go,' Sydney teased possessively, lying on the lounger opposite Avery.

In a stunning white costume, long limbs glistening in the

sun from a sweet-scented tanning oil, Sydney looked like a model.

Corrine smiled. 'I could teach you,' she said, 'but then I'd be out of a job.' She winked and returned to the bar that separated the pool and the tennis court behind it, from where Avery could hear the thwack of a ball being hit occasionally by a racket, and the scuff of shoes on the ground.

The sound of such exertion only made Avery feel more languid.

She lay back on the cushion-covered sunlounger. There were five of them dotted around the large infinity pool.

Archie surfaced from beneath the water. 'Morning,' he said to Hugo, who had just appeared, as he folded his arms and leaned over the side of the pool.

'Why are we here and not at the beach?' Hugo demanded sulkily as he collapsed into the lounger next to Avery.

'Because *Nora* doesn't like the water, remember?' Archie said, with a shit-eating grin.

'You're *in* the water,' Hugo pointed out, as if Archie was incredibly stupid. Well, not Archie, Avery realised. It was a dig at Nora. 'In fact, aren't we closer to the water here than we would be on the beach?' he asked, looking to her and Sydney for support.

Avery should have known it would be like this. Archie, Sydney and Hugo were, when they got together, either the absolute best people in the world . . . or the worst. Separately they were a lot more— Well, actually, they were a lot *less*. Dialled down and much more manageable. But together they could spin wildly out of control. And that was either the most fun you'd ever had, or your worst nightmare. Being with them was like walking on a tightrope, fearing which side of the line they'd fall.

'Where is she anyway?' Archie asked, wiping the water from his face.

'On the phone to her mum,' Avery said, frustrated that Hugo was being difficult.

'And we're here because when she's done, she *can* join us,' Sydney pointed out.

Avery smiled, thankful – if not a little surprised – to at least have Sydney's support. Sydney reached down for her water bottle, saluted Avery and took a mouthful, Avery belatedly realising that she hadn't been drinking.

'How did you two meet?' Archie asked, as if it were almost inconceivable that they'd be friends.

'She's my college roommate,' Avery explained, thinking that he knew that already.

'And that gets her an invitation to the island?' he asked, surprised.

'She's my *friend*, Archie,' Avery said, getting a bit tired of constantly having to defend either herself or Nora.

'Yeah, that or she's got something on you.'

Avery swallowed.

'Oh my god, she has! Good Little Avery Finch has a secret,' Archie accused.

'Back off, Archie,' Hugo said, his tone light but still a warning.

Archie shrugged it off and ducked beneath the waterline.

'You OK?' Hugo asked, turning to Avery, and she wished it didn't irritate her. Wished it didn't make her feel guilty. Because she knew he wanted to talk to her. But there was nothing more for her to say.

Except the truth.

That he'd made her feel like a trophy instead of a person.

'Yeah, fine.' Avery dismissed his concern, feeling the weight of Sydney's gaze, until it shifted to something over her shoulder. Turning to look behind her, Avery saw Nora coming their way with a drink in one hand and her phone in the other, waving happily.

'Hi, guys,' she called out.

'Hi, Nora,' they all called back unenthusiastically, and Avery hoped Nora hadn't heard any of their conversation.

HUGO

Christ, Hugo wished Nora would just *leave*. Acting like she hadn't just overheard their conversation about her. He'd seen her standing there on the path a little way back, pretending to check her phone, so he knew damn well she'd heard at least some of it.

He looked away from her and out to sea, not seeing the beauty of the island any more. He hated that Avery couldn't, *wouldn't*, talk to him. Hated that things were so different to last year.

'Dude, get in and swim it off,' Archie said for his ears alone. 'She's never gonna change her mind if you keep scowling like that. It ruins the pretty.' He waved a hand in front of Hugo's face.

Hugo laughed. Archie was right. He sighed and slipped into the pool easily, relishing the touch of the cool water against his hot skin. They just needed to have some fun. Because so far there had been very little of it.

Avery and Nora had been doing spa shit for the last couple of days, Leo had been working – *weird* – so it had just been him and the twins. They needed to spend more time together. He breaststroked over to the far end of the pool. It wasn't that far, not like the Olympic-sized pool at the Big House, but it was far enough for the buzz of irritation at Nora to dull a little.

'So, *you're* Hugo,' he remembered her saying when he'd met her for the first time. Hugo had travelled across the USA to visit them for a long weekend in California, and from almost the first moment they'd met things had been *off*. There was judgement in her gaze and disdain in her tone and he'd liked neither. And when Avery had gone to get them drinks, Nora hadn't said a single thing to him. And when he'd tried to speak to her, she'd pulled her phone out and tapped away until Avery returned, then behaved as if nothing had happened.

Which it hadn't, but . . .

She'd completely ignored him and then acted like she hadn't. And it wasn't just the once either. It had been the entire visit. And Avery hadn't seen any of it. He turned around to face the island, his arms stretched out across the invisible poolside, feeling the stretch of muscles across his back. His island. His domain.

And still he was tense. But it wasn't just Avery and Nora.

'How's art school, Archie?' Avery asked, taking a drink.

'Yeah, pretty cool. It's awesome not being carded anywhere.

And Camberwell is a bit like Brooklyn, but I'm staying just by the river in Tower Bridge.'

'Oh my god, have you seen it go up and down yet?' Nora asked. 'I've always wanted to see that.'

Feeling the touch of Avery's gaze, Hugo resisted the urge to roll his eyes, and instead swam over to join them.

'Not yet. Apparently, it doesn't actually happen that often.'

'Have you met up with Leo?' Avery asked.

'No,' Archie said, shrugging easily. 'Not yet. No time.'

'Is it strange living so far away from your family?' Nora asked.

'Are you kidding? I love it!' he cried, slapping the water for punctuation. 'I can do whatever I want, and the night life in London is epic.'

'You don't miss him at all, do you?' Nora asked Sydney.

'Nope,' she replied with a pop of her lips.

'What are you studying in London? Tech? Following your dad's footsteps?' Nora pressed.

'God, no. I'm doing art. *Syd's* the one that will take over from Dad.'

It had taken Archie ages to get his father to take his interest in art seriously. Hugo remembered how rough things had been for a while, the snide comments and the back chat that had caused tension over shared meals. But clearly distance, and perhaps even Archie's perseverance, had worked in their favour.

'Really?' Nora turned her full attention on to Sydney, which she would absolutely hate, Hugo thought with no small amount of glee. 'Where are you at?'

'Caltech.'

'Oh, not that far from us at UC Berkeley? Why haven't we—'

'She starts in the fall,' Archie teased.

'Why *did* you take a year off?' Avery asked frowning.

Sydney had been insufferable last summer, Hugo remembered now. She'd been all, *Caltech* this and *Caltech* that.

'To travel around Europe, obviously,' Nora said, grinning, no one in the group sure whether she was taking the mick or not.

'How do you know that?' Sydney asked, peering over the top of her glasses in surprise.

Nora shrugged. 'Your Insta account. You've posted so many pictures of the places I've always wanted to see. That café in Montepulciano looked a-mazing.'

'The coffee there was sooo gooood,' Sydney replied, relaxing back against her lounger as Hugo pulled himself out of the pool, water dripping off him as he grabbed his towel. He knew it was petty, but he didn't want Sydney and Nora to get on. He didn't want *anyone* to get on with her.

He unwrapped the towel and immediately regretted it. *Go Crimson* appeared as the lacrosse team towel unrolled, printed in golden yellow across the burgundy. It was just another thing he had to crawl back from the last godawful six months. He'd been kicked out after an altercation with another teammate. The last in a string of warnings from the coach.

But he'd get back on it. Just like he'd get Avery back.

'So where were you before that?' Nora asked innocently. *Too* innocently to Hugo's ears.

'What do you mean?' Syd replied.

'Before Italy. You got there in spring, so what were you doing before Christmas?'

Archie looked uncomfortably towards his sister, the move

snagging Hugo's attention. The tension in the air suddenly whipped up out of nowhere.

Sydney looked blankly at Nora.

Avery went to say something when Sydney finally said, 'Rehab. I was ...' She trailed off, then took a deep breath, preparing to dive right in. 'It was decided that I should spend some time really thinking about myself and what I wanted to do with my life.'

The words sounded parroted, as if she was repeating something one of her parents had said.

He knew that they all drank and partied hard, but even so.

'*Rehab?*' Nora asked.

'There may or may not have been an incident involving a little too much alcohol and the Lavender Ladies,' Sydney replied tightly. It must have been an utter car crash to get her in so much trouble.

Archie barked a laugh. '*May* have?'

Sydney sat forward on the lounger, pulling off her sunglasses and shrugged elegantly. 'It is *not* my fault they couldn't take a joke.'

'Well, *I* thought it was funny,' Archie replied.

'OK,' Sydney said as if willing to concede. 'So, I may have made a tiny scene over lunch with the Lavender Ladies—'

'Who are the Lavender Ladies?' Nora asked, on the edge of her seat, fascinated by Sydney's story.

'Oh, you know,' Sydney dismissed with a wave of her hand. 'Just the local Daughters of the American Revolution type, who probably didn't quite enjoy my very strong feelings on their more conservative leanings.'

'No, it wasn't that,' Archie said. 'I *think* it was the fact that you called them all a bunch of old dried-up terfs who probably hadn't had sex since the previous century.'

Sydney winced. 'In my defence, it is at least true.'

Archie howled with laughter. 'You should have seen Mother's face.'

'Oh my god, she looked like she was going to have a coronary.'

'How can you even remember? You were *so* drunk,' Archie accused.

'I was a *little* drunk,' Sydney admitted.

'Soooo. Drunk,' Archie repeated.

Sydney shrugged again. 'Anyway, I did a *little* time in a rehab centre in Europe and decided that, since I'd missed the start of college, I'd defer for a year and do some travelling instead.'

Everyone around the pool was staring at her wide-eyed.

'Guys, it was fine. And I mean, seriously, look at my skin,' she commanded. 'No alcohol, and my face looks nearly ten years younger!'

'What did your dad say?' Nora asked after a moment.

Sydney gave her a funny look. 'What does that have to do with anything?' she asked Nora.

'Nothing,' Nora replied.

'But, Syd, are you—' Avery started to ask.

Hugo was pretty sure Avery had been about to ask if she was OK, but Sydney cut her off.

'Guys. Seriously, it was nothing. Mother overreacted, and it was only for three months. And, god, was it worth it. Yoga, therapy, gorgeous food, the centre was *divine*.' Sydney made a chef's kiss with her hands and the others all laughed except for Nora, whose smile didn't reach her eyes.

'And what about you, Nora?' Sydney asked, managing to turn the piercing heat of everyone's attention back on her. 'What's *your* deal?'

'Not much to tell, really,' Nora said with a shrug, squinting up into the sun. 'Mum raised me on her own in Brooklyn, holding down a couple of jobs at the same time. I worked hard enough to get a scholarship to college, and luckily ended up rooming with Avery.' Nora bumped shoulders with her where they shared the lounger. If Nora noticed Sydney bristle, she pretended not to, Hugo thought.

'Your dad?' Archie asked.

'Died when I was four,' Nora said with another shrug.

'Damn. Sorry,' Archie said sincerely.

Even Sydney backed away from being a bitch about it. 'Yeah, sorry about that.'

Avery reached out and placed a hand on Nora's thigh. Nora leaned into her side. 'It's OK. I was young. We're good, though, me and Mum.'

Eyes bright. Smile fixed. Sounded like a company line. And Hugo would know.

'What are you studying?' Archie asked.

'English.'

Hugo frowned. He'd thought she was studying journalism. It wasn't a huge difference, but he was pretty sure that Nora knew they'd be less comfortable around her if she'd said as much.

'That's cool. I like English,' Archie said, bobbing his head, missing the way Sydney was staring at him.

'*WTF?*' she mouthed, distracting Hugo, who couldn't help but grin. This was Archie in flirt mode and Sydney was going to hate every single minute of it. Of course, knowing Archie, it was probably more to tease his sister than because of any attraction to Nora.

Oh, he could get in on this. Annoying Sydney was an Olympic sport and one that was more a marathon than a sprint.

But the problem was, Sydney could get mean when she was pissed. They needed to get away from their parents. Off the island for a bit.

'Hey, why don't we go back to that club on the mainland?' he asked.

'The one from last year? That was so much fun!' Avery said with an eagerness that seemed a little overly bright.

'Yeah. That's the one,' Hugo replied.

'Nice,' Archie said, grin spreading.

'Cool. I'll let Leo know,' Hugo said, hoping that he'd take the olive branch after the cock-up at the welcome dinner.

Sydney nodded once, as much of an acknowledgement as they'd probably get. And if he was lucky, he might actually be able to get Avery alone. And then he could try to convince her just how wrong she was to break things off with him.

CHAPTER FIVE
AVERY

'I mean, rehab. Really? Was Sydney's drinking really that bad?' Nora asked in their en suite, sweeping her hair over her shoulder and passing the mascara wand over her eyelashes.

Avery tapped her finger against her thigh.

'I mean, kind of?' Avery admitted. She felt terrible. She'd had no idea things had got that bad. Syd hadn't reached out once. And then, after not hearing from her for three months, Avery hadn't reached out either.

'I'm just surprised it didn't make the news, that's all. I can't imagine how much money Dennis must have paid to keep *that* quiet.'

'Nora,' Avery warned.

'What? I'm just saying. It's weird that they're all so disconnected from each other. I mean, her dad not saying *anything* about her going into rehab? My mum would have said A. Lot.'

'I feel awful,' Avery confessed, playing with the little white cubes on the friendship bracelet she'd kept with the rest of her unworn jewellery. The colour of the letters was the only difference between the matching bracelets. There hadn't been an argument over who had which one when they'd bought them, even if she *had* wanted the pink one. Syd had decided that Avery would have the blue. But she felt childish having not worn it now, as if they were back in school and she'd sulked because her friend hadn't talked to her.

Nora put down her mascara and swept an arm around Avery's shoulders.

'Aves, no. That's not on you. You didn't know,' she said.

'But I *should* have,' Avery insisted. 'Maybe I should have asked. Messaged or something?'

'You'd just started college, your mum was being so difficult, remember? Hugo wasn't exactly a barrel of laughs.' Nora ticked the list off her fingers. '*And* you were thinking about switching majors. You had *so* much going on.' The comfort Nora offered was something Avery desperately wanted to take. 'Besides, it sounds like she's fine? I mean, surely the Devereuxs wouldn't have sent her somewhere *awful*. It was probably full of hot yoga instructors, masseurs and food prepped by a Michelin-star chef. Actually,' Nora said, cocking her head to one side, 'do you think they'd send me there if I cause a scene? I could do with three months of being looked after.'

Avery laughed, because she knew that was what Nora had wanted, but it didn't really lighten the feeling of guilt pressing on her chest. She should have known. Sydney had been her best friend.

'You don't think she's downplaying it?' Avery asked.

Nora shrugged. 'You know her better than I do. Is she the type to downplay things?'

Avery huffed out a laugh. 'No.' Syd had never downplayed anything in her life.

'There we go then.' Nora returned to the bathroom mirror to put on a fourth layer of mascara. She caught Avery's eye in the reflection. 'Want me to tie that for you?' She pointed to the friendship bracelet Avery was still running through her fingers.

Did she?

Avery shook her head. It would be too obvious to wear it now. And it was exactly the kind of thing that Syd would notice.

'I'm sorry,' Avery said, thinking back to that afternoon. 'About earlier. About all the questions about you. If it made you feel uncomfortable.'

Nora bobbled her head, shaking off the apology. 'S'fine.'

'It's not, though.'

'Aves, it's fine. One day, all this,' Nora said with a sweep of her hand, 'it'll be *mine*. Not given or borrowed. I'll have earned it by being the best journalist the world has ever seen. I'll have my own talk show, my own island, my own broadcasting company. And it won't matter where I came from, because no one will remember,' Nora finished with defiance and determination, and Avery knew that if will alone would get her there, Nora would make it happen.

God, she wished she had even half the conviction that Nora had. When Avery thought about her future, she didn't see anything. She'd never been able to tell her parents that she didn't want to take over the family business. She wasn't like Sydney. She wouldn't last three seconds in that world. She just didn't know what she *did* want to do.

And then Nora winked at her in the mirror, bringing her back from her thoughts. The powerful dark sweep of liner across Nora's eyes made her look sexy and daring. If Avery tried that, she'd look like a panda. It was one of the downsides of being friends with Nora Miller. It left Avery feeling just a little *less* somehow. Less pretty, less clever, less quick, less *sexy*.

Avery hadn't missed the way that Archie had totally been checking Nora out at the pool. What had also been blatantly obvious was the tension between Nora and Hugo. She knew that Hugo didn't like Nora and she was pretty sure the feeling was mutual but whenever she'd asked Nora about it, she'd always shrugged and said, *I don't know what you mean. He's great.*

The other problem with being friends with Nora was that Avery couldn't tell when she was lying. She'd seen her lie to a waiter about not bringing her a glass of wine that she'd literally just downed and hid beneath the table so well that he'd apologised profusely and taken it off the bill. If Nora said the sky was green, the sky was green. Which was why, although Nora had promised never to say anything about Avery cheating on her midterms . . . she couldn't ever be one hundred per cent sure.

'Oh, hey. *Now* can I borrow that dress?' Nora asked, a wicked glint in her eye.

Avery smiled. 'Of course,' she said, knowing that she'd lost the dress to Nora forever. Which was OK. It would only really ever hang in her closet, never being worn. And Nora would look amazing in it.

She mentally scanned the rest of the clothes she'd bought with her. All familiar. All things she'd worn loads of times. Things that Good Little Avery Finch would wear, she thought, remembering the way that Archie had called her by her old nickname.

This summer was supposed to be about fun. She *wanted* to go to the club. She wanted to dance with her friends. She wanted to look pretty and *sexy*, like Nora.

But when she thought of actually doing it, she recoiled. Her mother's voice loud in her ears, Hugo's silent disapproval. He'd never really liked her dressing up, saying that she looked so much better when she looked *natural*. In the end, she chickened out and decided on a long-sleeved shirt with a deep V neckline.

Nora emerged from the bathroom, finally happy with her make-up and Avery followed her out into the bedroom, still clutching the friendship bracelet.

'What are you going to wear?' Nora asked. 'Let me guess, those denim shorts,' she said, pointing to the ones Avery was wearing, 'and a long-sleeved top?'

The look on her face must have said everything because Nora laughed.

'Oh, Aves. You've got to stop dressing in the clothes other people want you to wear.'

'That's not what I'm doing,' Avery lied.

It was totally what she'd been doing.

'That's it! I'm not going to allow you to dress like a nun any longer,' Nora announced, pushing Avery gently on to the bed. She opened her mouth to complain but Nora cut her off. 'It's time to unleash your sexy self for the world to see.'

Avery let out a laugh. 'My sexy self?' she repeated.

'She's in there somewhere. Hold on, if you listen closely you can hear her.'

Nora stopped, a finger to her lips, and they listened to the silence, until Nora whisper-yelled, 'Help, let me out, I wanna be sexy,' in a high-pitched, very un-Avery voice.

Avery laughed. 'Nuns don't dress like this, you know.'

'They do in Brooklyn.'

'Kinda feel like that might be sacrilegious.'

'You don't mess with a nun from Brooklyn,' Nora said, crossing herself and offering up a Hail Mary, before throwing a dress at Avery that she'd pulled from her own bag. 'Do us all a favour and change into that.'

Avery dropped the friendship bracelet in order to catch the dress and slipped into the bathroom to change, a smile on her face as she laughed at what Nora had said. Maybe Nora was right. Maybe it was time to dress the way she wanted, to *be* the way she wanted. Avery pulled the dress on.

Ruched on one side and a hell of a lot shorter than she was expecting, Avery looked in the mirror and felt . . . a burst of giddy excitement. She looked *OK*. Good, even. The clingy material was black with a zillion gold dots, making it shimmer whenever she moved, her tan glowing. It still had long sleeves, and a dramatic V neckline, but it pressed against her body in a way that made her feel protected.

'Niiiiiiiccceee,' Nora whistled from the doorway, nodding to herself. 'Yup,' she pointed at Avery. 'That's the one,' she said, before disappearing back into the main room.

'The one, what?'

'The one that will have their tongues hanging out of their mouths. You have an ass, Avery. You should use it!' she called from the bedroom.

Avery felt the boost of confidence zap into her veins. This was the other part of Nora. The one that made you feel special, and fabulous and high with happy.

She looked at herself in the mirror and liked what she saw.

Would he?

Leo had got the night off and was joining them. Leo, who had only ever seen her on the island, and certainly not like this. And just the thought of it made her pulse skitter. He'd been working ever since they arrived and she'd not seen him since the first night.

'Hair down or up?' Avery asked.

'Down,' Nora commanded. 'Swap.' Nora pushed past Avery into the bathroom as Avery came out into the bedroom, crossing over to her jewellery box and picking up some dangly gold earrings that would be fabulous with the dress. Maybe she could actually be a little freer this evening. Leo's rich amber gaze filled her mind again and she bit her lip, remembering the way that it had sparked two years ago, the night that they'd watched the sun rise together. The night she'd thought that maybe—

'I have the shoes to go with the dress too,' Nora said, calling through from the bathroom.

'Great.'

Shaking off her thoughts, Avery went over to Nora's bag and, without thinking, dug in between a few T-shirts, a bag of toiletries, some more make-up. Her fingers brushed against a book, which she pulled out without thinking.

It was a book on Dennis. An unauthorised biography from a few years ago. Weird.

'It's rude to go through someone's things.' Nora's voice was sharp as a knife and cut to the bone.

'Nora!' Avery exclaimed, thinking she was joking. *Surely* she was joking. But the laughter died on her lips when she saw Nora's expression.

'No. It's not OK, Avery. Leave my things alone,' she said, snatching the book out of Avery's hands and throwing it into the suitcase.

'But the shoes . . .' Avery tried to explain.

'*I'll* get them.'

It was such a hot and cold reaction. Avery shivered, feeling like she'd done something wrong.

'Nora, really, I'm sorry,' she insisted.

And just like that, Nora switched back to how she'd been moments earlier. 'It's OK, Aves,' she said with a smile and a shrug. 'Just don't do it again.'

Avery felt so bad that she didn't even think about how many times Nora had gone into her wardrobe or bag and just taken what she'd wanted; didn't think how unusual it was for Nora to be so territorial about her *own* things.

Nora kicked her bag back to the side. 'Anywaaays,' she said, sitting down on the bed to put on her shoes, 'we're going to have fun tonight, Avery Finch.' She threaded the buckle on the last shoe and declared, '*Fun!*'

She grabbed Avery in a bear hug and squeezed until they both laughed, making Avery forget about the book.

Pushing Avery to sit on the bed, Nora played Prince Charming and put her shoes on Avery's feet. They then checked themselves in the mirror one last time and headed to the door.

'One sec,' Avery said, running back to the bathroom to grab her phone. She scanned the vanity for her friendship bracelet, but couldn't see it.

'You coming?' Nora called out.

'Yup,' Avery said, already forgetting the bracelet as they headed out to meet the group at the jetty.

HUGO

Hugo checked his watch. Of course the girls were late. Impatience grew in him as the jetty bobbed on the tide, the birds screamed in the air and Archie, complaining that they were going to be late, kicked his foot against the bow of the boat.

Leo came towards them from the staff paths wearing sunglasses, a dark-navy shirt and a pair of jeans. Hugo nodded, glad he'd agreed to come and still feeling crap about the welcome dinner.

He held out his hand as Leo approached. Leo shook it, accepting the silent apology Hugo offered, and hopped on to the speedboat where Archie greeted him with a fist bump and a slap on the back. Hugo remained on the jetty, his gaze hugging the path which the girls should be coming from.

'Come grab a beer, dude. They'll get here when they get here,' Archie yelled, tossing a bottle over to Leo, who took a seat beside the driver, and stretched out to shake his hand.

'Thanks for the ride,' he heard Leo say to the guy, which grated on Hugo a little. The idea that Leo knew the staff member, connected them together, made it harder somehow. More awkward.

But that thought stopped in its tracks the moment he caught sight of the girls.

Archie let out a low whistle and he thought he heard Leo curse.

They all looked great, but Hugo only had eyes for Avery. She'd not worn *anything* like that when they'd been dating. He saw . . . too much. Too much skin, too much of everything. The dress clung to Avery and made her look older, made her look *different*. His pulse raced with anger and discomfort, irritation scratching his skin as Sydney applauded and Nora curtsied, Archie howled and Leo whistled. Hugo gritted his teeth and forced a smile to welcome them aboard the speedboat, firmly keeping his gaze at eye level and his scowl to himself.

Barely an hour later and they were being ushered through to the VIP section of the full club on the mainland by a bouncer who had greeted Hugo by name. As they arrived at their table, a bottle of champagne was delivered to them and the owner came to pour it. A small part of Hugo was satisfied by the awed look in Nora's eyes as she gazed around the club, which was, even he had to admit, impressive.

Spread over three floors, half of the club was inside, beneath a rooftop terrace – where they were currently – and the other half extended out over the sea. A DJ he recognised from a headline set in Ibiza was slowly turning up the heat on the decks.

Sydney pouted and told the waitress she wanted a mocktail

and Leo asked for a beer. Nora passed Avery a glass before he could, blanking him in a way that made him want to growl. Because it wasn't an accident. It took *work* to ignore someone that well. He would know. He'd been trying to do it with his dad for months. So he *knew* what she was doing. Just not *why*. She certainly didn't seem to have the same problem with Archie or Leo. And even though Sydney was giving her a bit of a hard time every now and then, Nora wasn't ignoring *her*.

Archie was looking at Nora like she was his next meal, not seeming in the slightest bit put off by the way she shifted away. Avery saw and frowned, before turning to say something to Syd, who shrugged and turned back to the club.

Leo was scoping out the rest of the club and would probably disappear sooner or later. He'd be back before they left, but he'd find some girl for a while. At least, that's what he'd done last year. Not that Hugo had really noticed. He'd been too busy with Avery, until Archie had got so drunk they'd had to take him home before the bouncer threw them out. He'd spent the entire boat ride back to the island throwing up.

'Bye, bitches,' Sydney called, downing the last of her mocktail and weaving between people to get to the dance floor. The fixed look in her eyes warned that she was on a mission. Hugo swallowed the last mouthful of champagne irritably. They weren't supposed to be splitting up. They were all supposed to be having fun together. Then maybe Hugo would have a chance at winning Avery back.

'Can I get you something else, sir?' a waitress asked.

'No,' he dismissed, his eyes tracking Avery's movements, missing the way his curt words sent the waitress scurrying. Avery was heading towards the outdoor area and he was halfway out to join her, when Nora bounded over to Avery and pulled on her arm, saying something he couldn't hear that made Avery laugh. He backtracked, frustrated, realising that now wasn't the time.

He felt Leo's gaze on him, but he just shrugged and took a sip of his beer, leaning back in the seat, his eyes on the crowd, as if Leo hadn't just seen the sheer awkwardness of it all.

Archie muscled over, slinging one arm around Hugo's shoulder.

'You know what this night needs?'

'Shots,' Hugo replied with a grin that was more a grimace.

'Shots!' Archie yelled at the top of his voice bringing Leo and all the girls back to the table. A bottle of sambuca appeared with a tray of glasses and Archie grabbed the bottle and poured.

Hugo downed the shot and just for a moment the sweet sticky taste of the alcohol reminded him of *before*. Before Avery. Before his dad. Before college. When everything had been amazing, when the future looked like it was blessed and he'd thought he was the luckiest guy alive.

He'd had it all planned out. Summers on the island, his degree in government, perfect girlfriend on his arm, captain of the lacrosse team. After graduating, he'd go to work at his dads' company, then start working in local government, get married and then at thirty he'd apply for the senate. He'd have the connections, the power and the money. Things no one could take away from him. Ever.

Hugo grabbed another shot as his eyes grazed over Avery, vaguely registering a whoop from Archie, and as he swallowed he let the beat of the music roll over his skin and pull the darkness away. Just for a moment. The song merged hypnotically into another, rolling beats and harmonies until Sydney recognised the next track and practically screamed, pulling them all on to the dance floor.

She wove them through the dancers and found a spot in the middle, managing to evict anyone from where she wanted to be. She was good at that. When Syd was on a mission, no one messed with her.

Nora started dancing with Avery. Close. And it was attracting a *lot* of attention. Sydney was doing her best to ignore it, Archie was doing his best to get in on it and Leo was standing just a little way off to the side – but Hugo barely noticed because he only had eyes for Avery.

Nora spun Avery round so that Avery's ass was in her lap, her hands on her waist. Nora whispered something in Avery's ears, making her head fall back and *Christ* . . . This was ridiculous. It was just asking for trouble. They were making a scene and it should stop. They'd had their fun.

Avery put her hands in her long dark hair, lifting it off her neck and letting it fall and someone shouted 'more', goading them on. Hugo shook his head. This had to stop. She needed to go back to being Avery. *His* Avery. Because then everything would go back to normal. He could handle his dad being a bastard if he had her back. He could maybe even get back on the team at college. He just needed . . .

'Avery!' Sydney yelled across the floor.

Hugo watched as Sydney beckoned Avery over. The flicker of Avery's gaze to him was enough to have him following, worried about what kind of trouble they'd get into. They stopped a little deeper into the dance floor, the press of people more insistent, urging him closer to where the girls were dancing.

Avery had her back to him and a break in the crowd allowed him to get a little closer. It – this – was all too much. He had to get her out of here. Had to talk to her. She'd become his anchor and she didn't even know it. She didn't know how much she meant to him. And he needed to tell her.

He reached out to pull at her arm but she flinched and shifted away from him.

Hugo frowned. Why was she behaving like that?

'Avery,' he called.

She pretended she hadn't heard him.

'Avery, please,' he said, reaching out for her shoulder.

Nora appeared out of nowhere, placing herself in between him and Avery, shaking her head like he'd done something wrong.

'Avery!' he shouted angrily, but she still ignored him.

'Lighten up, dude,' Nora told him.

Shame and fury poured into him like an avalanche.

'Piss off, Nora,' he yelled, leaning over her.

'Back. Off,' she hissed in warning.

Archie pulled him back and Leo was suddenly between him and Avery.

What the hell? All he was trying to do was make sure some guy didn't crash into her. And they were all looking at him like *he* was the problem?

'Take a beat, man,' Archie said in his ear.

Screw this. He shrugged Archie off and walked away, past

the bar and the VIP section, following a corridor until he found the toilets. He flung open the door, startling some guy at the urinal.

'Get out,' Hugo ordered.

'What—'

'Get the hell out!'

The guy zipped up his trousers and raised his hands before rushing out.

Hugo made sure the cubicles were empty before he slammed one of the doors.

Shit.

He slammed it again and when that didn't help, he punched a dent in it, the cracking of the wood enough of a release to clear his head.

Shit.

And there it was. The nausea he knew would come. The acid burn in his throat. The roil of his gut and he only just made it to the sink in time.

CHAPTER SIX
LEO

Leo's pulse raced as he watched Hugo storm off to the bathrooms, taking only some of the tension he'd created with him. The way that Hugo had looked at Avery made him instinctively stand between them. Leo might not have understood what he saw in Hugo's gaze, but he hadn't liked it one bit.

Leo didn't remember ever seeing him like this. Last year Hugo had been in a near state of bliss, glued to Avery's side. And now? It was as if he were a wildfire, switching with the wind and ready to take down anything in his path.

Leo wondered if something more was going on – beyond breaking up with Avery – but he knew that Hugo, who had always been closed off to a point, was unlikely to say anything. Certainly not now that Leo was working for his dads.

The reminder put another brick in the wall between him and them.

Leo had been touched when Hugo had reached out to him to invite him tonight. Touched enough to want to join them. To want it to be like before. But it wasn't. Not really. The only thing this evening was reaffirming was that it would never be like that again.

He kicked the floor. It wasn't really their fault. They weren't doing anything wrong or different. The change was in him. In how he now saw things. His father had – intentionally or otherwise – fully ripped the scales away from his eyes and all he was left with was a yawning gap between what he'd had and what he could look forward to.

So maybe rather than fighting it, he should accept it. Face it as his last summer on the island and give in. Have some fun while he could.

He took a sip of his beer and watched his friends dancing to the music – Sydney's grace as she twisted herself around some guy, Archie trying to dance up on Nora, who was tolerating him at best. He'd seen her the day before, on her own heading down to the beach, and wondered if she felt like he did. Like he was on the wrong side of an invisible line between himself and the others.

She turned and caught his gaze on her, threw him a smile and then rolled her eyes when Archie tried to slip an arm around her waist, which she artfully twisted away from. His friend's obliviousness made him laugh, and that's when Avery's gaze lifted to his.

He'd always felt sparks when she looked at him. But now, he felt the smile slowly disappear from his lips. He saw the uncertainty in her eyes, the hurt that Hugo had put there. And despite the anger he felt twisting his gut, that Hugo had done that to her, he offered her a reassuring smile. The corners of her lips lifted, and he felt it like a punch to the chest.

He drifted closer to her as she turned to make room for him where they were all dancing. Just the closeness of her made his breath hitch.

That *dress*.

He'd nearly choked when he'd first seen her coming towards the speedboat with Nora. He'd never seen her looking like that before and she looked . . . amazing. Her skin glowed against the coppery shimmer of the material that clung to her skin.

Avery had always been beautiful. That she hadn't seemed to realise it herself had always been a mystery to him. But tonight? Tonight, she looked . . . sexy. Powerful. Standing just a foot below his height, he'd thought that she might just be perfect. She'd been enjoying herself and that had been a damn delight, until Hugo had gone and ruined it.

Leo's breath stuttered in his chest as she shifted closer and closer towards him, her long dark hair falling in waves down her back, an accidental graze of her hip against him, the back of her hand against his. He watched, unable to look away, as she swayed in time with the deep base line, his body unconsciously moving in time with hers, barely an inch away from each other.

And just like that, he was back on the beach again, two years ago. The air had been warm, the stars bright and all the others had passed out on the blankets and chairs around them. But not Avery. She'd been stubborn all the way into the morning.

Leo shook his head trying to dislodge the memory, but he couldn't. It had taken hold.

I want to see the sunrise.

And he'd been utterly helpless to refuse. So he'd sat there, arm-to-arm with her, thigh-to-thigh. She'd asked him questions. About his life. About what he wanted to do. About what he cared about. She'd been interested. And he'd been *fascinated*. Sunk. Hook, line and sinker.

What had been friendship turned molten under the desire he'd suddenly felt for her. But he'd been unable and unwilling to risk what he'd just found. Because for the first time since he'd been coming to the island, Avery Finch had made him feel like he belonged. Not a hanger-on, not just someone to laugh at their jokes or agree with their wide, sweeping statements.

And it had been too precious for him to risk for a drunken kiss. So, he'd sucked it up, pushed down everything he'd wanted, everything he thought she *might* have been offering.

And when she'd came back the year after on Hugo's arm, he'd told himself he'd done the right thing. But after what had just happened, he wasn't so sure.

Avery lifted the long chestnut strands of hair from her neck, and he saw the damp tendrils curling from the sheen of sweat across her skin.

'Bro!'

A near violent slap on the back knocked him to one side, and Leo turned to find Nick Dawson, drink in hand, staring at him with a grin. A small circle of groupies stood just behind him, all staring at the one-time tennis champion with big doe eyes. Nick flashed him a cheesy grin, the club lights picking out his startling white teeth. Leo didn't even bother to resist the urge to roll his eyes.

'When did you get here?' Leo asked with a laugh, forcing his thoughts back to the present.

'I came over earlier,' he said, turning his back to the line of pouting women behind him. 'I was planning to head back, but maybe I'll stick around with you guys instead.' Nick's eyes flickered between Avery and Nora. 'Are they spoken for?' Nick shouted over the music, apparently uncaring if they heard him.

'Which one?'

'Either? Both?' he said with a shrug. 'They looked pretty good when they were dancing earlier.'

Leo gritted his teeth so hard, he nearly broke one.

Nick just laughed. 'No, but seriously. The Finch girl, she's not with Hugo any more, right?'

'No, she is not,' Leo bit out.

'You got dibs?'

'She's not a damn toy, Nick,' he spat.

'So, she's free then,' he said, nodding to himself, an eager grin on his features and ignoring Leo's reprimand with another laugh. 'You need to get laid, my friend. Come on,' he said, slapping Leo on the back again and pushing into the middle of the circle where Avery, Nora and Sydney had been dancing.

Nick was greeted like a long-lost friend. Especially when he grabbed a passing waitress and ordered a bottle of whiskey, because clearly more alcohol was what everyone needed.

By the time the shots were poured, Hugo had returned from the bathroom, seemingly calmer, but not enough to convince Leo that he was completely over whatever had crawled up his arse. Leo ignored the offer of the whiskey and grabbed another beer.

For a while there was a subtle awkward tension, as if everyone was slotting into new positions in relation to each other, everyone just slightly out of sync, not quite in tune.

Nick moved closer and closer to Avery, who shot Leo one last unreadable look.

Tension pulled across his shoulders as he saw what was about to happen. Yeah, he wanted to be that close to Avery. He wanted to be the one who pulled her back against him, the one who wound his arms around her. But what did he have to offer her? Nothing like what Hugo or Nick could. He bit back a curse. If he was honest with himself, he'd admit that he'd come to the island as much to see her as his dad. But if he'd thought that there'd been a gap between them before, what the hell was there now that he was *working* there?

It was too much. Too far.

And because of it, he stepped back, turning away from where Nick danced, half draped around Avery, frustrated with himself, with Nick, with everything.

The beat was building in the club and in his ears, sinking into his skin and vibrating in his chest, faster and faster.

Out of the corner of his eye, he saw Archie grab Nora's hip, but she twisted away and, instead, pulled some random guy in front of her into an open-mouthed kiss that had people around them whistling and screaming encouragement.

Hugo looked disgusted, but Archie just threw his head back and laughed.

Risking a last glance at Avery, Leo was surprised to find her looking at him. But her expression was unreadable, as if a wall had come down between them. An insurmountable one that he'd never be able to scale.

AVERY

Avery watched Leo turn away and slip into the crowd. She'd given him every opportunity to close the distance between them. She'd wanted *so much* for him to take the unspoken invitation she had given him.

And just like it had been two years ago, it hurt when he didn't take it. She wouldn't, couldn't, put herself out there like that again. She bit down on her lip, unwilling to admit how much that had cost her, and unable to show even a hint of it in this present moment. Nora frowned at her, angling her head at Hugo.

It was far better for Nora to think him the cause of her upset than to turn her attention on to Leo. Avery shrugged and forced a smile to her lips.

Shake it off. You have to shake it off.

She closed her eyes and moved to the music, trying to force herself out of her head. But it wasn't working, her thoughts just kept returning to Leo. When he'd stood in between her and Hugo she'd thought . . . She'd thought that maybe . . .

She opened her eyes to find Nick Dawson barely an inch away from her.

'Hey there, gorgeous,' he said in a smooth Australian drawl.

'Hey there, yourself,' she said, watching his eyes rake from her head to her toes and back again. It was obvious. Blatant. And honestly, right now? It was all she wanted. She was so tired of Hugo making her feel *bad* and Leo making her feel *foolish*. Something told her that Nick wouldn't.

Sydney winked at her and Avery tried not to smile. Nick was hot. Undeniably. That was part of the reason for his reputation. That and the scandals. Just before the accident that ended his last attempt at Wimbledon, he'd been caught by paparazzi leaving a hotel bleary-eyed and bed-headed just after the wife of an English aristocrat. It hadn't been the first time, and unlikely the last.

And despite being Good Little Avery Finch, she wasn't *naive*. She knew he wasn't after anything other than the obvious. But he was looking at her. Seeing *her*. In her dress. And he wanted her. And that meant so much. *Too* much.

For too long, she'd tried to be what other people wanted her to be. The perfect daughter, the perfect girlfriend. And along the way she'd lost little pieces of herself. The girl who'd once loved silly animal videos so much she'd watch them on repeat. The girl who had wanted to be a veterinarian when she grew up.

How and when had she forgotten that?

Avery shook her head from side to side, coming back to the present, steering away from the things she didn't want to face and into the music. Into Nick. Nick and what he wanted, clearly written in his gaze.

She'd thought that Hugo had wanted her. But she wasn't so sure. They'd had fun, they'd flirted and kissed, but she'd never felt that he *wanted* her. And he'd always tried to get her to do things just slightly differently. Laugh a little less loudly, dress a little more conservatively. And she could never shake the feeling that his interest wasn't about *her*. He wasn't seeing *her*. At least, not the way she saw herself.

Nora was like that sometimes. But there were certainly others who didn't see *her*. Like her parents. *Always*.

Avery bit back a curse. She just wanted to be *seen*. It was a soul-wrenching cry from deep within. It was there now, rising, a sob in her chest.

She felt someone stroke her arm.

She opened her eyes to see Syd staring back at her; understanding shimmering in her gaze. Sydney pulled her close, pressing her forehead against Avery's.

'It's gonna be OK,' Syd said, having somehow sensed her desperation.

'Oh god, I'm sorry about the rehab. I didn't know,' Avery said, not realising just how much she'd needed to say it. Ridiculously, she found herself almost on the verge of tears.

'Don't be silly. I could've called and didn't.'

'Was it awful?' Avery dared to ask.

'It was terrible, but don't tell anyone I said that,' Syd warned, the sweet pop of her perfume rising between them. 'Ignore Hugo,' Syd said, pulling back from Avery and the moment. 'He's an asshole, but he'll get over it.'

'And screw your parents,' Avery said with a wobbly smile. 'They're assholes, but they'll get over it.'

Sydney threw her head back and laughed.

Avery felt Nick move closer, pressing his body against her back.

'Can I join in?' he yelled, and Sydney just laughed, but neither she nor Avery pushed him away.

After a while, they moved outdoors, so that they were dancing beneath the stars, bodies pressed tight together, moving to a rhythm that transcended sound and slipped into bones – something primal, something instinctive – and Avery let the emotion pour out from her entire being.

She tugged Nick closer with a hand around his neck. Nora and Archie came to join them and even Hugo was joining in. Sydney had found some guy and Leo was out there somewhere, but she ignored the thought of him with a ruthlessness that was necessary for her fragile sense of self.

Eventually she didn't need to fake it. Relaxing into the beat of the music, her friends around her, Avery clung on desperately to every single moment of happiness she could get. Time lost meaning. UV lights picked out bright neon colours and someone passed around glow stick bracelets that were both the height of tack, but stunningly beautiful.

And then, Avery just let herself *sink* into a slow-rising euphoria that filled her with an abundance of love for everyone to the point where it spilled over and didn't stop. It just kept coming and coming and coming and it was *marvellous*.

Or was that the song?

Did it matter?

They danced until the sun peeked over the horizon and the last of the music petered out. Sleepy, danced out, stretched, blissed – but most importantly *happy* – they tripped their way down to the marina where the speedboat was waiting for them to take them back to the island.

'Was this what you wanted?' Nora sleepily asked her. Despite the tension of earlier she had one arm slung around Archie, who was so drunk he could barely see straight.

'It was *everything* I wanted,' Avery replied truthfully, holding her shoes to her chest, not even feeling her feet on the rough pavement.

Leo and Hugo were up ahead chatting about something she couldn't hear, Sydney dancing in between them, weaving around them, lost in her own world. *This* was what it had been like before. Everyone happy, everyone together, no one arguing, no one jealous or bitter. If she could just hold on to this, just for a moment longer . . .

They piled on to the boat, as the sun streaked easy pinks and warm golds into the first moments of the dawn. Archie collapsed on to the white canvas seating and promptly passed out. Sydney threw a blanket over him, before tucking herself in beside him. Leo sat on the deck, long legs stretched out in front of him, leaning back against a seat beside Hugo, who had fallen asleep, his head bowed, hands clenched in his lap.

Nora skipped over to where the boat's driver was chatting to Nick, dressed in the same Mokani Island uniform that Leo would be wearing either later that day or tomorrow. And for the first time, Avery wondered what that must be like for him.

What that meant for their friendship. She'd wanted things to go back to how they'd been before, but she realised that was impossible now. Things would never be the same.

She risked a glance at him, only to realise that he was staring at her. And this time neither of them looked away.

CHAPTER SEVEN

LEO

It had been two days since the night out at the club and Leo still couldn't get the way Avery had looked at him on the boat back to the island out of his mind.

The phone rang in the staff centre and his dad answered it. They'd just finished having lunch together. A rare moment of peace between them as he'd helped his father make an easy carbonara for them to share.

If his dad had noticed anything about his knife skills, or the way that Leo had moved around the kitchen, he hadn't said anything. Just before the phone had rung, he'd almost done it. He'd almost told his dad that he hadn't gone to law school like he'd said he would. His mum had supported his decision, knew how difficult the choice had been for him. But telling his dad? That was too much. Too much to risk.

Because how did he tell the man who barely gave him the time of day that he wanted to be a chef? That when he wasn't on the island – when he was back home – he spent almost his entire time in the kitchen, trying new recipes, getting his mum to taste them. Enjoying her delight when something went right, and laughing with her when it went wrong.

How could Leo tell the man who prided himself on having learned at the hands of masters that he had chosen to go to culinary school; something his father laughed at and belittled and berated junior chefs in his kitchen for doing.

But thankfully the phone had rung and he'd been saved from his brief moment of craziness.

'Yes, I'll send him down,' his dad said.

Leo's body tensed. Bracing for what he feared was to come.

'They need you to cover Corrine at the tiki bar.'

'No,' Leo said, already shaking his head before his father had stopped speaking. He regretted it instantly, but that didn't change the fact that he couldn't, *wouldn't*, take a shift down there. His *friends* were there.

'What did you say?' His father's voice had gone the kind of cold that sent shivers down his spine.

'Dad, I can't—'

'You think this is a free ride?' his dad demanded.

'No, sir,' Leo said, biting his tongue.

'You think you're better than everyone else here? Better than me?'

Leo's stomach dropped. Is that what his father thought he thought? About him?

'No, I—'

'Get changed and get down there. Now.'

His dad turned his back on him and Leo knew he'd been dismissed. Angry, frustrated and just a little confused, he slammed the door of the kitchen behind him.

Stalking to the bunk house, Leo entered his small one-bed unit that was identical to the other staff rooms on the island. Well, not Nick Dawson's – he got a larger suite as a perk for giving the occasional lesson to whoever wanted one. He kicked off his trainers and jeans, and within minutes was dressed in the khaki trousers and white shirt worn for guest service. Gut full of the kind of restless energy he disliked, Leo made his way to the poolside bar. Once out of the bunk house, he immediately slowed his pace, aware that while on duty all staff members had to present the 'guests' with their best behaviour.

Leo kept the main part of the buildings to his left, sticking to the staff areas of the island, where the grass was just that little bit drier, the flowers a little less colourful. Here there were rubbish bags piled up – flies already buzzing over whatever feast they might contain – waiting to be taken to the incinerator, which was intentionally as far away from anywhere an unsuspecting guest could get. The maids' buggies – kitted out with everything needed to ensure the villas were picture perfect every single day – were lined up ready to go for whenever the guests left their villas or requested a clean-up.

Leo huffed a laugh. They were so good at getting rid of dirt they could have worked for the government. Or the mob.

He turned the corner towards the pathway that led towards the pool and tennis courts, when he suddenly stopped.

'Listen to me, you little shit, I will have you fired, do you hear me?'

He recognised Dennis Devereux's voice immediately.

Leo risked a peek around the corner.

Mr Devereux, red-faced and growling, had backed Domingo

up against the wall and had him by the neck. It was vicious and ugly. Alarmed, Leo went to intervene, but Domingo caught his eye and shook his head in a clear 'no'.

Dennis, so consumed with anger, didn't even notice.

'Sir, absolutely. I can only apologise.'

'Not just fired, destroyed. You'll never work anywhere again. And when that's done, I'll find your family. Siblings, parents, aunts, uncles. A visa and a green card won't even help you when I'm done. You know what ICE is like. They don't even need an excuse.'

'I understand, sir.'

'It was your mistake. Your screw-up. And I expect it fixed by the time I'm back.'

'Yes, sir.'

'And don't think the Vandenburgs won't hear about this. Because they absolutely will.'

With one last shove, Dennis – skin glowing bright red, sneer across his face and hands in fists – stormed off, without having seen Leo standing there.

'Jesus, Dom, are you—'

'I'm fine,' Dom said, visibly shaken but holding it together.

'But you—'

'I said I was fine, Leo,' he snapped.

'Nothing about that was fine,' Leo said, furious that Dennis thought he could get away with behaving like that. 'He can't treat you like that.'

Dom laughed. 'Are you for real? Do you even know what goes on on this island?'

Leo stared back in shock.

'Listen, you've been working here for *weeks*. And you get special treatment 'cos you're the chef's son and you played with their kids, OK? We get it. You get to come here, earn some money, pretend to slum it with us and pretend to play with them. But you need to get it too, dude. Because this? This was *nothing*,' Dom said, shoving hard into Leo's shoulder as he walked away, leaving Leo reeling.

He'd never seen Dennis behave like that, but then – as Dom kept reminding him – he'd never been on 'this side of the island' before. Not really.

He thought about where he was headed. To the pool. Not to hang with the guys like he had done in the past. But to work. To make drinks for them, while they lounged and laughed and played, without even one iota of the work that went into making them, and keeping them, so blissfully happy.

And when he got to the pool, for the first time he didn't see his friends. He saw the entitled children of the rich guests staying on the island.

Sydney occupied the large square sunlounger on the far side of the pool, sprawled across plush pillows in a cream bikini held by gold hoops that glinted in the midday sun. As he came down the stairs, he watched her wipe her hands on a napkin and just toss it to the floor. The plate of food, half eaten and discarded, had taken his dad nearly forty-five minutes to prepare, the ingredients having been flown in from halfway around the world, and she had barely eaten it. Corrine bent to pick up the napkin off the floor and take away the unfinished meal, and Syd didn't even look up from the magazine she was flicking through.

Nora, sitting at the bar, gave Corrine a grim smile, and Leo knew that Nora got it. Her mum was a waitress. In any other universe, Nora would have been working with them, not being waited on by them. Which was probably why he'd seen her hanging around at the back of the staff centre the other day.

Archie ambled over from the pool to sit beside Nora at the bar, shaking the water from his hair, drenching her. She screamed and tried to push him away, but Archie just laughed and threw an arm around her. The move looked a little unwelcome to Leo.

The thwack of a ball and an energetic grunt drew his attention. Nick Dawson was giving Annalise Finch and Carol Devereux a joint lesson, while Jonathan Finch was fast asleep in a white chair at the side of the court, his head tipped back in a way that would be painful when he woke. But that was the least of his problems from the way that Annalise was backing up into Nick, who had his arms around her showing her a 'better grip'. They were both smiling but when Leo looked at Carol, he shivered from the mean glint in her eye.

Eventually he turned to where Avery sat perched on the edge of her sunbed, shaded by the linen canopy fluttering in the gentle breeze, checking her phone. As Corrine passed, taking away her plate – with the knife and fork neatly paired and the napkin rolled up – he heard her say 'thank you' and offer a smile for Corrine that she seemed to return genuinely. They stopped to have a short conversation, another thwack of the ball making it hard for him to hear.

Then there was Hugo. And while he was wearing sunglasses, the angle of his head couldn't have made it any clearer that Avery was his sole focus. There was something tense about him. Angry. Reminding him of Dennis.

The violence and threat burning the air around him.

Did Syd and Archie know that their father was like that?

Was he like that with them?

Were they *like that?*

He watched them all for a few minutes from the shadows. Nora fending off Archie, whose arm had lingered a little too long. Hugo's jaw locked angrily as he watched a completely clueless Avery.

And he saw it. For the first time he saw what money bought.

Whatever they wanted.

Sick to his stomach, he wished he was anywhere but there.

AVERY

'Yo, Leo,' Archie called from the pool, making Avery turn, shading her eyes as she peered up to where Leo was standing in the shade.

'Look who it is,' Hugo called. 'Come to hang?'

'Not this time,' Leo said, lips in a thin smile. Avery watched him nod to Corrine, who smiled and waved goodbye as Leo went around the bar.

Avery swallowed, trying to ignore the way that her body reacted to seeing him. He looked smart in the staff uniform, but despite that there was always something *more*, just beneath the surface. As if he were wearing it *his* way, in a defiance she found she wanted a little bit for herself.

Her heartbeat fluttered, and her cheeks flushed. She tried to cling to the sting of his rejection of her at the club, but that didn't seem to diminish her ability to observe the way that the white shirt was filled out by muscles that hadn't been there a year before. The way that his features were all clean lines that drew her gaze around his face, his high cheekbones, the scatter of dark freckles across his cheeks and the bridge of his nose.

She swallowed, forcing her gaze away when she felt Hugo's eyes on her. It raised the hairs on the back of her neck and made her feel uncomfortable. Skin that had been hot just a moment ago now flushed with ice, and she shivered despite the heat.

He'd given her a bit of space since the club, but she was beginning to think he was working up to try to approach her again. Instead, she looked at her phone.

She felt stuck out on a little island on her own, the tensions that had been briefly buried by the night at the club already returning to the surface. Sydney was being snippy and short, and Avery couldn't tell how much that had to do with her sobriety or her dislike of the dynamic that Nora created in the group. Archie wasn't getting the hint about Nora *not* being interested, and—

Her chain of thought was broken by an incoming email.

> Change in timetable to next semester's Sustainable Business Model course.

Avery's stomach dropped. She'd been trying not to think about it. Her course, the midterms. God, she'd been so stupid. She'd thought that if she could just pass, just get through to the second year, things would be different. Better.

Which was why, when a guy from the year above had approached her after class a week before the exams, she'd been secretly thrilled. He'd been so laid back about it.

'Heard you were struggling.'

A shrug.

'I've got an in on the exam. It's there if you want it. Just let me know.'

And it had seemed so easy. The solution to everything; to not failing her first year, to not being an embarrassment to her parents, to not making her mother *angry*.

'It's there if you want it.'

And she'd really wanted it.

And then Nora had found her one night, having fallen asleep trying to learn the test paper she'd paid for.

'It's OK, Aves. I won't tell anyone. I understand. You have to do what you have to do, right?'

But it hadn't been right. Good Little Avery Finch wasn't cut out for cheating, and ever since, she'd felt something awful coming for her on the horizon. Something dark.

Sick to her stomach with the thought of being found out, and knowing that she wouldn't have passed without it, the thought of returning to the same studies in September made her truly miserable.

Her mother and Carol's voices cut into her thoughts as they left the tennis court. Her mother seemed totally unaware of how much distance Mrs Devereux seemed to want to put between them. Carol cast a steely glance in Avery's direction and Avery automatically smiled, but Mrs D gave her a cold glare.

Avery watched as her mum turned back to Nick and placed a hand on his arm for too long. She squirmed in embarrassment. Urgh.

Nick flicked a glance to Avery and smiled ruefully, and it made her feel both better and worse at the same time.

Avery flung her phone aside and fell back on to the daybed, squinting up at the cloudless brilliant-blue sky. Clean. Unmarred. She wished she could be like that again. For a moment, she even wished she could go back to being Good Little Avery Finch. When things were easier, when she hadn't dated Hugo, when hangovers weren't a thing, when she hadn't lied and cheated and risked messing up her entire life.

'Aves?'

Nora loomed into her vision, wearing one of Avery's bikinis and a cheeky smile that Avery wanted to trust.

'Drink this. It'll make you feel better,' Nora insisted.

She waved a large glass, full of ice and red liquid and, from the smell, a *lot* of booze.

Avery felt herself smile, and reached for the glass as Nora lay on the sunbed beside her.

'Jeez. These people,' she whispered to Avery. 'They're so rich they have four-poster beds. *Outside*.'

'You know whispering in company is rude,' Sydney sniped from the other side of the pool.

'So's being a bitch,' Nora said under her breath.

Sydney might not have heard, but she got the idea as she glared at Avery like it was her fault and purposefully looked away. Avery wished Nora wouldn't do that. And she wished Sydney wouldn't either.

'Do you think she gets it from her father?' Nora asked Avery as she turned on to her stomach away from the gazes of the Devereux twins.

Avery shrugged, frowning a little, but trying to mask it from her friends. She just wished Nora would leave it alone. She squinted into the sun and watched Archie and Syd goof around on the lounger.

Nora reached out to play with the bracelets on Avery's wrist, as if they were hers.

'He's watching you, you know?'

Nora was talking about Nick. She'd felt his presence ever since her mother and Carol had left the tennis court.

'I know,' she said quietly, a small smile playing at the corner of her mouth. Nick was easy and uncomplicated. And it had been nice. Dancing at the club.

Just then, Archie hurtled towards the pool and cannoned into the water, sending a wide arc of water over Sydney, whose scream of outrage was almost enjoyable. Everyone laughed, while Sydney hurled curses at her brother – even Leo cracked a grin from behind the bar.

'Little Finch,' Nick Dawson said, plopping himself down on the daybed behind them.

Nora's laugh was easy, and she welcomed Nick with a raised eyebrow.

'I think I'll just leave the two you of you to get *reacquainted*,' she said. *Subtle*.

Embarrassment painted Avery's cheeks in a flush.

But Nick just laughed and waved her off.

'And where have you been hiding the last couple of

days?' he asked with a grin as he sat himself down on her daybed.

But actually why *should* she be embarrassed? She wasn't a child any more, she thought defiantly, ignoring the way only moments before she'd been regretting recent life choices.

Avery relaxed into the daybed's mattress and grinned at Nick as he peered down at her over a dark pair of sunglasses.

No, he didn't make her feel the way that Leo did, but at least he was interested in her, right? Nick was hot. Built and easy. No complications, no ulterior motives, no *judgement*. And she wanted the escapism he was offering. She wanted to be free of the guilt and the shame. She wanted to be *fun*.

'I've been right here, all this time. And you didn't come to find me,' she pouted.

He grinned, biting his lip. 'I didn't realise that was the kind of game we were playing.'

'Well, now you do,' she taunted, leaving the ball in his court.

He opened his mouth to speak but Nora's shout cut him off.

'I said *no*, Archie!'

Everyone turned to look as Archie staggered back from where Nora had clearly pushed him.

'Hey, it was just a joke,' Archie said, his hands raised in the air.

'It wasn't funny,' Nora insisted.

'If he said it was a joke, it was a joke, *Nora*,' Sydney said.

'Look, seriously. I meant no offence,' Archie tried.

'You took it too far,' Nora replied.

'You're the one blowing this out of proportion,' Sydney interrupted. 'Just chill. There's no need to make such a scene.'

'Why are you defending him?' Nora demanded. 'I've been telling him for days that I'm not interested.'

'It's OK,' Archie said. 'I've got the message. I really am sorry,' he said, backing away from the two of them.

'Like he'd be that interested in you anyway,' Sydney dismissed.

Nora's eyebrows were practically in her hair. 'Are you *kidding* me?'

'I personally wouldn't touch you with a barge pole, so kidding? Nope,' Sydney replied.

'Hey—' Nora went to reply.

'Syd—' Avery tried to cut in.

'Oh, don't *you* start,' Sydney shot at Avery, making her gut churn and her cheeks burn. 'Go back to flirting with Nick.'

'I think it's time to get back in your box, Ms D,' Nick deflected.

Sydney shrugged, grabbing a drink from her water bottle as Nora picked up her things and walked past Syd.

Avery got up to follow her, but Nora turned, walking backwards and said, 'Don't worry about it, Aves. Stay here, with your *friends*.' She turned on her heel, leaving Avery feeling completely lost.

CHAPTER EIGHT

HUGO

The tension in Hugo's gut unwound as he watched Nora leave, his gaze going to where Archie slunk into the pool and swam a length underwater.

Hugo took another sip of his beer and returned to his phone. He dismissed a weather alert for the area about some storm that would never hit and returned to Nora's profile on Instagram. He wasn't in the least surprised that she was willing to cause a scene and then leave the rest of them to deal with the fallout. Syd was now in full sulk mode and they all knew what that meant. A headache for the rest of them for the next hour at least.

Not that he was going to lose sleep over any tension between Avery and Nora.

He glared at his phone, flicking to Facebook, more and more convinced that Nora was hiding something. It was like a silent alarm, tripped in the back of his mind, that he just couldn't quite pin down. It was something to do with her family.

She had lied about something. He *knew* it. He just needed to find it, and then he could show Avery what a brat Nora really was. It was bad enough that Nora was causing problems in the group. But once he had proof, Avery would realise how she'd been played, and she'd be thankful.

And then she'd maybe – finally – allow him to talk to her properly.

Sydney downed the rest of her water, glaring across the pool to where Avery sat on the sunbed with that tennis player.

Hugo ignored it. It wasn't serious. There was no way that Avery actually *liked* the guy. He was *nothing*.

'You coming in?' Archie asked.

Archie was always trying to distract him, trying to take his mind off her. And Hugo should be thankful. But the argument he'd had with his dad before leaving the Big House was still playing in the back of his mind.

Get your shit together, Hugo. If you keep behaving like this, Mark will know something's up. And then what do you think will happen?

The looming threat of 'what do you think will happen' was precisely what had kept Hugo on edge ever since he'd caught Darian out in New York. Because he *did* know what would happen. They'd reject him. Leave him. Like his birth parents.

Until he'd realised that it wouldn't be the same at all. It would be worse. Worse because he *loved* them. He loved Darian and Mark. He didn't care if people had made fun of them when he was younger. He'd been proud of them, of what they'd fought just to love each other. But what he'd loved had been a lie.

Getting up, Hugo crossed to the edge of the pool, looking down at the sun dancing patterns through the water. But he didn't see that. Instead, he was taken back to last winter, and saw his breath rush out of his mouth in streams in the frigid air as he unlocked the door of his parents' New York apartment. He had just ended a phone call with Avery, the words *I love you* on the tip of his tongue – but she'd hung up before he could say it. In his mind's eye, he walked through the apartment door, only to find his dad, Darian, smiling at a guy who looked about two years older than him.

That same shock hit now as Hugo dived into the pool, the cold a slap against his hot skin, the press of water just like the punch of emotion he'd felt then, making it impossible to take a breath.

And a kind of bewildered betrayal overcame him all over again. Because he'd not realised. He'd not known how devastating that single moment had been. Like the smallest of cuts that had nicked an artery, and unknowingly he'd been bleeding out this entire time.

Holding himself under the water, he knew that the betrayal went beyond the fact that Darian had been cheating on Mark. It went beyond the moment that Darian had sat him down to warn him that Mark would be devastated. How Mark would never be the same, their *lives* would never be the same. Darian was right; Mark *wouldn't* recover from it.

The betrayal wasn't even that Darian had offered to keep him sweet, offering an invitation for Avery to join them on the family ski trip at spring break. The Lamborghini Urus he'd been lusting after for months. Early access to the trust fund that they had put aside for his twenty-first birthday, if he wanted. *For being good*, Darian had justified. For being *so* good at keeping Darian's secret.

No. What had *truly* destroyed the foundations Hugo had

naively built his life upon was the way that Darian had *looked* at him. As if Hugo were a stranger and not his son.

As if he were a snake that would bite him.

Carbon dioxide burned his lungs, screaming in his veins. His eyes stinging from the chlorine in the water as he forced them open to see the blue. He wanted to stay here. He wanted to stay down here where there wasn't a Darian or a Mark or even an Avery. He wanted—

An explosion of displaced water and Archie landed right beside him, knocking him on to his side, cushioned by the water, but shocked by the suddenness of it. Hugo took a mouthful of water into his lungs and pushed, panicked, to the surface, coughing and spluttering, his throat sore from the violent expulsion of water from his body.

By the time he was able to open his eyes, Sydney, Leo, Archie – and even Nick Dawson – were all laughing at him. Only Avery was looking at him, but he couldn't tell whether it was concern or pity. Embarrassment twisted into shame and anger in the blink of an eye.

'Screw you, Archie,' he said, slapping water over him.

Nick was bent double with laughter.

'And I don't know what you're laughing at. Shouldn't you be teaching someone how to hit a ball with a bat?'

'There's a little more to it than that, but no worries,' the tennis player replied easily.

'Yeah, and I'm sure you could have shown those guys at Wimbledon that too if you hadn't twisted your ankle.'

'There was a little more to that too,' Nick replied, his tone cooling and hardening like lava. Nick squinted at him and something thrilling snapped through Hugo. This was someone he could spar with, could fight. This was someone he could lash out at.

'I guess we'll never know,' Hugo fired back as Avery shifted uncomfortably on the sunbed.

Nick laughed, easy and Australian, but there was still an edge there.

'I'll take you on any day, bro.'

'I'm not your *bro*,' Hugo snapped back. 'But let's do it,' he said, pulling himself out of the pool.

'You want a game?'

'Was I unclear?'

Nick held up his hands in surrender, peeling himself off the sunbed. 'You're the boss's son. But don't worry, I won't let you win because of it.'

Archie whooped and hollered; even Sydney pulled herself out of her sulk enough to cover up and come along to watch. Avery looked away to where Nora had disappeared, and back at the tennis court.

Come. Please come.

Hugo wanted her to be there when he wiped the smirk off Nick's face. He wasn't naive; it wouldn't be easy, but Nick didn't know how good he was. His friends *did*, which was why this was going to be more fun than not.

Avery reluctantly drew herself up, Leo following along a little more hesitantly, probably because he was supposed to be working.

Hugo shoved his feet into his trainers, not caring that his shorts were wet. They'd dry soon enough in this heat.

'Want to borrow a racket?' Nick asked him. *Patronising ass.*

'No need, I've got my own,' he said as Archie threw him the tennis bag he'd left on the stool at the tiki bar.

It was the first time Hugo saw the moment of doubt in Nick's eyes and it was like blood to a shark. Excitement, adrenaline, the rush of the challenge – it pushed out everything else. The pain, the doubt, the confusion, the insecurity. No, *this* was where he excelled.

He followed Dawson through the entrance to the court, the crunch of gravel satisfying beneath his trainers. Retrieving a ball from the bucket by the net, he grasped it, the familiar shape fitting in his palm perfectly. He'd always been good at sports. Naturally athletic, tall, built for speed and power – but it was the determination that drove him. To win. To be the best.

Hugo bounced the ball, harder than necessary, to get rid of the voice from his head.

'Best of three? First to two sets wins?' Nick called from the other side of the net, pocketing a tennis ball.

Hugo nodded.

'Why don't you serve first?' Nick said, his tone offering him an advantage.

'That's very kind of you,' Hugo replied, in a tone that told him to go screw himself, but took it anyway.

He tested the ball on the court floor a few more times, feeling the bounce. He'd know this court in his sleep. He'd been playing on it since he was old enough to hold a racket. He knew every inch. And he'd been taught by players who had actually *won* Wimbledon. Not ones that had just dropped out.

He rolled his shoulders and readied for the serve, relishing the movement of his body, the feel of the ball swinging up into the air, the way the racket carved towards it and met the ball with a *plung*.

Hugo sent the ball a foot to the left of where Nick was expecting it, and to meet it he had to crunch himself back and in, and the return was sloppy. He just made it, but it allowed Hugo to send the ball back over to the far corner with speed and accuracy.

'So, you do more than lacrosse, I take it,' Nick said, his tone a little more wary than it had been.

'Yup,' Hugo replied with a smirk.

'Good. That way it'll feel better when I kick your arse to Sunday,' Nick replied as he returned Hugo's next serve hard and straight down the middle, not holding back.

AVERY

Archie had pulled up a chair by the edge of the court to watch like a spectator. Sydney lounged at the end of it, sunglasses on and working really hard to ignore Avery, while Leo had hung back on the outside of the court as if he could, or would, return to the bar at any moment.

Avery remained in the entranceway – not committing to going on to the court. Partly because she wasn't sure that she actually wanted to see this. She'd wanted to go after Nora. She would have, if Nora hadn't told her to stay.

She'd seen that Archie had been a bit full-on, but she hadn't realised that it had got that bad. Flicking a gaze across to him now, grinning and taking a mouthful of his drink, it was like nothing had happened. In fact, it had been Syd who had made the scene. Even when she *wasn't* drinking. But maybe that was the problem. It can't have been easy being around them all drinking all the time and sticking to water. But that didn't give her a reason to be so awful to Nora.

Don't you start.

Or to her. The slap-down had been mean and painful. And the tension had only tangled tighter from there.

Archie cheered a point to Hugo, and Avery stared at the ground, the rough surface biting into her bare feet. She pulled her toes in, feeling the harsh surface, the gravel chips, stinging like she deserved it.

She wasn't stupid. She'd known that Hugo would be upset from her showing attention to Nick. But she hadn't wanted this at all. She'd just wanted him to realise that it really was over between them and she wanted to move on. And just maybe she'd also wanted a little something to make her feel better. And why was that so awful, she wondered miserably? Why was it bad to want something for herself?

'You shouldn't play with him like that,' Leo warned, for her ears only.

'I don't know what you mean,' she lied, his words vocalising the worst of her thoughts. She tried to shrug him off, tapping her finger against her bare thigh. The denim shorts she wore over her bikini had frayed at the edge and she rolled the cotton between the pad of her finger and thumb.

Leo leaned heavily against the wire cage that surrounded the entire court. He was watching her. But unlike the way it had been on the boat, this was different. He was *angry*.

'Don't give me that,' he said, turning his attention to the game and dropping her as if she were insignificant.

'You think this is *my* fault?' she prodded, wanting to argue, even though she agreed with him. She turned to face him finally. So angry. Angry with herself, angry with him. She could just make out Sydney say, 'Fifteen-forty to Nick.'

Leo raised his eyebrows at her.

'You *don't*?'

'I think they're both adults who can make decisions for themselves,' she snapped back, not wanting to take responsibility for their egos and their behaviour.

Leo looked down, nodded to himself and let out a bitter laugh.

'But they're not *equals*, Avery,' he said, looking back up and pinning her with his amber gaze, gold shards glittering in the sun.

She was caught off guard.

'No,' she said, pulling back. 'Nick is ranked in the top twenty players in the world. Of course they're not equals.'

'Deuce,' Sydney announced, as if trying to contradict them both.

'That's not what I meant, Avery,' Leo said, shaking his head and turning back to the game.

Avery did the same, feeling that she'd missed something important and resenting Leo for making her feel that way.

Nick lobbed the ball over the net, and Hugo slid across the court with a backhander that returned the hit, leaving Nick to careen towards the edge of the court to catch it with his own backhand. He pushed it straight across the net, with no time for Hugo to reach it, and won the point.

The game was becoming reckless and messy. Shoes skidded on the gravel, grunts filled the air and sweat poured down in the midday sun. Unlike the pool area, where there was shade if needed, the tennis court felt exposed. Avery felt her skin begin to burn and pressed a finger against her forearm to see how pink she was. *Too* pink.

Leo sighed and shrugged out of his shirt, holding it out to her to put on.

She felt her eyes widen as she took in the white T-shirt he was left wearing and the way it hugged his body.

'We both know your skin isn't up to this much sun,' Leo chided, having clearly thought her lack of reaction was because she needed convincing.

'Don't you need it?' she asked, finally taking the shirt from him.

'There's another one behind the bar,' he said, his gaze returning to the match.

She wanted to refuse it but that would make things worse. *And* she'd be burnt, so she slipped it on over her shoulders and tucked herself into the light cotton, trying not to get caught inhaling the scent of Leo that wrapped around her.

The shirt smelled . . . *familiar.*

Not sweet like Hugo or cloying like Nick.

Just . . . like Leo. A bit of deodorant, a bit of the sea and a bit of him.

'Deuce.'

Back and forth Nick and Hugo went, Archie cheering on Hugo, Sydney cheering on Nick to be difficult.

Leo felt an entire world away now, even though he barely

stood a metre from her. The breeze teased the ends of her hair, as if it was disturbed by the tension on the court, grazing a little over her sun-pink skin. She tried to see what Leo saw. The son of the island's owners playing against the tennis champion. Two of the richest kids in America cheering on opposite sides for fun, acting as if this was all perfectly normal. When it wasn't.

Nick volleyed, but Hugo was ready and slammed the ball back to the far end of the court just inside the lines to win the point. Archie cheered and Sydney was off her seat, coming towards the side of the net.

'Match point to Hugo.'

Avery flicked a gaze to Nick, seeing the moment he realised that he'd underestimated Hugo.

'I could just be letting you win, you know,' Nick said, breathing heavily.

'You said you wouldn't,' Hugo replied, aiming for nonchalant, but he was sweating and breathing just as hard.

'You're good. Who did you learn with?' Nick asked.

Hugo replied with several names of various number-one-ranked players who had stayed on the island either as guests like Avery and her family, or as visitors, like Nick.

'You didn't want to play?' Nick asked, genuinely curious.

'I like lacrosse. It's more violent.'

'I can see that,' Nick replied calmly, his poker face having been one of the things that had attracted the spotlight.

'Stop stalling and play.'

Leo turned to fully face the court and watch more closely.

Avery shrank further into his shirt, and the movement must

have caught Hugo's attention, because he looked across at her. His gaze snagged on Leo's shirt. The briefest frown turned to a glare and then back to the game.

She flicked a glance to Leo, who seemed to be focused on the court. Until . . .

'He won't like that,' Leo said.

Avery swallowed, knowing that Leo was right. Hugo had been possessive, which had been lovely at first. Hugo was such a powerful personality – gregarious, outgoing – and, before things had changed, there had been nearly a year when it had been amazing. Things had been easy and Hugo had been happy.

But then last winter something had happened and by the time she went on the skiing trip with Hugo and his parents at Spring Break, whatever it was had taken hold. And it had left her with a Hugo whose short temper had become a hair trigger.

He'd not been mean, not intentionally. Just more exacting, more demanding. As if he no longer had the energy or capacity to soften himself. As if he was getting closer and closer to a line neither of them wanted him to go over. And eventually she'd realised that what kept them together wasn't about her. He didn't *want* her. She was either a life raft or a trophy, and Avery couldn't be either.

Not for him.

'You know Nick isn't going to let him win,' Leo said, his voice low.

Avery swallowed.

'And how do you think Hugo is going to take that?' Leo pushed. 'What do you think he'll do? He's not the kind of guy to let that go, Avery. And these days? I don't think *he* even knows how far he'll go.'

'It's not *that* bad, Leo,' she lied to herself.

'Deuce.'

Hugo let out a scream of frustration, banging his racket on the ground.

Nick laughed, which was entirely the wrong thing to do, and the tension on the court was palpable.

'You can't play with people like this, Avery.'

And that was it. *He* was accusing her of playing with people? *Leo?* Who had spent an entire night talking with her until the sun came up. Who had leaned his leg against hers. Who had wrapped his arm around her when she had been cold. Whose lips had been close enough to hers to kiss. Just like at the club. When all she'd wanted was for him to see her as she saw him, to pull him against her and . . . She thought he'd wanted the same. She couldn't have imagined that he wanted her, could she? But he'd just left. He'd just walked away like it was nothing.

'You think *I* play with people?'

Leo looked at her and all she saw in his gaze was disdain.

She bit her lips together. 'You know what? Screw you, Leo. You've got a stick up your ass this year and you're walking around like we're all less than you.'

'You're less than *me*?' He bit out a laugh. 'That's a joke. This is literally what happens when you *actually are* less than people, Avery,' he said pointing at the court where Hugo and Nick were deep in a rally. 'It's like *Gladiator* and we're just here to entertain whatever whims you have.'

'It's *not* like that,' Avery said, feeling desperate, hating that he would think that of her.

'It's *always* been like that, Avery. We just haven't realised it until now.'

She stared up at him, her gut twisting and her conscience spiralling. He was putting them on different sides of the line. Him and her. Them and him. And she couldn't help but feel that he was blaming her.

She shook her head, unable to say anything to contradict him, fearing that he was right. And she turned away, missing the way that Hugo's eyes tracked her and, distracted, lost the entire match.

Over the pounding of her heart in her ears, Avery could barely hear the howl of fury that Hugo let out, throwing his racket across the court.

Nora. She wanted to find Nora.

CHAPTER NINE

AVERY

Collapsing against the tree stump between the forest line and the far end of the main beach, Avery blew out a breath. She'd searched for Nora for the last couple of hours and had not seen a trace of her.

She told herself that was fine, and tried not to notice how the misty grey sea reminded her of the frost in Leo's gaze as he had watched her walk away.

She hated arguing with him. Somehow, it felt worse than when she argued with Nora or Sydney. As if there was more to lose.

Her phone buzzed and she saw another alert with news about a storm that was skirting the Caribbean, and she wondered whether the edgy breeze she felt against her skin was part of it. The setting sun blasted rays of pink and purple across the skyline, the colours fading like a bruise.

She couldn't blame Leo. Or Hugo. Or Nora, who'd disappeared and not come back.

She *should* have told Sydney to stick it the moment she'd

defended Archie over Nora. She *should* have told Hugo not to be so mean, challenging Nick. She should have told Leo how she felt about—

Her phone buzzed with a Snapchat from Syd asking where she was, but Avery ignored it. She didn't want Sydney and all her passive-aggressive drama.

She wanted . . . She wanted . . .

She didn't even know any more.

She wanted Hugo to stop being so *angry*, she wanted her parents to get it together, she wanted to go back in time and not cheat in her exam . . . or . . . Was it just that she didn't want to have been caught by Nora? Because if Nora *hadn't* caught her, would she even be here on Mokani? Maybe Avery wouldn't have felt like she couldn't *not* invite her.

She makes you different. That had been Hugo's accusation when they'd broken up. *She makes everything different.*

'Aves, *there* you are,' Nora exclaimed from behind her as if she'd been looking for Avery forever. Which she hadn't been, because Avery knew Nora would have found her by now. 'I'm sorry for running off like that. I just . . . needed some time on my own,' she explained.

'Are you OK?' Avery asked.

'Yeah, course I am. Sydney was just out of order, that's all.'

'She was,' Avery agreed.

'But that doesn't mean it's OK for *me* to have been a shitty friend and to have left you alone with *all of them* all afternoon,' Nora said, coming to sit beside Avery, leaning her head on her shoulder.

'That wasn't being shitty!' Avery cried in defence, even

though she was touched that Nora had understood that she'd felt abandoned.

'It was! In fact,' Nora declared, springing back up and pulling Avery by the arm, 'I would say I've been absolutely, monumentally, abysmally, outrageously obnoxious in the last few days,' she performed for no one but Avery. 'But I have just the thing to make it up to you,' Nora promised, her eyebrows waggling for emphasis before she pulled Avery towards the forest that had been out of bounds for as long as she'd been coming to the island.

'We're not allowed in there,' Avery called out as Nora skipped ahead.

'So?' Nora asked, cocking her head to the side, a cheeky glint in her gaze. 'Come on!'

'I'm not sure about this,' Avery protested as she jogged to catch up, following Nora as she effortlessly wove through the trees.

Avery frowned, realising that Nora had changed clothes at some point. Avery was still in the ones she'd been wearing earlier, while Nora was now wearing a low-cut, cropped vest and a pair of high-waisted, high-cut shorts, the small butterfly tattoo on her ankle just visible above the straps of her sandals. Nora looked amazing, while Avery ... she winced at the thought of what she must look like; Leo's shirt over a bikini and a pair of old denim shorts.

Avery opened her mouth to suggest that maybe she should change for whatever this was, but Nora had disappeared into the thick canopy of leaves.

'Hey!' Avery called. 'Wait up.'

But there was no reply.

Avery shivered, feeling cold despite the warm Caribbean evening.

'Nora?' she called out hesitantly.

She paused, waiting to see if she could hear anything, her heart beginning to thud as the dense leaves and sticky humidity closed around her. Strange noises clicked and slithered, and for the first time on this island she didn't feel entirely safe.

'Avery!' yelled Nora. 'Over here!' An arm waved from the shadows.

A burst of relief drenched Avery from head to toe as she jogged over to where Nora danced beneath the fir trees.

'Where are we going?' Avery asked, laughing a little as Nora pulled her deeper into the forest.

'It's a surprise,' Nora whispered into her ear, sending little shivers across Avery's skin.

Avery had never been this far into the forest before. Here, the wind whispered secrets to the trees, and darkness shaded the dusk.

'Aves, babes, seriously. He's not worth it,' Nora said.

'I'm not sure what you mean,' Avery replied, hastily scrambling to hide how badly her earlier exchange with Leo had hurt.

'I heard about the tennis match,' Nora said.

Oh. She was talking about Hugo.

'I didn't think you saw that.'

'I didn't *have* to see it. The whole island's talking about it.'

Oh god, that was just going to make things worse.

'But I think it's working.'

Avery looked at her blankly.

'Getting Hugo to realise that you've moved on?' Nora clarified. 'All you have to do now is to put the nail in the coffin.'

'What coffin?' Avery asked, a sinking feeling in her gut.

Up ahead an orange glow pierced the thick overlap of tree trunks and Avery could hear music. Fire. People.

Her heart thudded in her chest, excitement and that little bit of fear that always seemed to accompany her whenever Nora started acting secretively.

They emerged from the trees into a clearing; a bonfire was in the centre, loaded with wood and flames and snaps and sparks, hissing and cracking as if warning her away. A few people she recognised from the staff at the resort eyed them suspiciously, but eventually went back to their conversations when Nora waved at someone Avery barely knew and pulled them into a hug.

It didn't surprise Avery that Nora had made friends with the staff. Nora could make friends with anyone. But Avery stood there feeling awkward, until Nora remembered her and pulled her into the small circle.

'Domingo, this is Avery, and she is simply *the best*,' she said, her hand a graceful wave of introduction that turned into a mock bow. 'Domingo can get you whatever you need on this godforsaken island.'

Avery laughed, because she'd thought Nora was being ironic. Everyone knew that Mokani Island was nothing short of paradise, but when Domingo stared at her, she thought perhaps she'd been wrong.

'And you know Corrine,' Nora said, leaning into the French woman's side.

Avery tried to push away the small spike of jealousy that had risen from how close she seemed with these people and smiled, waving a hand awkwardly. 'Hi, guys.'

Corrine greeted her warmly, but Domingo just nodded his head and looked away.

'It's nice to see you,' Avery said to Corrine.

'Out of uniform, you mean?' Domingo said underneath his breath, before shaking an empty beer bottle and raising his brows at Corrine. 'Want one?'

Corrine nodded. 'Please.'

'Sorry. There's no *champagne*,' Domingo said insincerely to Avery. 'OK slumming it with beer?'

'Yeah, that'd be great, thanks,' Avery replied, her cheeks burning a little from the sting of his words as he stalked off towards a large black cool box.

She swallowed, wanting to object to the bitterness in his voice, but getting where it came from – probably not deeply or truly, but enough. She looked around her and realised that all the people here were staff. And she was the interloper, the odd one out. She was on the other side of the line now.

Leo's side.

Nora had wandered off to talk to another person she didn't recognise, leaving her alone with Corrine.

'I like your necklace,' Avery said, hoping that she didn't sound as awkward as she felt. But genuinely, the multicoloured beads had caught her eye, liking the way that little rounds of silver, beaten and textured, sat in between them.

'Thank you,' Corrine said with a genuine smile. 'I made it.'

'Oh wow,' Avery replied, surprised. 'It's really pretty. Sorry, that sounds silly, but I mean it,' she insisted.

'No, that's nice to hear. I'm hoping to study jewellery and fashion next year.'

'Really? That's so cool. Why not this year?' she asked, wondering whether if *she* had taken a year off, she might not have made so many mistakes. She might—

'Because,' Domingo replied, cutting off her train of thought as he came over to pass Corrine and Avery each a beer, 'she needed to earn the money to pay for it.'

The jab was pointed and Avery was left with little to do but nod. She'd been thinking of a year off, and Corrine had just needed the money. The difference was painfully obvious.

'And you? Are you at college?' Avery asked, trying to draw Domingo into conversation, to soften the discomfort between them.

He let out a huff of laughter. 'No. I plan on working for a living.'

'Dom,' Corrine chided, but Avery looked away, hoping that Domingo didn't see how hard his verbal blow had landed.

She glanced across the firelight, perhaps more surprised than she should have been to find Nick staring at her with a small smile lifting the corner of his mouth.

His eyes danced like the fire.

'Fancy meeting you here,' he mouthed across the distance.

Avery smiled back, thankful that at least *someone* was happy to see her.

Nora came dancing back at that moment, taking a swig from

Domingo's beer and winking at him in thanks. She threw an arm around Avery's shoulder.

'You're welcome,' she whispered into Avery's ear and pushed her towards the fire and Nick.

But as she stumbled forward, she collided with Leo, who came out of nowhere.

Stepping away from her quickly, hands in the air as if touching her was a fate worse than death, Avery felt stung. She waited for him to say something, anything, but he didn't.

He just looked at her with an unfathomable blank gaze and it hurt. The distance between them never having been more clear.

'It's always been like that, Avery. We just haven't realised it until now.'

Was that why he'd never made a move? Why he still hadn't at the club? Because of the line between them? A line that he could never cross because they weren't 'equals'? Trying to cover her disappointment, she pushed past him to where Nick waited with a grin, the offer of a drink and hopefully more.

'You're not supposed to be here,' Nick chided in a sing-song voice.

Avery looked around her and caught Corrine flashing her an awkward smile, while Nora greeted Leo with a gaze that burned red hot. Heart in her mouth, Avery watched as she pulled Leo into a hug, wrapping her arm around his neck and pressing her chest against him. She turned away before she could see any more.

'I didn't realise,' she said, unsure whether she was replying to Nick's statement, or Leo and Nora's actions. 'I should—'

Nick caught her wrist gently as she pulled back. 'Hey, don't worry about it,' he said drawing her to his side. He looked around and, finding what he was looking for, said, 'Let's get out of here? Find somewhere a bit more . . . private?'

LEO

'You shouldn't have brought her here,' Leo said to Nora as they joined Domingo and Corrine.

'But I had to, or she wouldn't have left me alone,' Nora pouted. 'You know what she's like,' she said, patting at his chest.

Leo did. He'd known Avery since she was eleven years old. And she wasn't what Nora was making her out to be. He looked at Corrine, wondering why she had invited Nora, but was more worried who else Nora might have brought.

'Are the others coming?' he asked, praying for her to say no.

'Why? Worried they'll ruin your street cred?' she teased. 'No, it's just Avery and she's fine,' Nora dismissed. 'Nick will keep her out of the way of your new friends.'

'They're not new,' he replied, irritated by her tone.

'But they're not old either,' Nora taunted, her overfamiliarity grating.

Leo looked back to where Avery was talking to Nick, and he pressed down hard against the sense of disappointment. Of betrayal.

'You need to decide which side of the fence you're on,' Nora taunted, being far too perceptive about his position not only within the group, but on the island.

He wanted to tell her she was wrong.

But she wasn't. Ever since they arrived, he'd been walking a line either side. Staff or friend, staff or friend. And despite what he'd said to Avery earlier that afternoon about there being a line between them, a power imbalance, they didn't make him feel bad about who he was. They didn't greet him with resentment, like Domingo often did.

No, his friendship with Hugo, Archie, Syd and Avery had been shaped over time, like a pebble on the seabed. Rough sometimes, but the smoothness left in its wake was warm and comforting to the touch.

At the club, his only real sense of discomfort had been around Avery and the way he felt about her – being here now, he realised the difference.

'I know which side of the fence I'm on,' he replied, for the first time seeing the truth of it.

'Yeah, what's that?'

'My own,' he said honestly.

Leo went to leave, but Nora reached out and caught his wrist, looking up at him with *those* eyes. The kind of eyes that got stupid people into trouble. But he wasn't stupid and he had no intention of getting into trouble.

'You're playing a very dangerous game,' he warned.

'I know. It's fun. Want in?' Nora said with a smile, leaning forward, her lips a bright crimson that looked both beautiful and like a warning at the same time.

He wasn't sure what Nora was up to. It was something to do with the strange places he'd seen her pop up over the island when she wasn't with Avery or anyone else. But he didn't like it. He didn't like the sense he got that Nora was using Avery.

And he trusted his instinct when it came to her. But while he was distracted, Nora closed the distance between them and draped her arms around his neck.

He swallowed and automatically glanced back to where Avery had been standing, but Nora reached up and pulled his face back to hers by his chin.

'Don't you want to play with someone who knows what they're doing?' she taunted.

'I'm not sure I'm ready to pay the price,' he said truthfully, looking down into her gaze long enough to see the flare of irritation that he wasn't behaving as she wanted him to.

'Oh, sweetie. I promise it won't cost you too much. What if I give you a sample?' she teased, leaning up to whisper in his ear. 'For free?' she goaded, dropping one hand from his neck to his chest – a nail scraping over his skin through the thin T-shirt as her fingers tiptoed their way across his abs and teased the waistband of his jeans.

There was something strangely involuntary about the way his body responded, *impersonal* even, and he railed against it.

'No,' he said, pushing her gently, but firmly, away from him.

It didn't matter if nothing was going on between him and Avery, or if nothing would ever happen between him and Avery. Nora was her friend – though god knew why at this point – and Leo wouldn't get in the middle of that.

He looked at her and saw anger glittering in her eyes.

'I don't know what you're playing at, but you should stop. Avery deserves better,' he said.

'Better, like Nick?' she taunted cruelly, and he realised that he'd not fooled anyone. His feelings for Avery had been seen.

He looked up to find Domingo and Corrine's gazes on him and shook his head.

Looking around one last time, he knew now that this wasn't where he belonged either. At least with Archie, Syd, Hugo – and even Avery – he'd spent years building up a friendship. Why was he going to let his father giving him a stupid job mess that all up? Yes, he saw the line between them a little more clearly. But they weren't the ones who made him feel unwelcome. He'd made *himself* feel unwelcome.

But here? Now? Domingo's gaze was full of judgement, and he felt a few more suspicious glances his way. He shook his head one last time before turning his back on them and walking away.

AVERY

Avery followed Nick further into the forest, more to get away from Nora and Leo than to spend more time with Nick. She'd seen Nora press herself up against Leo, curling her arm around his neck and she couldn't stay there to see what happened next. She couldn't bear it.

Pushing aside her hurt, she let Nick lead her further into the forest. The callouses on his palm felt rough against hers, but when he looked at her she thought she felt excitement. Escapism. She wanted this.

She bit her lip, secretly delighting in his open attraction to her. Something that Hugo had never shown, and Leo would never do. Would never *let* himself do, she realised.

Nick's gaze flickered from her eyes to her mouth and back again. And when she closed the distance between them, even in the darkness she could see the flush on his cheeks.

'Why are you here, Avery Finch?' he whispered, his breath puffs of air against her lips.

'I'm here for *you*,' she said, using unfamiliar bold words, wanting to be that person who could throw caution to the wind. Wanting to be smart, sexy and desirable.

Hadn't Nora brought her here for him? She'd told her as much. After all, this was what they'd promised each other that the summer would be, right? Fun, fabulous, fantastic?

Glitter exploded in Nick's gaze, a sharp inhale, as if she'd surprised him.

It was easy to rise to her tiptoes and kiss him. Here, she didn't have to be Good Little Avery Finch. Maybe this time she could be *bad*.

Nick's arm swept behind her and drew her against him, pulling her into his chest. Their breaths heaved in the night air. His hands pawed at her shirt to get to her bare skin beneath, his cool fingers casting a shiver down her body.

'What you do to me,' he panted against her mouth, shaking his head.

'Mmm?' she managed, not quite sure what to say

Avery shifted uncomfortably. She *did* want this . . . but it was going a little too fast. His hands a bit too hard, his grip a little painful. And he didn't even notice. She pressed gently against his chest, trying to move him enough to get just a little space.

But he didn't budge.

'Nick,' she said against the lips that were pressed hard against hers. 'Nick,' she tried again, but—

A scream tore through the air, cutting into her nerves, finally forcing him back away from her.

'What was that?' she asked, shaken by the sound.

Nick frowned, but shrugged. 'I don't know,' he said, coming back towards her for more.

'No, Nick,' she said, stepping away from him. 'I want to know what that was,' she said, trying to see into the dark.

'Who cares?'

'I do,' she replied, getting angry now that he wasn't listening, or even concerned.

He stepped back, hands raised, like Leo had done, but meaner somehow. 'Hey, what's the problem? Nora said you wanted this?'

Avery blinked, the ground feeling off kilter.

'I—'

'Whatever,' he said, shrugging as if she was the one with the problem. 'When you work it out, let me know,' he said, stalking back towards the party.

Avery swallowed, feeling miserable, embarrassed and shaken. *Nora had told him that she wanted this.* How far would he have taken it, she wondered, just before another scream filled the air. Only this time, it was followed by a group of people laughing. Somewhere deep in Avery's mind, it sounded like they were laughing at her.

CHAPTER TEN
AVERY

Avery pushed a piece of avocado around her plate, not hungry at all. She'd come to the pool to get away from her parents at the villa. It was the only place she could think to go. No one was there apart from the staff member working the bar. Someone that thankfully, she hadn't seen the night before.

Avery had smiled and said hi, but she felt awkward and uncomfortable in a way she'd not felt before. She'd ordered breakfast more as something to do, and gone to sit at one of the tables beneath an umbrella.

In the silence around the pool, Avery heard the echo of her parents' argument. They'd started early that morning, having finally decided that they didn't have to play pretend in front of their daughter's friend.

They hadn't seen her, just like they hadn't noticed that Nora hadn't come home last night. She'd planned to tell them that Nora had gone out for a run, even though the idea of Nora running was laughable. But it hadn't mattered in the end.

'We don't have much time left. You have to ask them.'

'I can't just come out with it, Lis.'

'Jesus. Don't you get it? If you don't ask them, if we don't get the money from them – either of them, both of them, whatever – we're done. All of it. The company. The house, the cars, the friends. Avery's college fund – it's all gone. There will be nothing left. Nothing.'

'It's not my fault.'

'How is it not your fault, Jonathan? How didn't you notice what was going on under your own nose?'

Avery had snuck out at that point, not wanting to hear how else her world would fall apart, as her mother continued to list her father's numerous failings.

All last night she'd felt painfully aware of how rich and sheltered she was. Of how rich and sheltered they *thought* she was. And no one had a clue. *She'd* not had a clue. Until a man from the FBI had turned to up to speak to her father.

He'd been devastated when they'd arrested his business partner for fraud and discovered the loss of millions from the company accounts.

And while her mother had tried to pass it off as 'having some difficulties', Avery knew that it was so very much worse than that.

They could lose everything, and there she was, unable to think beyond where Nora had spent the night.

Avery's head hurt with all that it was trying to contain. Her parents, Nora, Hugo ... *Leo*. She tried to ignore the way thoughts of him and Nora together made her feel angry. So angry. And that mixed horribly with the fact that Nora hadn't even bothered to let her know she wasn't coming back to the villa, which made her feel unimportant. Invisible. To both Leo *and* Nora.

And then she felt guilty and wretched for being so self-obsessed.

She squinted into the thousand different shades of blue across the horizon, feeling deeply uncomfortable about what had happened last night.

With Nick.

Avery swallowed. She'd thought he'd been what she wanted. But she'd been wrong. Yes, he wanted her, but it wasn't *her*, her. He just wanted sex. A hot fumble, nothing more. And she'd tried to convince herself that would be enough.

But it wasn't. She wanted *more*, Avery finally realised. She wanted what Hugo had never seemed to want to give her.

She didn't know whether to believe that he'd wanted to wait. It didn't chime with what she'd heard from all her girlfriends, whose boyfriends would do anything to get them into bed. But Hugo had always found some excuse. Either they'd been too drunk, or he hadn't wanted to rush things or they were in his dads' house. And slowly, bit by bit, it had eaten away at her self-confidence. It had made her feel unattractive. Undesirable. Unwanted.

In her mind she saw Leo make a beeline for Nora last night . . . and the way that Nora had looked up at him, flirtation on her lips.

And Avery couldn't compete with that. With her. Nora was bright, and funny and *sexy*, and Avery was awkward, and failing and flailing and messing everything up.

She hated being jealous of her friend, hated comparing herself to Nora in the first place. But what she really hated, Avery thought as hot wet tears pressed against the backs of her eyes, was that she'd brought her here.

The sound of flip-flops slapping against the ground yanked her out of her thoughts. Only one person walked with that much energy.

Nora careened into the chair on her left, her careless energy cutting painfully into the tranquillity of the surroundings. She looked bright, and cool and . . .

'Oh. My. God. You won't *believe* what happened last night,' she exclaimed.

Avery braced herself for *I slept with Leo*. It would hurt, of course it would, but—

'Corrine and some of the guys went out up to the cliff to try and climb it.'

'Wait, what?' Avery's mind screeched to a halt. 'Climb the cliff? But that's—'

'I know!' Nora replied with her eyes wide and thrilled. 'But it all went horribly wrong and Corrine fell and scraped her leg and hand really badly.'

'Oh god, is she OK?' Avery asked.

'We had to take her to the island's doctor at, like, *three* in the morning,' Nora grimaced. 'He stitched her up, but said that she needs to go to the mainland for an X-ray to make sure she's not broken anything.' The words poured out of Nora at a million miles an hour.

'That's awful,' she said thinking of Corrine's hand, of her jewellery making. She must be terrified and hurting. 'Is there anything we can do?'

'No, I don't think so. They're just figuring out how to get her there now. It was so bad,' Nora said, shaking her head. 'There was blood *everywhere*.'

Avery shivered, her skin feeling suddenly overly sensitive.

Sydney pulled out the chair on the other side of Avery, the screech of legs making Avery jump.

'What happened?' Sydney asked, dressed in a silk kaftan, her hair twisted up in a half-knot, her face failing to hide her simmering anger. Avery felt herself brace for what would surely be another fight. 'Because last night,' Sydney exclaimed archly, 'I did absolutely nothing. What about you?' She turned to glare at Avery.

'Corrine and some friends went exploring and she fell,' Nora explained instead.

'Who?' Sydney asked, and Avery felt irritation crawl up her spine.

'Corrine. The girl who makes the mocktails you really like?' she replied, flushing with something close to anger when Sydney just shrugged her shoulder.

Archie loped along the side of the pool and called out to Sydney.

'Dad's meeting with the Cayman Island bank got pulled up so he's heading out. He's planning to drop off the girl who hurt herself on the mainland on the way,' he explained.

Nora jumped up. 'I'll head down to the jetty.'

'Why?' Sydney asked, voicing Avery's silent question.

'Well, I've got some things I wanted to pick up from the mainland and I'll keep Corrine company at the same time.' Nora shrugged, but Avery noticed something stilted about the way she was talking. 'And if Mr D's already going, one more won't hurt, right?'

'Too late,' Archie said.

'What?'

'Look,' he said, pointing over his shoulder to where the boat was just leaving the marina.

Nora masked her disappointment quickly, but not quickly enough.

'Didn't realise you two had got so close,' Sydney snipped.

Nora shrugged off Sydney's comment as she sat back down, shoving her hands into her pockets.

Sydney glared at Nora for longer than was necessary, the tension one-sided as Nora remained completely unaware of her. At least, it seemed that way. Eventually Sydney got bored and left to go and speak to Archie, who was on the phone to their mother.

In the silence, Avery's thoughts turned back to last night and she told herself not to ask. It wasn't her business what Nora and Leo had got up to. Not really.

'So,' Nora said, finally bringing her attention back to Avery. 'How was it last night with Nic-o-*las*?' she teased in a sing-song voice.

Avery frowned. 'Actually, it wasn't that great.'

'Oh,' was all Nora said. 'Shame.' She pulled out her phone and started tapping away.

That was it? That was all she had?

'What about you?' Avery asked, feeling anger rise to the surface. 'Where were *you* last night?'

'I was with Corrine and the guys. I said.' Nora didn't even bother to look up.

'No, you didn't.' Avery dug her heels in.

'I didn't what?' Nora looked at Avery as if she were being

confusing. But she wasn't. She knew what Nora had said, and she hadn't said that.

'You *didn't* say that. What happened with Leo?' Avery asked instead, because her patience was wearing really thin.

'Nothing much,' Nora said easily.

'What's that supposed to mean?' Avery demanded.

'What's the problem, Avery?' Nora asked, looking at her as if she were causing a fuss. Avery's cheeks pricked with pink. 'I thought you liked *Nick*?' Nora said almost accusingly.

'*You* were the one who decided I liked Nick,' Avery said, pushing back in her chair.

'Avery, I—'

'You *lied*, Nora Miller.' Hugo's accusation came out of nowhere.

Avery turned to see him stalking towards them, his phone out displaying something she could hardly see.

HUGO

Hugo relished the look of shock on Nora's face. It was far better than that cocky grin she usually wore. It had taken more hours than he cared to admit, but he'd finally found proof that Nora was lying. A two for one, as it had not only distracted him from what was going on with Darian, but it also meant that if Avery had any sense left, she'd put Nora on a flight back to the States and get the college to change her roommate.

And if she didn't, then Hugo would personally help Nora off the island himself.

'What are you talking about?' Nora asked. There was confusion, yes, but there was also fear. The fear of being found out. He could see it. He could practically *smell* it. After all, he knew what that looked like himself.

'Is that why you've been so interested in Mr Devereux? Daddy issues?'

Nora blinked and Avery gasped.

'I'm *not* interested in Mr Devereux,' she hit back, the flush on her face telling Hugo that was *another* lie.

Hugo raised his eyebrows. He'd overheard Leo's dad telling Sven that she'd been asking some of the staff about him.

'Hugo, what the—' Avery tried, but he just glared at her, enough to cut her off.

Nora lurched out of her chair. 'What the hell is your problem?' she demanded. 'That's disgusting.' She looked at Avery and then to where Sydney and Archie were beginning to pay attention.

'Really? I mean, I just thought you might have been looking for a father figure, because yours is dead, right? *Right?*' he said again for emphasis.

Nora blanched. And he relished every single moment. Because when Nora was finally revealed to be the liar that she was, everything would return to normal.

'Hugo, seriously—' Avery demanded.

'I mean . . . he *is* dead, right?' Hugo asked Nora. 'And not living in South Carolina with a gorgeous wife and three, from what I can tell, absolutely *adorable* children,' he pushed.

Hate gleamed in Nora's eyes. He could see it. An anger that nearly matched his own. She was furious, but so was he. And he had proof.

'What are you talking about?' Sydney asked, coming over with Archie to join them.

'I'd tell you to ask Nora, but I don't recommend believing a word that comes out of her mouth.' He folded his arms across his chest, satisfied by the silence coming from Nora. 'Well?' he asked. 'Are you going to tell them that it's all a complete lie?'

'Hugo—' Avery's tone held a warning note that he didn't pay attention to.

'No, I won't stop. I want to know who is *in my house*. On *my island*. And the only thing I know about you is that you're a liar.'

He was vaguely aware of Sydney laughing and saying, 'This is just great.'

'Hugo!' Avery tried again, but his sole focus was locked on to Nora.

'Care to explain?'

And then calm descended in Nora's gaze and for the first time, he felt a little unsure. But he didn't have to be. Three hours of internet stalking and he'd found Nora's aunt on her father's side on Nora's mother's Facebook profile. He'd then searched through a few years of photos to find one of the aunt and her brother. The brother that was Nora's father. The one that she'd told everyone was dead.

Who did that? Who lied about their dead father?

Someone sick, that's who.

'I didn't lie,' Nora had the audacity to say. But there was no more shock, no more fear.

And Hugo didn't like that at all.

'Like hell.'

'I. Didn't. Lie,' she repeated. 'He *is* dead.'

Hugo scoffed, but he caught the look on Avery's face and, yes, she was pissed but it wasn't at Nora. Avery was glaring at *him*.

'To *me*,' Nora stressed. 'He was dead to me the day he walked out on my mother leaving her saddled with one hundred and fifty thousand dollars of *his* debt that she had co-signed because she thought he loved her,' she explained, slowly and clearly and determinedly.

'My mother,' she pressed on, taking a step towards him, forcing him to uncross his arms in order to avoid touching her, and to avoid taking a step back, 'was forced to work three jobs, just to cover the damn interest.' Nora continued, cocking her head to the side, her eyes taking on a mean glint. 'He walked out on us and straight into the arms of another woman. The gorgeous wife? A woman who doesn't even know about us. Because when my mum contacted him, he denied my paternity.'

'Jesus,' Archie winced, sinking into the chair and wiping a hand over his face. Hugo looked at Sydney. Even she was looking embarrassed.

How the hell had this turned on him so badly?

'I didn't—' he tried, but his words were lost as Nora continued.

'My mother didn't even have enough money to fill the fridge. Let alone pull together enough money to take him to court,' Nora explained, her laugh bitter and angry.

'So yeah. My dad is dead. To *me*,' she said pointedly. 'I'm sorry, Hugo, that I wasn't as lucky as you, to have been chosen by two rich daddies who can waste billions on you, you dick,' she said, shoving him hard in the chest, her words striking home far more brutally than her finger.

'Dude,' Archie said at the same time as Avery said, 'Nora—'

'No, it's OK,' Nora said, raising her hand, still staring at him. 'Thank you, Hugo, for airing that for me. I'm sure that you can imagine I was just *desperate* to tell Avery's friends all about how I was rejected and abandoned by my father, and how we grew up dirt poor because of it. I'm glad there are no more *secrets* amongst us,' she said, emphasising 'secrets' in a way that made him decidedly uncomfortable.

She pushed past him to walk away, but turned back just at the last minute, her voice dropping low for his ears only.

'And by the way. This isn't *your* house, or *your* island. It's Daddy's and Daddy's. Don't mistake their power for yours,' she warned, and with that, she left.

Shit.

Shit.

'Not cool, dude,' Archie said as Avery ran off after Nora.

'Avery!' Hugo called out, but she was gone.

'Jesus, Hugo, give it a rest,' Sydney said, dropping into her chair with a disgusted sigh.

Hugo's head was spinning. 'But she lied about it.'

Archie shook his head. 'Yeah, but you can understand why, right?'

No. Yes.

Shit.

'But she lied.'

'You need to let it go,' Archie said, turning back towards his villa.

'Where are you going?' Hugo asked.

'Mum needs help with something.'

Sydney sighed and stood up to go with him, leaving Hugo standing by the pool all alone. It wasn't supposed to have been like this. Nora was the one who was supposed to have been alone. On the outside looking on.

Damn it.

CHAPTER ELEVEN

LEO

> **Archie Snapchat:**
> You should have seen it. Hugo totally lost it.
> And ended up face planting right into a shitstorm.
>
> Party at Luna Beach tonight. Be there!

Leo's phone vibrated against his thigh. He didn't have to check. It would be Archie. *Again.*

He rolled his shoulders as discreetly as possible, standing back from the dinner table that stretched out on the deck between the villa the Devereuxs were staying in and their private beach.

He wondered if it was strange for Mark and Darian to be invited for dinner on their own island. Four large fire torches had been staked into the sand just off the wooden deck area and were flickering dangerously in the winds that had picked up. There was of course still hope that the storm would miss the island, but as of an hour ago it was heading straight at them.

Everyone's attention was on Carol, who had stepped inside to take a phone call from her husband.

'Well, Dennis made it to the Caymans and back to the mainland,' she said, closing the sliding glass door behind her as she came back out on to the deck. 'But the captain has said they can't come back tonight; the sea is too rough. They're hoping for a moment of calm tomorrow before the storm hits so that they can return,' Carol announced, returning to her seat.

A frown flickered across Leo's brow. Domingo was chartering the boat, and Leo knew for a fact that the man could pilot that boat back in the middle of a tornado if he'd been asked.

'And the girl?' Annalise asked.

Leo flinched at the careless, casual mention of Corinne.

'What girl?'

'The one who got herself hurt?' Darian clarified for Annalise.

Because she'd done it on purpose, Leo thought sarcastically.

'Oh? Dennis didn't say.'

Because it wasn't important enough. God, he hated these people.

Carol tapped the top of her half-drunk glass and Leo gritted his teeth and swept up the bottle of sparkling wine flown in from Scandinavia just for the Devereuxs. He hadn't even known they made wine in Scandinavia. His father had tracked it down, deciding it a perfect match to salt-cured scallops, garlic mustard leaves and shaved turnip. Leo thought it had more to do with the fact that it was the most expensive wine he could find. He'd watched his dad plating up just before service, watching his discipline and impossibly high standards. Things that he wanted to aspire to, but also the very thing that kept a wall between them a mile wide.

'Mark, what do you think?' Annalise asked.

'About the girl?'

'No, the storm. Do you think we'll avoid it?'

'Of course,' Darian interjected.

'But we will prepare all the same,' Mark insisted in a reassuring tone.

'We've been so lucky. All the years we've been coming here, and not once have we been caught by one,' Annalise said, eyes a little too shiny.

Leo backed away from the table and replaced the bottle in the fridge in the back of the catering van, once again parked discreetly out of sight.

Something hard hit the back of his head and he flinched, brushing it away. Then it happened again and he turned to find Archie, Avery and Nora, all waving at him from behind the villa's garden wall a few metres away.

'Bring that with you when you come,' Archie whispered.

Leo tried to shoo them away, but Archie just pulled a stupid face. Nora pulled up her T-shirt to flash him – thank god she was wearing a bikini top – and Avery covered her mouth trying not to laugh. Leo bit back his own laugh and mouthed 'piss off' at them before anyone could notice.

He caught the raised eyebrow of one of the staff and the attention of another as his friends made the most stupid amount of noise while trying to be quiet. Someone must have stepped on a foot, as Archie squealed and Avery started to laugh again.

This was what he'd missed. The silliness, the laughter. And the fact that they had come here, for *him*.

Ignoring the silent judgement, he bit his lips to prevent a smile from taking hold.

'Get out of here, guys,' he hissed before they could get him into trouble.

Finally, they left for the beach on the other side of the island where Luna, the villa undergoing repair work this summer, was far enough away from prying eyes. And he realised, with a sense of ease, that he was actually looking forward to seeing them later.

'This is just what we needed,' Annalise said, unconsciously echoing his thoughts, while nudging her husband with her elbow. Only there was something about her tone that was overly forced. 'Isn't it, Jonathan? So restful.'

'Yes,' Jonathan Finch agreed, sitting up in his chair a little taller. 'Especially because things have been a little difficult recently. And—'

'Oh, *darling*, they've been difficult everywhere,' Carol interrupted. 'I mean, just look at the politics.'

'Let's not, shall we?' Mark said, laughing.

'Just the other day I was hearing from a friend that they were having to let go several of their house staff. I mean, how shocking. That people are having to make do like that,' Carol said. The sheer audacious privilege of her ignorance had Leo's ears near ringing in shock. 'But *you're* doing OK, right? I mean, the resort in Verbier and the new project in Manhattan?' Carol asked, angling her question away from the Finches and turning to Darian.

As if she really didn't care about Jonathan and Annalise. To Leo, it sounded like Avery's parents' business was in trouble.

'Oh, that's going well, actually,' Darian answered Carol. 'We've managed to secure investment from . . .'

Leo let their voices go over his head, thinking he'd ask Avery about it . . . and then remembering that he couldn't. Not after the harsh words they'd exchanged the other afternoon. And especially not after he'd seen her walk off with Nick.

His thoughts drowned under the crash of the surf brushing relentlessly against the shoreline and he looked out to see clumps of seaweed and sea-foam sprawled across the sand. All he could think was that one of them – one of the *staff* – would have to clear that up in the morning before the guests were up.

The wind was erratic, bringing an unholy energy to the evening. He might not spend his year on the island, but he'd been here long enough to know that, unlike in the UK, the storm threat here was serious.

He eyed the large fire torch staked into the ground warily. It would be a miracle if they made it through the dinner without that collapsing and setting fire to the table.

'Oh, for the Carpenters? I've heard they're lovely,' Annalise said, trying to interject herself into a conversation that was purposefully trying to exclude her.

Leo cringed and caught Jonathan shaking an empty glass in his direction.

Taking the wine and the sparkling wine, Leo wondered if he'd wanted something stronger.

'Nick Dawson!' exclaimed Darian. 'What are you doing here?'

The Australian stood just on the other side of the villa's perimeter wall, jaw line and dark brow picked out by the flickers of the flame torches.

'I was just passing,' – unlikely, Leo thought – 'and wanted to let you know that, weather permitting, I'll be heading to the mainland tomorrow for physio.'

'Oh no, have the lessons been exacerbating your injury?' Mark asked with concern.

'Not at all. Just a routine part of my recovery plan. Though I know for a fact that being here has done wonders,' he said, his gaze lingering on Annalise in a way that turned Leo's stomach.

'I'll be back the day after, though,' he said, with two fingers in a lazy salute.

'Well, we hope the session is good and has you back fighting fit as soon as possible.'

'But not so soon that you'd leave us,' Darian said with a smile that was worryingly close to a threat.

He was pretty sure that Nick saw it for what it was, despite the grin plastered on his face as he headed down a pathway that Leo recognised was *not* the one that would take him back to his villa.

An agonising two hours later, and Leo could finally call it a night. Sven arrived and sent half of them away, knowing that tomorrow would be an all-hands-on-deck situation to prepare the island for the storm.

Leo loosened the tie and undid the button at his neck, fishing his shirt from his trousers hoping the others hadn't finished all the alcohol. After that dinner, he needed a drink.

He turned on to the back path and stopped. He'd thought he

heard something ... He waited. Nothing. He was about to move on when he heard it again. Harsh whispers in the dark.

'Oh. Oh yes.'

He blinked, instinctively understanding what he was hearing and half worried what he'd see if he looked too hard.

'Oh yes,' he heard again.

Oh god.

He'd recognised the voice the first time, he just wished he hadn't. But now he knew that Annalise had slipped off with Nick Dawson, as if he hadn't spent the night before with her daughter!

Angry and frustrated that he could do nothing with his anger, he turned, knowing that he'd have to tell Avery. It would be horrible, and awful, and difficult after everything they'd talked about, but she needed to know. He couldn't watch her get hurt. Not again.

AVERY

The moon shimmered on rough waves as the sound of the music beat a drum in Avery's veins. They'd needed this. *She'd* needed this.

Earlier that day, she had managed to talk Nora down. She'd been threatening to leave and even though Avery had almost wanted exactly the same thing that very morning, she didn't want Nora to go. Not like that.

Hugo had been a complete ass. And if he'd just come to her first, she could have put him straight. She'd known about Nora's dad from very early on. It wasn't some secret, it never had been, and Avery had completely understood why she'd told the rest of them that he was dead. For all intents and purposes, he was.

Avery had convinced Nora to stick it out, even just for a day or two, and see how she felt. Then when Sydney had come to find them, she'd proved why, sometimes, on very rare occasions, she was absolutely one of the best people to have in your corner.

'You don't get a monopoly on shitty parents,' she'd told Nora, 'but you *do* get an afternoon of the Sydney Special to prove that we're not all *complete* assholes. I promise, we do have our good moments.'

'Do I want to know what the Sydney Special is, before I agree?' Nora had asked.

'Trust me, you want this *bad*,' Avery had insisted.

'We're going to spend the next six hours with Marta's magical fingers—'

'I don't swing that way,' Nora had gently insisted.

'Neither does Marta,' Sydney had said without missing a beat, 'but her massages are legen-dary. Then we'll have Mitchel Walker's amazing spa ceviche menu, then we're going to party on the beach –, if you're OK with that – and we're going to forget Hugo even exists. Just for today. Then we'll get over it, and tomorrow will be a new beginning for all of us. *Together*.'

Not wanting to ruin the moment by pointing out that, in all probability, a storm of epic proportions was due to hit the island tomorrow, Avery had simply nodded her head in agreement.

And they'd done just that.

Nora had declared loudly and widely that Marta was so good, she should work for the CIA. 'She can have all my secrets, my firstborn – and my last if she wants it!'

They'd spent the entire day getting massages, facials, waxed, scrubbed, exfoliated, hydrated, hydrated some more, moisturised, buffed and lounging beneath the swaying palm trees on the spa's private beach, Sydney conceding to stay further back from the water than she would normally.

They'd gorged on champagne and delicious food, and every single whim that could be conceived of by Sydney's *very* lavish mind was indulged. Including, but not limited to, several pieces of clothing from the LVMH collection that hadn't even been released yet. Syd had them flown in from New York by private jet for them to wear that evening.

Even Avery had balked a little at that.

'Don't worry. It's on Daddy's tab,' Sydney had said, and Avery wondered how long she was going to punish her parents for, for making her go to rehab. A lot, probably.

They had got ready at the Finches' villa, a process that had completely trashed Avery and Nora's room. But Avery didn't care. Because for the first time that entire holiday, she had both Sydney *and* Nora with her. Friends. She felt it and she *loved* it.

They'd gossiped, swapped clothes, shared make-up. It was everything she'd wanted. Even her parents had managed to stay quiet as they'd got ready to go to the Devereuxs and the girls had got ready to go to the beach at Luna.

And now that they were here, Avery was still riding high on happiness.

'Here,' Sydney said, passing Nora the bottle of vodka she'd taken from Archie without having any herself.

Archie was busy messing around with the speaker system,

while Hugo was over by the small bonfire they'd dug into the sand to try and protect it from some of the wind.

As promised, he had been well and truly ignored for the entire evening. Whether Sydney had told him of her plan, Avery didn't know, but he seemed to be content leaving them to it and taking their snub with a patience that wasn't like him at all. His gaze landed on hers for a moment and skittered away. But not before she saw regret and shame in his eyes. A part of her felt for him. She knew that he wasn't being himself, that he wasn't this angry, frustrated guy. Instinct told her that something else was going on, but after what he'd done to Nora, it was too little, too late.

Avery turned away, not shutting him out but definitely closing him off, as Nora danced in between her and Sydney, who was spiralling her arms into the air in time with the music, singing along to words that Avery could barely make out.

Syd was still wearing the friendship bracelet, and Avery made a mental note to have another look for hers. She hadn't seen it since before the night at the club, but now she wanted to wear it.

Then Leo arrived, seeming to take in the bonfire and them with a sweep of his gaze, until it locked on her with a frown.

Unease spiked in her gut. Was he still upset about the other day? Or was he wondering about Nora? In all the fuss with Hugo and Nora, she still didn't know what had happened between them.

He made his way towards her with a focus that made her feel awkward.

'Hey, can I have a word?' he asked, his nod gesturing away from the fire.

She frowned, looking across at Nora and Sydney. Sydney shrugged and Nora just looked away.

'Yeah, sure,' Avery replied, sounding very *un*sure even to her own ears.

She pulled her jumper around her shoulders and headed just a little bit away, further from the flames and deeper into the shadowed darkness that fell across this part of the beach.

'Listen, I wanted to say,' he said at the same time as she said, 'I was hoping to—'

And then they both half laughed awkwardly.

Leo looked at the floor and then back up at her. 'Listen, about Nick.'

'Nothing happened,' Avery rushed to tell him. She wasn't telling him because she wanted to change whatever was going on with him and Nora. But she did want him not to think badly of her. And the thing between her and Nick, that hadn't been right at all.

She'd come here hoping to escape, but what she really needed to stop doing was making silly mistakes. And Nick was nothing more than that.

'Oh,' Leo said, and she wondered whether she was imagining the relief in his gaze. 'That's good,' he said, nodding.

And she nodded too, and then he smiled and she smiled too. Until she remembered Nora.

'I guess I should let you get back to Nora,' she said reluctantly.

'Why?'

'Oh, it's just that I saw you two—'

'Noooo, nope, not a thing,' he said quickly, shaking his head.

'Really?' she asked, horrified that she'd sounded so hopeful.

Embarrassed that he might have heard that. 'Oh, OK,' she said, trying to style it out and feeling like a complete idiot. Especially when she couldn't stop smiling. She turned away, hoping that he hadn't seen.

Will you get it together!

But it was so hard when she now knew that nothing had happened with Nora.

'I guess we should . . .' He trailed off as if the last thing he wanted was to rejoin the group.

Instead of saying anything else that would hint at how she really felt, she nodded and headed back to where Nora and Sydney were dancing, all the while conscious of Leo's attention returning to her again and again.

He accepted the bottle of beer Archie held out to him and took a long pull. Avery found herself hypnotised by the way he swallowed it, the flames licking shadows over his skin and face. She forced her gaze away before he could catch her watching him.

'So, we're all gonna meet at the annex tomorrow, right?' Archie asked, looking to Hugo. It was, after all, *his* island.

Avery frowned. 'What's this?'

'For the storm, tomorrow. In case it hits, we're all meeting there.'

'If we're going to get locked down, there are few better places to be,' Hugo conceded.

He was right. The annex had everything: a billiards table, a cinema even, and most importantly, its own generator.

'Sure,' Sydney said. Nora shrugged and Avery nodded.

She felt Leo's gaze on her . . .

Until Nora passed her a bottle of vodka and she took a mouthful, feeling alcohol slip into her bloodstream and lull her into the music. As a group, they chatted about things from last year and made loose plans for the next. Avery tried to anchor her thoughts to the present – her future, miserable and impossible between her course and her parents' troubles.

Hugo drifted closer, but stuck to talking with the guys. Over Archie's shoulder, Avery saw Leo try and make conversation with Hugo and although they looked OK, it was clearly an effort. Eventually Leo returned to where they were dancing and her entire body responded to his proximity. She rolled her shoulders, trying to shake the millions of sparks across her skin, hoping that no one had noticed her reaction.

Archie offered Nora a drink and, after a pause, she accepted it, everyone breathing a sigh of relief as she did. Nora took a mouthful and accidentally offered it to Sydney, before wincing.

'Sorry,' she said to Sydney, who raised her hands.

'No worries. I've got my trusty water. It's sooooo delicious,' she replied, but without any of the bitterness or nastiness from the previous day.

Electricity danced on the air. Stars blinked in and out, winking from behind clouds passing so fast that Avery could barely keep track of them. The firelight warmed everything.

As the music swelled around them, they all began to dance, swaying in time with the music; hands in the air, around each other, across shoulders. She felt him at her back the entire time. *Leo.* Just out of reach. But different to the last time they had danced at the club. This time, something had shifted.

She turned in a circle, sweeping closer to him, testing herself, testing *him*, her heart racing. She took a step closer and his hand brushed against her hip. Subtle, small, so brief anyone else would have missed it, but it sent a shower of sparks into her chest and out across her skin.

She turned, her gaze catching his, the way that they flared into gold as he caught her looking, his hand on her hip again. Longer. One heartbeat. Two. His fingers flexed, and he came even closer. Impossibly aware of everyone around them, but unable to think of anything but him, her heart thundered in her chest. It was as if this was secret, invisible, *stolen*. His face barely inches away, her breath locked in her chest, her arm on his to keep her from falling and—

'You coming?' Sydney asked Nora, the question cutting through the haze that Avery had fallen under.

Her eyes widened as she realised how close she was to Leo, who instinctively pulled back, cheeks glowing with a faint blush.

'Ahh, that's still a no from me, guys,' Avery heard Nora say as she turned to look at the others. 'But go for it. I'm gonna make it an early night.'

'Nooooo!' they all shouted, and Nora laughed gracefully.

'Seriously. No worries. Have fun!' she said, turning away with a wave, and although Avery was a little regretful, she was also just maybe a little pleased.

Avery's attention was pulled back to Syd when she suddenly and inexplicably pulled off her top.

'What are you doing?' Avery asked with a laugh.

'Swimming!'

'Now?' Avery said, wondering if Syd had finally lost it.

'*Now*,' she said with a glint in her eye.

'Hell yeah!' Archie cried as he too started to remove his clothes.

'Oh shit,' Leo said, laughing, and soon they were all stripping down to their underwear and running for the sea.

A thrill snapped through her body. The electricity sparking on the breeze bit at her skin as she peeled off her dress. Racing for the water as beams of moonlight forced their way through the clouds speeding across the night sky, they screamed as the cool water hit them, laughing and jumping into the waves. Water swept across Avery's skin, the shock, the *life* in it, filling her up with an energy she'd never felt anywhere but here. Currents pulled and swayed, but not enough to disband them. The boys splashed each other and Sydney swam in lazy circles around her.

Her mind buzzing and her body humming, Avery turned her back on the firepit and the glow of the white sand in the moonlight and stared out into the darkness. Unformed shapes shifted around her, water lapping against her skin drowning out everything but her. She felt as if she'd been plucked from this earth and put into the middle of the galaxy. Space surrounded her; space and nothingness and peace and—

On a half-inhale, something tugged Avery sharply beneath the water. Fear seized her mind as her lungs sucked in water that shouldn't be there. She kicked and struck out but whatever it was held her ankle tight, and her scream was swallowed by the sea.

Terror was a jagged streak across her body and suddenly she found herself hauled back out of the water and pressed against Leo's body.

His arm secured her to him, but his face was furious and glaring behind her.

'Jesus, Archie, that wasn't funny,' Leo growled.

'Come on, it was just a joke.'

'Not funny,' Leo snapped again, looking down at her as she spluttered to catch her breath.

'Whatever,' she heard Archie say behind her, and felt him swim away.

Leo guided her back to shore and led her over to the fire, rubbing her shoulders while she tried to get the trembling in her body back under control.

She shivered when he put his arms around her, pulling her into the warmth of his body for an entirely new reason and, just for a moment, Avery wanted to close her eyes and pretend that they were alone. On the beach. The same beach they'd waited on for the sun rise two years before.

'It's OK,' Leo said. 'I've got you.'

And Avery so desperately wanted that to be true.

CHAPTER TWELVE

HUGO

Hugo leaned against the back wall of the staff centre. Mark had woken him up after barely three hours' sleep, *after* having heard the noise on their way back from the Devereuxs and breaking up the party. Mark had told to him get dressed and be ready for the staff meeting at 7.30 a.m.

Overnight, the storm had been categorised as Tropical. As the island was outside the Hurricane belt, they usually missed things like this, but the weather had been getting more and more erratic each year.

Mark was briefing the staff on what needed to happen. He'd made Hugo come with him so that he could see what was needed, and help where possible. He knew Mark was trying to involve him in the *family* business, not because he wanted him to take over, but because he wanted him to feel connected. Mark just hadn't realised that for Hugo, that felt close to impossible these days.

'Sven,' Mark was saying, 'you're in charge of the guests. Can you do the rounds, make sure the villas are prepped, that they know the drill; no wandering around, no funny business. Stay away from doors and windows. Remind them: all the villas have storm-frame windows so we know they'll be entirely safe, but it's best to be prepared.'

'What about the bunkers?' one of the staff asked.

'There's nothing to indicate the storm is going to be that bad, but make sure everyone knows their locations just in case. Mitch?' Leo's dad nodded. 'You're in charge of the staff. Head counts, safety, roles, etc. Drains and drainage channels need to be checked.'

Mitch nodded, and Hugo took the time to look at Leo's dad a little closer. The tall Caribbean man sat on the opposite side of the room to his son. His expression was stern; Hugo wouldn't want to mess with him. Leo had less of his father's severity, but all of his intensity. But Hugo couldn't help but jealously trace the kind of familial similarity that he'd never have with Mark or Darian. He'd witnessed some of Mitchel Walker's outbursts, though, and was still surprised by how contained Leo always was. As if he were older than them, or above them in some way.

Or maybe he was just pissed at Leo for how he'd been with Avery last night.

'Tidal and Luna villas need to be locked down. Tidal is empty, but Luna is midway through construction, so that's the priority. The storm's not due to hit until this afternoon, so we have a few hours. So, let's use them wisely.'

'Yes, sir,' was the unanimous response.

Everyone thought that Mark was the laid-back one, but really, when it came down to it, Hugo thought that he might have been the most in control of them all.

Mark dismissed the staff and beckoned Hugo over.

'Hey, kiddo,' Mark said. He'd been saying that more in the last few months. As if the further Hugo retreated, the more Mark wanted to keep him a kid. 'You've got the others, right?' he asked of Hugo's friends. 'You have to step up and make sure that they're safe.'

'We're going to bunk down in the annex.'

'Good plan,' Mark said, his arm slinging around Hugo's shoulder, the pride and assurance in his tone filling Hugo with a comfort that made him miserable. He hated Darian for doing this, but he hated himself more. For keeping Darian's secret. For betraying Mark every single day.

'You OK? You know you can talk to me. I can't imagine it's easy with Avery—'

'I'm fine, Dad,' Hugo said, shaking Mark's arm off his shoulder, stifling the guilt that rose from the flash of hurt Mark tried to hide.

'Really. It's all good,' Hugo lied.

It was anything but, but he didn't want Mark to know that. Hugo bit back a curse, knowing that he was messing things up and making it all worse.

Mark had some things to finish up at the staff centre, so Hugo left to make his way back to the Big House. He'd grab his stuff, everything they'd need for the storm and then head back out to the annex.

Maybe, now that they were all going to be locked down together, he could finally get hold of Avery. Apologise. Tell her what was going on. Not about his dad, but at least about Nora. Try to explain maybe.

He made his way back out via the path that skirted the inner crescent of the island. It was a little longer, but he wanted that time to himself. Away from the prying eyes of everyone. Paranoia whispered that they were all staring at him, that they all thought he'd lost it.

It's like I don't even know you any more.

Avery's voice crossed in a loop with Archie's.

What is wrong with you?

Hugo wasn't sure he could answer that any more. He felt like he was on the verge of exploding and everyone could see it when they looked at him. He came to the soft green slope that looked down on to the marina.

The boat that had brought Mr Devereux and the girl, Corrine, back from the mainland was moored up on the jetty being rocked by unsettled waves, as if it was trying to throw them off its back.

Dennis was talking to the captain, as Corrine made her way to the side of the boat, stepping off it awkwardly and nearly falling. She gathered herself and the coat she wore around her shoulders and swept a leg over the side of the boat. The other leg was bandaged, but she placed her weight on it easy enough. It was just that...

Hugo squinted.

The two men, still talking on the boat, did nothing. Not even acknowledging her as Corrine hurried awkwardly away from the boat. Something about the way she moved caught Hugo's eye. It reminded him of how he was after a particularly brutal lacrosse face-off.

He watched her go, his mind struggling to make the

connection it wanted to, when in the corner of his eye he caught a flash of red.

Nora. Her bright shirt tucked into denim shorts. She'd been watching too. There was a look on her face that he couldn't read, her gaze flickering between Dennis and Corrine, before she jogged down the pathway after the injured girl.

Hugo huffed out a bitter laugh. Maybe Nora was the reason she was hurt. He doubted they would have been on the cliff without Nora. The staff had never done anything like it before she'd arrived on this island.

Just then a gust of wind slapped at him, nearly pushing him off his feet, and he turned back towards the house. He needed to get everything in place for them to hunker down at the annex. His dad had put him in charge, and for Hugo that was the least he could do for Mark.

Three hours later, Hugo tossed the rucksack packed full of snacks and alcohol on to the sofa in the annex. He'd made a serious raid on the Big House stores, knowing his parents wouldn't notice, let alone care. The wind had seriously picked up and it was getting difficult to stay standing upright out there. Three trips it had taken him to get the annex set up for the lockdown. There was enough food to feed an army. And as for entertainment? There was the projector, the billiards table and a new VR suite.

They had anything and everything they could want. He was just putting the walkie-talkie on to charge, when Syd came down the stairs.

Set underground, the entire space was probably the safest place here aside from the more industrial hurricane bunkers dotted around the island. He was just happy that the parents were staying put in their villas. The idea of having to share the annex with them was horrifying enough to send a shiver down his spine.

Syd pushed up her totally useless sunglasses into her hair and collapsed into the sprawling sofa set that was large enough to accommodate at least ten people and then some.

'Where's Archie?' he asked, throwing a bag of crisps at her.

Syd pulled it open. 'He was on his way, but Mum was on the phone with our grandmother, who wanted to speak to him.'

'Favourite grandchild?'

'And don't you forget it,' Syd said with a vein of bitterness that hadn't been there last year. Whatever help she'd received at the centre clearly hadn't worked through whatever tension was now between the siblings. But he couldn't help but wonder if some of it had helped. Talking to someone.

Hugo was about to ask when Avery came down the stairs, blinking in the brightly lit room, taking all his attention. Relief settled in his veins having her here.

'How bad is it out there?' he asked.

She grimaced. 'Bad. And dark,' she said looking around. 'Where's Nora?'

'Nora?' Hugo echoed, not sure whether he wanted to tell her about seeing her earlier or not.

Syd shook her head. 'Not here. I thought she was with you?'

'No, she left earlier. She said she'd meet me here,' Avery said, rubbing her arms.

'She didn't say where she was going?' Hugo asked, promptly regretting it when Avery turned a flat gaze on him.

'She'll be fine,' Syd dismissed, and Hugo knew at least to hold his tongue.

Avery squinted. 'I'm not so sure. She really should have been here by now,' she said, her gaze flicking to the clock on the wall.

'If you want,' he offered, 'I can radio in to see if anyone's seen her?' Yes, he'd seen Nora with Corrine but that was three hours ago. And if he told her that *now* . . .

'Maybe, I don't know,' Avery hedged, shifting her weight between her feet.

Avery's phone vibrated, Sydney's beeped and Hugo's trilled.

He grabbed his phone, scanning the text alert from Sven. They were locking down the island because the wind speed had picked up too much. No one was to leave, and if anyone was out, they had to find shelter immediately.

Sydney's laugh cut awkwardly into Hugo's alarm. This was serious, didn't she *get* that?

'What's so funny?' he demanded, annoyed.

'Archie . . . he's got stuck at the villa with Mum and Dad. Poor baby,' she said, laughing again and wiping a tear from her eye. 'What?' she demanded when Hugo simply stared at her.

He looked over to Avery for support. But Avery was gone.

LEO

Leo had half expected to be on lockdown duty, but his father had decided that his 'lack of experience' on the island would make him more of a danger than not. So, Leo had bitten his tongue, reminded himself he'd already made plans with the guys last night and aimed for the annex, *not wanting to be a danger to anyone.*

He shifted his rucksack on his back and pressed into the wind. He'd just received the alert and knew he had to get out of the storm soon.

The trees were being pushed into unnatural angles, their branches bearing the brunt of the forceful wind. Bits of trash from bags that had escaped lockdown rolled across the floor and flew into the air. But really all he could see was last night's stars, firelight and flames, Avery and . . .

'Avery?' he yelled into the wind, realising he wasn't imagining her bursting through the treeline.

She stopped when she saw him. 'Have you seen Nora?'

'No, why? Isn't she with you?'

Avery shook her head as wind pummelled her clothes against her body and messed with her hair. It was getting dangerous to be out here.

'We need to get indoors,' he shouted to her.

'Not without Nora,' Avery said shaking her head.

Leo cursed. That girl was more trouble than she was worth.

'We don't have time for this,' he said, closing the distance between them. He wrapped his hand around Avery's arm, and when she tried to pull free he held on tighter. 'We—'

His words were cut off when a table slashed across their path, Leo pulling Avery out of the way just in time.

'Fuck. We need to go. Now.'

'But—'

'No buts,' he said, calculating the distance to the annex. It was too far for them to get to now. He tried to think of the nearest shelter. 'This way, come on.'

'But the annex—'

'No time,' he yelled over the sound of winds that were picking up speed every second that passed.

Something flew low over their heads and Avery screamed, scraping her knees as she dropped down to avoid being hit. Leo pulled her to her feet.

'Can you run?' he asked, noticing her bloody knees.

Avery nodded, her lips trembling.

'Good. We run,' he shouted above the noise of the storm. *'Now.'*

With his arm around her, he hurried them towards the track that led to Tidal. It was by far nearer than either the staff centre or the annex. His only hope was that his staff card would let him into the unoccupied villa. Because if it didn't, they'd be stuck out here in the middle of a tropical storm.

They hurried down the path, the wind pushing and pulling at them, making their descent slow. In the distance he could see the way the waves whipped up against the shoreline, white frothing beasts attacking the island.

By the time they reached the villa, they were breathing hard. Leo retrieved his key and passed it over the keypad. The red light flashed, and he knew there should have been a beep, but the sound was swallowed by the wind.

He cursed as he swiped the card again. And again, no dice.

Avery pulled the card from his hand and held it against the keypad. After two seconds it turned green and she pushed into the building, Leo hot on her heels until they slammed the door shut and collapsed in the hallway, shaking, breathing hard and, in Avery's case, bleeding.

'Are you OK?' he asked her.

'No,' she said, pushing up off the floor. 'I'm *not* OK.' She turned against him and shoved at his chest with her hands. 'Nora could be out there, hurt. She could be . . .'

Avery trailed off with a sob as if imagining a thousand different terrible ways Nora could be hurt.

'That girl has nine lives,' Leo dismissed under his breath before saying louder, 'She'll be fine.' He stalked towards the villa's kitchen and started opening the drawers beneath the sink. The kitchens were primarily for show, even though every single one was one hundred per cent fully functional and top spec. He reached for the large green box he knew would be under the sink.

'What are you doing?' Avery demanded.

He turned to her, putting the first aid kit on the side and lifted her up before she could say or do anything, placing her carefully on the island counter.

'You—'

'Shh,' he said, opening the box and retrieving the antibacterial wipes. He tore one open and wiped his hands with one. Then reached for another.

'I—'

'Shhh,' he said, tearing the fresh antibacterial wipe packet as he looked at her knee. It didn't look too bad, but it did need cleaning, ointment and covering.

'What—'

He stopped what he was doing, looked up and glared at her until she was quiet.

'This may sting,' he said, and pressed the wipe over the graze on her knee. He heard the sharp hiss of her inhale and clenched his jaw. He swallowed. 'And again,' he said as he did the same to the other knee. He dabbed at the grazes, making sure that they were as clean as possible before applying the ointment carefully.

He was reaching for a plaster when the walkie-talkie in his backpack crackled.

'Leo, are you there?'

He picked up the walkie-talkie. 'Yeah.'

'Where are you?' Hugo asked, the line heavy with static.

Leo's eyes met Avery's, both knowing that he wasn't going to like it one bit that they were here and he was there.

'We're stuck at Tidal,' he replied, cutting the connection of their gaze.

'We?' Hugo asked.

'Me. Avery.'

The silence on the radio made him want to wince, but he gritted his teeth together instead.

'It's not safe to head back out,' Leo forced out. 'We'll stay here until the storm passes.'

'Fine.'

It was the only answer they got. He tossed the walkie-talkie on to the counter.

'He's not going to like that,' he replied.

'That is not my problem or responsibility,' Avery replied.

'Just like Nora isn't mine,' Leo pointed out as he peeled the back off the plaster.

'She's my friend, Leo.'

'Is she? Really? I doubt she's cared about anyone other than herself her entire life,' he said, thinking of how little she seemed to behave like a friend to Avery.

'Is this because of what happened between the two of you at the staff party?' Avery asked.

'Nothing happened at the staff party,' Leo replied honestly. 'There is no "two of us". And even if there was, why would you care?' he poked, digging into the frustration that was burning between them.

Because, he realised, she *did*. The memory of last night on the beach, before the party was broken up by the parents ... The *almost* thing that was developing between them.

Avery scoffed, which turned into a gasp as he pressed the plaster carefully over the scrape on one knee.

'I don't care,' she denied, as he picked up the next plaster, nudging her leg out to the side so he could get better access.

He placed the plaster on her knee and straightened, realising that he was in between her legs. He took her in – the whole of her. The way the sun had picked out golden highlights in her long dark hair. The way the freckles she hated spread out across her nose and touched her skin with gold. The way her lips were pink and lush, and just a little open, until she bit down on the bottom one with her teeth.

'What if *I* did?' he asked, unable to stop himself.

'Did what?'

'Care.'

'About Nora?' Avery asked, her voice catching.

Leo reached up to cup her jaw. 'No.'

This wasn't about Nora. It was about *them*. And she knew it. He saw the way her eyes changed in realisation.

She swallowed and looked down.

'Why now?' she whispered, as if not sure she wanted to ask. As if half afraid of the answer. 'Why not . . .'

'Two years ago?' he finished, knowing that this was where they'd always come back to, that *this* was what was between them.

'Was it me?' she asked, voice quivering, eyes glistening.

'God, no,' he rushed to reassure her.

And she bit a trembling lip, finally leaning her head into his palm, the contact sending a flare through his chest. His thumb brushed over her cheek.

'That night,' he said, inhaling a sigh, 'it was . . . *everything* to me.' He gently angled her face to his, so that she could see the truth in his eyes. 'The island had always been fun – games with the boys, swimming, then partying when we got older. Seeing my dad whenever he had the time, but mainly it was about all of you guys.

'But that night . . . that night we talked about things that I'd never said on this island.'

'You told me about your mum.'

'You *asked* about my mum. You asked about,' he shook his head, remembering, '*everything*. What I wanted to do after school, if I wanted to travel, did I want to come here and work with Dad, did I want to go to university.'

'You said no,' she remembered.

'And I still don't.'

'But you *are* working on the island.'

'I didn't know that until I turned up here.'

'Oh, Leo,' Avery said, her eyes shining bright. 'That's . . . awful. I'm—'

'I don't want to talk about my dad right now,' he interrupted her gently. They'd tap-danced around this for two years. He didn't want to waste another minute on anyone else, as hope and fear and something else drove him on.

Her.

'That night, for the first time, I'd found someone who made me feel like I *fit*.'

'Are you calling me a jigsaw?' she teased hesitantly.

'A little?' he confessed, smiling only because she smiled. 'And it felt so good that I didn't want to mess it up.' Looking back he realised that he'd been scared. Terrified of losing someone who meant so much to him. Who had made him feel like *all* of him was right. Not just parts of him like his father or his mother – or Hugo and the twins just seeing him the weeks they spent together.

'And I hadn't wanted to risk losing that feeling. But by the time I'd realised what a monumental mistake I'd made, you . . .'

'Were with Hugo,' Avery finished, looking down again.

'And honestly?' he said, pressing on. 'You seemed *good* together. And he could give you all the things that I couldn't.'

'Like what?' she asked him, her hand on his wrist. 'What could he have given me that you couldn't? You think all I wanted was gifts? Nights at the club? Skiing holidays?' She shrugged in confusion. 'Fancy jewellery?'

'You *deserve* all those things,' he insisted.

She looked at him and shook her head. 'If you thought that, then you don't know me at all,' she said, turning away.

Leo's hand slipped out and circled her wrist, holding her in place.

'I didn't want to give you things because I thought you wanted them, Avery,' he said, pulling her hand to place it against his chest, where she would feel his heartbeat. 'I wanted to give you things so that you'd know I wasn't with you for something. So that you knew I was with you for *you*,' he said. 'Because I *do* know you, Avery. I know you better than I know anyone else in the world.'

'That's just it,' she said, tears welling in her eyes, shocking him. 'You don't. You don't know what I've done,' she said with a sob.

CHAPTER THIRTEEN

AVERY

Misery welled from somewhere so deep, it felt bottomless.

Leo was pressed in between her legs, but she wouldn't move him. Couldn't. He was finally here, with her, telling her that he wanted to be with her . . . and he didn't know her at all.

He thought she was still Good Little Avery Finch.

'Speak to me,' Leo begged. 'Tell me what's wrong?'

Everything. She wanted to tell him but was so terrified of what he'd think, of what she'd see in his eyes when he looked at her. Judgement. Disappointment.

But she couldn't start anything with him, with a lie hanging over their heads. She just couldn't.

'Whatever it is, Avery, it can't be that bad.'

She swallowed. But it was.

'I . . . this year . . . it was tough,' she started, wanting to pull him closer, wanting to bury her head in him, to feel his warmth wrap around her. But if she did that, and he pulled away . . . And then Leo made the decision for her, pressing in closer, his arms coming around her to hold her. To hold her *together*.

'Things are tough with my parents. There are problems with Dad's company. It's made Mum *extra* . . .' Extra stressed, extra mean, extra demanding. 'And college, well. It was such a step up from high school. So much harder than I thought. Within months I was struggling, and by the second term I was failing,' she admitted. 'And if I failed, then I couldn't take over the family business like my parents want me to, like Sydney will do for the Devereuxs. And I hate it. I hate business. I hate my degree. That's why I'm failing. And because I'm failing . . . I cheated,' Avery whispered, eyes closed, shame burning her cheeks. 'On my midterms. And Nora caught me, the night before the exam. Told me not to worry. That I was doing what I needed to do. But . . . it's just . . . everything has felt wrong and horrible since then. So,' – she wiped away a tear from her cheek – 'you see? You don't know me at all.' She looked up at him, braced for horror, for disgust.

But all she saw was an understanding that stopped her heart with hope.

He shook his head. 'I'm so sorry. About your folks. About how hard that must have been for you.'

She tried to look away, not ready to believe his words, seeking the familiar hurt and fear that was closer to hand.

'But I *do* know you, Avery. And I know that you're more than just that one thing, that one decision.'

She wanted to scoff, to deny it, but the intent in his gaze froze her to the spot.

'I know that stupid Insta reels about silly animals makes you laugh. That, and unlikely or inappropriate swearing,' he said with a lightness and a shrug that stole away some of her heart. 'That doing something you think is naughty – but not mean – makes you giddy and excited. Like the time we stole the jet-skis at midnight three years ago.' She remembered that. She'd laughed and squealed as they'd raced around the bay in the moonlight.

'I know that you can't watch a film with animals in case they're hurt and no one can tell them why, and you'll cry because that's the saddest thing you know, and that when you were younger you wanted to be a veterinarian,' he said, his words striking deep into her heart, making her want to cry all over again, but this time for completely different reasons.

'I know that you like the quiet more than you like the noise. That your favourite snack is some weird-ass Canadian chocolate-chip cookie, and you inexplicably like paprika-flavoured crisps, which is *not* a flavour by the way,' he insisted, pulling on her arm, bringing them closer.

'And I know that you don't like laughing first because you're afraid that Syd or Archie will take the piss. Which they will, so I get it. I know that you *did* like Hugo,' Leo said with a swallow, 'that he wasn't just someone you used. But he used *you* and that's why he'll never be good enough for you. And that's why he hurt you the most.'

Avery felt the tears well in her eyes, and despite the way they smudged the outline of Leo, she felt the truth binding her to him, making her feel seen.

'I know that you're amazing, Avery Finch,' he said vehemently. 'You're smart, funny, beautiful. And I know that you'll find the right way through what happened with the midterms, whatever that is. And one day, you'll find something you do want to do, and when that happens, everything will fall into place and make sense. And then you'll be unstoppable,' he said, pressing his forehead to hers, not aware how much his words had healed a broken part of her. How much she wanted those words to be true.

'So no, nothing you've said makes me feel any differently. I want *you*. I want to be with *you*,' he confessed in a voice that sounded like surrender.

Shivers rippled over her skin; her heart pounded in her chest, in her ears.

His gaze was like a touch everywhere his eyes landed, her cheek, her hip, her toes scrunching in her trainers. Her breath caught in her lungs, and a flush of heat burned her cheeks.

She bit her lip and his hand reached up, the pad of his thumb gently leveraging it free. But even after its release, his hand stayed against her jaw, cupping her cheek. His gaze was golden, swirling like the winds of the storm outside, his breath soft against her damp lips.

Her inhale was a gasp, her body arching into him, wanting – needing – to feel him against her. His head was bowed, his lips barely an inch from hers. All she had to do was reach—

He met her halfway and kissed her.

And suddenly where there had been silence and subtlety was movement and noise and *everything*.

Oh god, it was incredible.

His hands reached up to frame her face as he pushed her back against the counter, as if he wanted to lean into her as much as she wanted him to.

He pulled out of the kiss, his dazed eyes still on her. 'That's ... You're ...' He swallowed and she liked that she'd done that to him. That she'd made him speechless. Hugo had always been so controlled, but Leo . . . he just let it show. Let her see.

She bit her lip. 'You are too,' she said with a smile, giggling when he swept in for a short kiss as if he couldn't stop himself, until something hit the window, scaring the life out of her and making her jump.

'Let's get somewhere safer,' he said, pulling her away from the kitchen window and towards the hallway.

His pace slowed as he hesitated about where to go next. Taking over, she dismissed the smaller bedrooms off the hallway and guided him out into the glass-sided walkway that led to a different section of the villa.

It was an entire bedroom suite, fully furnished, with a free-standing tub and a chair in the corner of the room facing the larger than imaginable bed. She flipped the switch, but nothing happened.

'Guess the power is out,' Leo said.

'Guess so,' Avery replied, her voice shaky, because her heart was pounding. She went to sit on the end of the bed, Leo coming round to face her. He was looking at her in that way – intent, intense – like he had on the boat. Like he had two years before. Then and now collapsed together and it was as if last two years hadn't happened. It was as if this was the logical, the *only*, end to the night they had spent talking for hours. It was even as dark as that pre-dawn moment had been, where everything was quiet and it was just the two of them.

Eyes on his, heart in her mouth, Avery slipped out of her T-shirt, revealing the bikini top she wore beneath. Leo's gaze raked over her skin, leaving light touches in its wake. The muscle at his jaw flexed, but she knew he wasn't angry. He was holding himself back. And she didn't want that. Not any more.

Once again, he bent to kiss her, gently pressing her back against the beautiful bed.

She grabbed at his top, and he stopped kissing her just long enough for her to pull his T-shirt over his head and throw it aside.

There was only one thing that occupied her thoughts now.

Leo.

HUGO

'Leo? Come in, Leo,' Hugo said into the walkie-talkie. 'Leo?' he tried again and . . . nothing. He pressed his forehead hard against the bar's countertop until it hurt.

'It's not worth it, H,' Sydney called from where she was halfway down her second bag of crisps, on the sofa pretending to watch one of the DVDs he'd found after hooking it up to the projector. The power had flickered for a while until it cut out and the generator kicked in. But the generator didn't cover the Wi-Fi.

At least it hadn't knocked out the walkie-talkies. Mark had checked in with him just moments ago. Which was why he was so mad that Leo wasn't answering.

Hugo barely restrained the urge to hurl the walkie-talkie across the room.

This wasn't how it was supposed to go. He dropped down on to his haunches, ducking behind the bar, not wanting Syd to see him like this.

Christ, he was going to start crying like a little girl. He clenched his fists trying to hold on to himself, and failing.

'They did this thing, you know, at the centre. Whenever we got stressed or . . . whatever,' Sydney said, her voice drifting over to where he hid behind the counter. 'Box breathing.'

'Syd,' he warned, not in the mood.

'You breathe in for four, hold it for four, out for four, hold it—'

'For four. I get the picture, Syd.'

'Anyways, I thought it was a load of bull,' she said, then he heard the crunch of crisps. 'But apparently,' she added, swallowing, 'the seals do it.'

'Seals?' Hugo asked, despite himself. 'How do they know—'

'*Navy* SEALs, dude. And if it works for them, I thought, why not give it a go?' she said, followed by more crunching of crisps.

The sound of which, he realised, would cover the sound of his attempts at this breathing thing.

He bit his lip and cursed silently. He couldn't hold on to all this anger. It was pouring out of him in ways he couldn't control any more.

So, he inhaled. Counted to four.

He felt like a fool. An idiot. But he stuck to counting, breathing, holding, until eventually he started to feel less angry. Less urgent. Less out of control. Finally coming back into what felt more like himself than he'd done for a while, he sat properly on the floor, his head falling back against the side of the countertop.

After a while, the silence between them settled.

'Did it work for you?' he asked, looking at the fridges but knowing she'd hear him all the same.

'I dunno. I never tried it.'

Hugo couldn't help the laugh that burst out of his chest. 'You bitch,' he said without heat.

'Grab me a can of soda?'

He reached forward, grabbed a can from the fridge and pulled himself off the floor. Rounding the countertop, he threw it to her as he sunk down on the sofa beside her, catching the bag of crisps she tossed him in return.

'Mum's worried I'm going to get fat,' Sydney said, popping the can open. 'But she'll probably just find me another rehab for it.'

Her tone was amused, but Hugo wasn't completely convinced.

Side by side they both stared ahead at the muted TV, neither really watching.

'How was it? *Really?*' Hugo asked, finding some kind of ease talking about someone else for a change. Thinking of something else for a change.

He felt her swallow.

'Pretty awful. Not ... *good*,' she said, as if choosing her words carefully. 'Part of me didn't want to be there because I didn't think I needed to be.'

'And the other part?'

'Terrified of turning into one of the repeats. The people that had gone out, come back, gone out and come back again.'

She shook her head, her lips wobbling as if she was trying to stop herself from tearing up.

'They all had this look, you know. Like a wounded animal ready to bite off its own foot to escape. And to go back out there, to what?' she said, throwing another handful of crisps into her mouth.

'I'm sorry. I didn't know it had got that bad,' Hugo confessed.

Sydney shrugged. 'I didn't either.'

'Are you on, like, steps or something?' he asked, feeling like a complete tool.

'I'm kind of struggling a little with the first one to be honest,' she said blowing out a breath. 'I don't *want* to have a problem. I don't *want* to be different. I don't want to be around you guys when you're all drinking. It's hard when you're all together getting wasted.'

Guilt twisted in his stomach. 'We shouldn't—'

'Don't be silly. You can't all stop just because I'm . . . *not*. Life doesn't work like that, does it?'

No, it didn't, he thought, rubbing the ache in his sternum. For a short while, there was nothing but the sound of fizz from the soda can and the crunch of Sydney's crisps. But he knew what was coming. He knew it wouldn't be that easy.

'What is it?' she asked, sincerely for the first time, putting the empty crisp bag down on the table. 'What's up with you? Because I know it's not just Avery,' she said, pinning him with an unreadable gaze.

His breath shuddered in his lungs. And he didn't want to do her the disservice of lying. Not after what she'd shared.

'What if . . . what if it wasn't *me*? What if it was my dad?' he said, his hands gripping his thighs. Instinct not to speak almost gagged his words before he could get them out. The fear of saying the thing that would detonate his entire life. But he couldn't keep it in any more. It was like it was finding ways to get out, to ruin him anyway.

'What if it was my dad with some guy barely two years older

than me, and it was clear they'd been . . .' Hugo trailed off, not able to actually say it.

Sydney let out a soft gasp, understanding without him having to verbalise it.

'And what if, instead of being sorry, or apologetic, he was . . .' Hugo swallowed and looked at his hands. 'Angry. Mean. And he stopped looking at you like a son, and instead looked at you like a threat. And what if he blackmailed you into silence? Promised that it was better that way. Promised that you could have whatever you wanted, and no one would need to be hurt. No one's life would be upended. No one would lose anything. They'd only *gain*.'

God, he really was going to be sick. Because he'd agreed. He'd gone along with it. He'd wanted it.

Because he hadn't wanted his life upended. Because he *did* want everything to stay the same. Because he'd been genuinely terrified that he would lose everything he'd ever loved. And it was happening anyway.

'I *hate* secrets,' he said, as tears formed in his eyes.

'Is that why you went after Nora?' Sydney's voice was gentle, but curious.

'I went after Nora because she deserved it,' he said, his thoughts shifting instantly. 'She was the one who made Avery split up with me. Whispering in her ear. Ever since they met, Avery's been acting differently. *Nora said* this. *Nora said* that.'

'Maybe people change when they go to college. I wouldn't know,' Sydney hedged.

'Yeah, maybe,' he said, not really meaning it.

Avery had gone from careless and fun to something else.

She'd accused him of keeping things from her, but she wasn't exactly being honest either. Things were going on with her folks – he'd heard his parents talk about it. But more than that, it was this *thing* between her and Nora. Like knowing looks. As if they had their own secrets.

Sometimes, he wasn't even sure that they liked each other.

'Look, Nora is hardly my favourite person. But you need to let it go, or you're going to push Avery too far.'

'She shouldn't be here,' Hugo said, ignoring Sydney's warning. 'And she's up to something too. I just *know* it. She's always sneaking off and then suddenly appearing when you don't want her to. And she's always asking about your dad.'

'Is she?' Sydney asked, sitting up straighter. 'I don't—'

'Not to you, obviously. But she was asking Archie about him the other night on the beach. And she wanted to go to the mainland with him and that girl.'

'What girl?' Syd asked with a frown.

'The—'

The projector burst back into life in the middle of an action scene.

Hugo's heart pounded, and even Sydney yelped.

'Jesus.'

'Oh my god.'

The two of them descended into giggles at their shock. The moment was broken and it was almost impossible to imagine going back to the intimacy of before. Instead they spent the rest of the lockdown willingly distracting themselves with terrible action flicks and all the crisps and treats they could get their hands on.

'Syd...'

She turned. 'I won't say a word. Promise.'

He really hoped that was true.

Six hours later and he'd just dropped off the walkie-talkie at the staff centre and was heading back up to the Big House.

Mark and Darian were out there with Sven, checking on the island. There were some minor bits of damage, but it was already in the process of being fixed. Luna had suffered the worst because of the on-going construction, but nothing irreparable.

Archie had found him and Syd as soon as they emerged from the annex, complaining bitterly about the lecture he'd received from his dad about getting a 'real job', and how his mother had forced him to play cards for three hours straight, while Dennis locked himself in his study. 'Presumably so he didn't have to play cards with Mum,' he'd said, before punching Sydney in the shoulder.

'What was that for?' she'd asked.

'Abandoning me to them.'

'You don't get to say that any more. Not after last year,' she'd said, her tone sharp. The look Archie had given back was unreadable.

Leo and Avery had joined them by the pool, Avery still asking if anyone had seen Nora. Neither would meet his gaze, but Nora was consuming the conversation even without being here.

'She'll turn up,' Syd had said before heading back to her parents' villa. 'Like she always does,' she added, almost inaudible on the still frantic breeze.

Archie and Leo had offered to help look for Nora and as Avery had headed towards the Finches' villa, they'd gone to the beach, while Hugo had come back to the staff centre.

Hugo passed a couple of staff, who bobbed their heads in acknowledgement, but rounding the corner of the bunk house, his feet came to a stop when he heard heated voices.

'Enough. I told you already. I don't want to do this.'

Hugo frowned, recognising the French accent. Corrine. But it was the person she was talking to that surprised him the most.

'Please, C, I've only got one shot at this. *We've* only got one shot.'

'You think I don't get it? You think we all don't get it?' Corrine demanded. 'We let them take what they want, and in return, if we're lucky, we take what we can get. And he's offering a hell of a lot more than you are. I could finally go to college.'

'Yeah. You could. And that's a big offer for *now* maybe,' Hugo heard Nora plead as he edged towards the corner of the building. 'But once he's exposed? Once everyone knows? There'll be a hell of a lot more to take from him then.'

Who was Nora talking about?

'All you have to do is get him admitting it on tape,' Nora pressed.

'I have to go.'

'Corrine—'

'I have to go,' Corrine repeated, and he heard the beep of a key pad and slam of the bunk-house door.

Footsteps coming his way had him pressing into the wall, not wanting to be seen by Nora, having overheard whatever the hell that was. He watched her walk back towards Coastal, where the Finches were staying, uneasiness settling into a hard stone in his gut. He should probably tell Avery. But Sydney's words rang in his ears and he knew it would only make things worse. No. This was one secret he'd be happy to keep.

For now.

CHAPTER FOURTEEN

LEO

Leo roughly dried himself off after getting out of the shower, then grabbed his shirt and a pair of jeans, in a hurry to get the hell out of the bunk house.

Yesterday had been . . .

Yesterday had been *incredible*.

He'd not really allowed himself to think about what it would be like if Avery returned his feelings. So, he'd been completely unprepared for how amazing it had been. He'd not even known that sex could *be* like that.

And for the first time that summer, he didn't care that his dad had only wanted him here to work. He didn't care that the staff treated him differently, or that he was different to his friends.

Because he had Avery. And she was all he could ever imagine wanting right now.

He pushed out into the sunshine – bright and harsh after the darkness of the storm yesterday. He blinked, taking in the debris and mess the storm had left in its wake.

The bins had tipped over at the back of the staff centre and spilled their contents on the pathway. Everyone was too busy putting the guest areas back to rights to worry about here. Leo stopped and shovelled what he could back into the broken sacks and into the storage containers. Grimacing, he went to wash his hands at the outside tap.

'You're not fooling anyone with that smile, boy,' his dad had said with the jab of his finger. 'You make sure Sven doesn't find out. I'm not losing my job because you couldn't keep it in your pants.'

He'd been surprised that his dad had even noticed, but he just couldn't bring himself to care, nor could he stop smiling as he made his way down to the beach at Tidal where he'd agreed to meet Avery before they'd left yesterday.

The beep of an electric cart surprised him, yanking him from his thoughts and Leo was forced to jump out of the way to avoid being run over. Domingo and Nick cat-called him as they passed, Nick clearly having only just got back from the mainland now that the travel ban had been lifted.

'Piss off,' Leo yelled without much heat.

Dom locked eyes with him in the rear-view mirror and flipped him off, causing Nick to howl with laughter and Leo grinned as they disappeared off towards the staff centre.

He came to the end of the path and saw Avery sitting on the wall that hugged the entrance to the villa, swinging her legs and knocking her heels against the brick. And he took a moment – just a moment – to soak her in. She looked like sunshine and every sweet thing he'd ever wanted.

She smiled before she looked up, as if sensing him. It was a secret smile, the kind that he wanted to kiss on her lips.

'Hey,' Avery said, lifting her gaze to his, grinning at him as he finally closed the distance between them.

'Hey,' he replied, probably grinning back like a maniac. His hands went straight to her hips and pulled her down, off the wall and into his arms for a kiss. Avery put up a terrible show of fake resisting.

'Come on, let's head down to the beach,' he said, knowing that if they went into Tidal, they'd not want to leave.

She took his hand in hers, threading her fingers through his and he liked it. He asked about her folks as they followed the side path from the villa down on to the beach.

'They're—*Oh*,' Avery gasped.

Further on down the beach, closer to the other villas, staff had already cleared much of the debris, but down here, it was a mess. Broken tree branches, leaves, human rubbish, broken bottles and wood. There was a half-broken sunlounger, one of the staff ones, plastic and jagged.

'I didn't realise it had been this bad,' Avery said, stepping delicately in between the debris.

'I don't think that's a good idea,' Leo said, wondering how dangerous it was, and worrying about the flip-flops on her feet. They didn't look like they'd protect her from anything sharp.

Further out, the sea was still a stormy grey but the sky was blue and cloudless like nothing had ever happened.

'Avery—'

'Oh god,' she said, her hands flying to her mouth in shock.

Leo rushed over to where she stood and immediately stopped.

A bird was lying there, neck broken, wings matted and feathers dirty. Ants were already crawling all over it, out of his eyes and beak, and at least two crabs were scuttling over the carcass, picking at whatever they could find.

'Come on, there's nothing we can do for it,' he said, gently pulling her away, back towards the cleaner part of the beach, his gut twisting in disgust.

'Sorry, I'm being silly,' she said, trying to shake off the horror she clearly felt.

Leo pulled her into his side. 'That's OK,' he said, and turned her to face the villas.

'Was it all bad? The storm . . .' he asked, trying to distract her, but also – not so unconsciously – wanting to know.

Did she regret it? Was it just a one-off? He hated feeling insecure about it, but it was so new, so precious and they'd not really been able to properly talk about it yesterday. Once the all-clear alert came through, they'd been worried that someone, *Hugo*, might try to come and find them. So, they'd hastily scrabbled back into their clothes and headed out to the pool just as Archie had been coming out of his parents' villa complaining that they were now old enough to have their own villas and shouldn't have to be forced to share with their parents.

Avery leaned back in his arms, blinking up at him, with a beautiful smile on her lips. 'No. Some of it was *amazing*,' she said in a whisper, as if it were a secret just between them. He preened beneath her words, relief staked his heart and he probably could have died happy right in that moment.

And when something clouded her gaze, he almost wished he had.

'I'm just . . . not sure that I'm ready for everyone to know yet,' she confessed.

He got it, he did. It wasn't as if people knowing would make his life any easier. But a part of him, instinctive and involuntary, wondered whether it was because he was just the son of a cook and—

'Stop,' Avery said, shaking her head. 'It's not what you think. It's not *that*.'

He nodded and rested his head against her forehead.

'It's just that when the others find out, it won't just be you and me. And I kind of want it to be you and me for a while. I don't want the comments, and the jokes. I can't even imagine what Hugo would be like. And I just want to enjoy *us* for a while.'

'I know. And I get it. My dad's the same,' he explained. And if the staff found out, it would make things a million times worse. 'I just . . . I really hate secrets,' he said, frustrated with the situation. Maybe if Hugo had been less over the top about the whole thing, and if his dad wasn't such a hardcase . . .

'Are you sure? Because if you're not . . .' she asked, looking up at him with those deep-brown eyes.

And, smiling, he rolled his own and said truthfully, 'Yes, of course.'

AVERY

Avery swallowed her sigh of relief. Yesterday had been incredible, and better than anything she'd experienced before. And he *still* wanted her. A part of her, an old part, had worried that he might change his mind. Or that she might not have been . . . good enough. But that wasn't the case and it warmed her as much as it thrilled her. She bit her lip and looked up at him, struck by how handsome he was.

She hated the fact that if people found out about them, it would ruin the rest of the holiday, but they didn't really have much time left.

And after the holiday?

Thoughts about her midterms, her parents' business, her degree – they rose like a darkness on the horizon. And she didn't want that. Couldn't think about that now.

So, instead, she rose on to her toes and pulled his face down to hers. She pressed her lips against his, relishing the way it felt to be in his arms. Safe, protected. *Wanted*.

'This is hardly discreet,' he teased against her mouth, laughing.

That was what she liked most about him. He was *happy* with her. Hugo was demanding, Sydney obnoxious, Archie was just a joker and Nora . . . Avery wasn't really sure what Nora was. But Leo, she thought as she looked up at him and pushed away from him to skip down to where the warm tide met the shore, Leo was happy.

She picked her way through the waves, but the sea foam had picked up dirt and seaweed and bits of rubbish torn by the ocean. It was strange to see it like this. Especially when the sky was a perfect clear blue.

'Was there much damage to the island?' she asked as she toed the foam on the tide.

'Bits and pieces,' Leo said, watching her. 'Luna was worst hit, but that was because it wasn't as watertight as the rest. The renovation work had opened up a part of the building, and that didn't do it any favours.'

Avery nodded, thinking of how he'd known that, of how weird it was that he was working here. And then remembered what he'd said yesterday about his dad.

'Why *are* you working here this year?' she asked, looking up at Leo as he squinted to the horizon.

He took a breath and blew it out hard.

'We don't have to talk about it,' she rushed to tell him, taking his hand in hers, but he was already smiling at her, to let her know that it was OK.

He shook his head and scrunched his nose. 'I didn't know I *would* be,' he admitted, pulling on his earlobe. 'Dad called about a month back? Said he wanted me to come out a week early. And . . . And I thought this was it. *This* was the year that I'd get to spend some proper time with him.' His fingers flexed in hers. 'That maybe *this* was the year he'd take me to meet my grandma, my aunties. They live on an island about an hour from here.' Leo swallowed. 'He'd always said he was too busy in the past. But last year, at the end of the trip, I forced myself to actually just ask. Ask to meet them, and he said, we'll see.'

Leo's steps slowed to a stop, and she leaned against him, already hearing the hurt in his voice.

'So, when he called wanting me to come a little earlier, I thought that this was it.' He bent to pick up a stone, rolling it in his fingers, before hurling it into the sea. 'And then maybe, once I'd met them, I wouldn't feel like . . . like he was ashamed of me.'

Avery hugged herself back into his side, devastated for him, and then felt sick to her stomach that she'd asked to keep him a secret.

'We're telling everyone!' Avery announced, and he laughed.

'I'm serious,' she insisted.

'I can see that,' he replied. 'But that's not necessary. I *do* know that these two things are very different. It's just . . . It's weird having this whole family out there that I'm linked to by blood and not knowing who they are. What they're like. How they live, even. For all I know, they don't even care.'

Avery looked at him, struggling to find the right thing to say. But all she could say was, 'I'm so sorry. For your dad to just . . . put you to work. That must have been devastating.'

Leo bit his lip and just nodded.

'Did you tell your mum?' Avery asked.

'No. She'd be . . .' Leo frowned. 'She'd be worried about me. She'd know that it would have hurt. And she's worked so hard to keep some kind of connection between me and my dad going, especially as it's not just about him but that whole side of my family – my identity. Things Mum just couldn't give me, no matter how much she might want to,' he said, kicking the sand. 'But at least I'm getting paid, right?' He grinned, trying to lighten the feelings brought up by their heart-to-heart.

She sensed that he was bringing the conversation to an end, and she didn't want to push him. He'd tell her more when he was ready.

So instead, she replied, 'Yes. And what exactly are you planning to do with your millions?'

He picked her up, twirled her around and put her back down. She laughed.

'They're already spoken for, I'm afraid. They should take a nice chunk out of my student debt.'

'When I first met you, I don't think I'd ever have guessed that you'd end up studying law. What's it like?' she asked, her footsteps slowing as Leo drew to a halt, wincing with a pain that didn't look physical.

'I'm not. At law school,' he said swallowing. As if he was nervous.

'No?' she asked.

He shook his head.

'Then what are you doing?' she asked, confused.

'I . . . I'm at culinary school,' he said, kicking the sand on the beach.

'Really?' Avery asked, excited, *knowing* that it fit Leo far better than law ever had. And then she realised. Realised why he'd been so hesitant telling her about it. 'Does your dad know?'

'I never told him about switching my course. He doesn't think that culinary school is the *right* way to learn how to cook.'

Avery pressed her lips together, understanding parental disappointment. After all, wasn't that why she'd got into the mess she was in?

'Do you like it?' she asked, curious.

He looked at her and she saw. She saw the way his eyes just *lit up*.

'I *love* it,' he confessed. 'I love everything about it. I love the precision, I love the order. I love the creativity. I want to go to Italy and learn how to make pasta, I want to go to Spain and learn how to make paella. Korea! I want to go and learn how to make bibimbap!'

And that kind of excitement, enthusiasm . . . It was wonderful.

'What did your mum say?'

'She was a little worried. Worried that I was doing it just to try to impress Dad. But then when I started cooking for her, making her things when she'd get caught up in a painting sometimes and forget to cook, I realised that I liked feeding her. It was like paying her back in a way. Not that she'd ever wanted that or expected it. But still, I enjoyed it, caring for her.'

Avery could see that. She was fascinated by his passion.

'Would you . . .' She hesitated, but told herself that it was unnecessary. That she was free to ask now. He wouldn't laugh at her or reject her. 'Would you maybe cook for me one day?'

The look of delight that passed across Leo's features made her feel a million bucks.

'Yeah. Yeah, I could. I'd really like that,' he said, picking her up and swinging her round again, their laughter stolen by the wind and swept away into the distance.

Leo smiled, kicking at the waves. He looked bashful and adorable, but when he hit her with that amber gaze she felt a kick to her chest.

'I'm glad your mum supports you. She's proud of you,' Avery said, having realised it from the way he spoke about her. Their love, that bond, it was something she was near envious of. He smiled that bashful smile again and she loved it.

'I don't know. It must all seem silly to you,'

'No. Not at all,' she replied. 'If I'm honest, I'm a little jealous,' she admitted. She just wished she'd found something that she wanted to do half as much as he had. Like Corrine had, Nora even. They all had things that they were passionate about. And she felt like the odd one out.

'Have you decided what you're going to do? About the midterms,' Leo asked.

She bit her lip and it was her turn to look out over the dull, white-capped sea.

'Yeah, I think so. I think I'm going to—'

'There you are!' Sydney shouted angrily, hurtling towards them from the treeline.

Avery turned, shocked at how angry Sydney seemed to be. With *her*.

'Yes?' she said, confused and then, trying to make light of whatever was going on, 'I haven't been hiding.'

'What the hell is your friend up to?' Syd demanded.

Alarm cut through any attempts to lighten the situation. 'What are you talking about?'

'Archie found Nora coming out of our villa this morning, acting all shady. Saying that she was looking for you. But I don't believe her.'

'Hold on a minute—' Leo tried to intervene.

'Back off, this has nothing to do with you,' Sydney warned with a pointed finger.

Leo held his hands up in surrender but moved closer to Avery all the same.

'Do you want to tell me why she was looking for you at my villa?' Sydney demanded, her anger totally disproportionate to whatever was going on.

Oh god, what was Nora playing at?

'I . . . told her I was going to try to meet up with you,' Avery lied and felt Leo flinch beside her as if knowing what she'd just done.

'Yeah, then why didn't I know about it? And why the hell is she so interested in my dad?' she said, hands on hips, glaring at Avery. 'Because apparently she's been asking around about him *and* my family.'

'Syd, I honestly don't know what you're talking about. She's not asked me anything about you at all,' Avery insisted but, despite that, Sydney's face darkened.

'You can't trust her, Avery. She has less than you. And because of that she's always going to want something more from you.'

'For god's sake, Sydney,' Leo said, but Sydney ignored him.

'I trust her more than I trust you.' Avery snapped forward recklessly.

Sydney's face darkened even more. The cut of her glare was deep.

'That girl is wrong. She's not one of us. She shouldn't be here and *you* shouldn't have brought her here. She came between you and Hugo and now she's come between you and me.'

'Oh my god, Sydney,' Avery shouted, finally losing it. 'Nora didn't come between me and Hugo. And *you* were the one that dropped *me*, remember? Or are you just used to bending reality to whatever you want it to look like?'

Tension whipped back and forth between them, Avery unsure of who was more shocked that Good Little Avery Finch had spoken back, Sydney or her.

'You don't see it, that's fine,' Sydney replied, shaking her head. 'It's not on me what happens next. But just remember, when you wake up and realise that she's just using you to get something she wants, don't come crying to me.'

'Oh, just piss off, Syd. I'm done taking crap from you,' Avery said, finally having been pushed too far.

'Really? You're choosing her?' Sydney asked, near hysterical. '*Her?*'

'Yeah, I guess I am,' Avery replied hotly, even though her stomach clenched. She knew something was wrong with what Nora had been doing, but she couldn't help herself. Sydney had left every message she'd sent her on read. She'd ghosted her for a whole year, not just the three months she'd been in a rehab. Avery couldn't imagine how awful that must have been for her, but that didn't mean she got to go around making other people miserable by being so mean.

Sydney glared at Avery as if expecting her to change her mind, but she wasn't going to. She was tired of being pulled back and forth between the powerful personalities on the island.

'Come on,' Avery said to Leo, holding her hand out, not caring what Sydney saw or didn't see. And as they walked away, she felt Sydney's gaze on her back the whole time.

CHAPTER FIFTEEN

AVERY

It was dark by the time Avery got back to the villa, having spent the last few hours looking for Nora only to find her lounging in the hot tub on the deck outside their room. But before Avery could ask about what Sydney had said, her mother called them in for dinner ahead of their drinks at the Vandenburgs that evening.

Nora had swept passed her and into the living area where the large teak table had been set for four. If Avery didn't know better, she'd have thought that Nora was purposefully ignoring her. Avery took a seat opposite Nora and in between her parents.

'We only have a few days left on the island and I wanted us to eat together,' her mother had announced, missing the important words: *like a family*. Because of Nora. Because of the things going on with her dad's company. It was a performance by her mother for an empty auditorium.

A member of staff was on hand to serve each course and Avery was painfully aware of their presence. So much more so than she ever had been. Over the ten years they'd been visiting the island, she and her parents must have had more than twenty dinners like this in their villa with food brought to them by an unseen cook, served by staff who had been invisible. Until now. Until Leo.

Now it just felt wrong. Wrong to have someone wait on them. Wrong to have someone cook for them. Someone they didn't know. That didn't care.

The centrepiece on the table was almost obnoxiously ostentatious: a dark, twisting, leafless miniature tree from which hung glass baubles, some filled with cured fish and others with pomme soufflé filled with a scallop foam and truffle shavings. A braised wedge of cabbage had been plated for each of them, but no one seemed particularly hungry.

It should have been exquisite, but for the fact that the bare tree reminded Avery of the storm and the awkward silence was broken only by the sounds of cutlery scraping against their plates.

'Nora, dear, don't play with your food like that,' her mother snipped as Nora pushed her cabbage around the plate.

'Sorry, Mrs Finch.'

Avery's mother sighed; the noise rubbed up against the tension headache that was beginning to throb at the back of Avery's head.

Her mother persisted for another twelve minutes of painful silence until she finally gave up.

'Girls, you're excused.'

'Thank you, Mum,' Avery said at the same time as Nora said, 'Thank you, Mrs Finch.'

Avery followed Nora back to their room. As soon as they got there, Nora pulled off her jumper and kicked off her shoes.

'I'm going to jump in the shower,' she said, a towel clutched in one hand, phone in the other.

'Nora, I wanted to talk—'

The door to the bathroom closed, cutting her off at the same time as her parents' arguing resumed.

'Jesus, Jonathan. You had only one job this summer.'

Avery stood in the middle of the large room feeling incredibly alone and frustrated. She wanted to speak to Nora, to find out what Sydney had been talking about earlier.

Do you want to tell me why she was looking for you at my villa?

And why the hell is she so interested in my dad?

Sydney's questions sounded in her head on repeat.

She hadn't said anything to Leo, but she'd remembered the book she'd found in Nora's suitcase about Mr Devereux. Nora had shut her down by having a go at her for going through her things, but Avery had seen it. And it *had* been weird.

Why had Nora lied about what she was doing at the Devereuxs? And what *had* she been doing there?

Avery looked to the bathroom door. Even if she did get to ask her, she was sure that Nora would just fob her off. Avery needed to find out what was going on. Because if Nora started causing trouble, *she'd* be the one who got the blame. She was the one who'd brought Nora to the island.

You can't trust her.

She saw Nora's suitcase tucked into the corner, zipped up and out of the way. Avery heard the shower turn on in the bathroom, and before she could talk herself out of it she crossed the room and pulled out Nora's case. She flicked one last gaze to the bathroom door, praying Nora would stay in there.

Heart racing, dizzy from the fear of being caught, Avery unzipped the case and picked through the clothes Nora had chucked in there. Underwear, bikinis, T-shirts, shorts. More than one of Avery's vests and the dress she'd worn to the club were in there too. But she wasn't looking for clothes. She was looking for . . .

Avery's fingers brushed against her friendship bracelet, the one that matched Sydney's in every way apart from the letter colouring and that she hadn't seen since the night they'd gone to the club. Annoyed by that more than the clothes, she put the bracelet in her back pocket and pushed a jumper out of the way to reach for the book that she knew was at the bottom.

But her fingers brushed up against something hard, and Avery realised that there was something inside the sock she'd just moved. She picked it up and slid the sock down over the object. Avery was left holding a phone. An older one, a little beaten up, but definitely a different phone to the one that Nora had taken into the bathroom with her.

There were a couple of notifications on the top bar and, flicking a gaze to the bathroom door, Avery swiped down on them with her thumb.

ONE FILE UPLOADED: DEVEREUX PART 7 10.19

Sitting back on her heels, she stared at the notifications filling the screen.

VOICE NOTE SAVED 15.36

VOICE NOTE SAVED 17.42

ONE FILE UPLOADED: DEVEREUX PART 3, EDITED 17.58

The phone was violently slapped out of her hands and she snapped her head up to find Nora standing over her, with a face like thunder.

'What the hell do you think you're doing?' Nora demanded furiously.

Avery's heart pounded in her chest and static sparked across her skin. She was afraid, yes, but she was also angry.

'What is that?' Avery snapped back.

'It's a phone, Avery?' Nora replied sarcastically. 'Haven't you seen one before?' Nora's voice dripped with acid.

'Are you for real right now?' Avery demanded. 'I know what your phone looks like, and it's not *that*. Why have you got files with the name Devereux on them?'

There was a beat of mulish silence, until . . .

'Fine, OK. You got me,' Nora said, glaring at her. 'I'm writing an article on Mr Devereux.'

A sick feeling opened in the pit of Avery's stomach.

'What kind of article?' she demanded.

'Just a bio piece.'

'Is this what you were doing earlier? Is this why I lied to cover for you? Oh god, Nora, you were sneaking around their villa! What if you'd got caught?'

Nora's face turned defiant. 'I *did* get caught. And you covered for me, didn't you? So, it's fine,' she said with a shrug.

'It's not fine at all, Nora,' Avery said, not recognising her friend any more. 'Were you just using me? This whole time, just to get close to Sydney's father? Just so you could write some stupid article?'

'Aves, you really are blowing this whole thing out of

proportion,' Nora said, throwing the second phone back into her suitcase and dropping the towel from around her body.

Avery glared, knowing Nora had done that on purpose. She looked away as Nora started to pull on a pair of jeans and a T-shirt.

'I'm not overreacting, Nora. Do you know what Mr Devereux will do when he finds out about this?'

'He's not going to find out about it. Until it's too late,' Nora replied defiantly.

'Are you on another planet right now? Whatever newspaper or online site you think you have lined up for this will have to approach him for comment. And he'll *know*.'

'Good!' Nora exclaimed. 'He deserves it. He deserves to know who did this to him. Because that man, Avery – he is not who you think he is. He is not who he pretends to be.'

'Yeah, right. So, what, this is all altruistic for you?' Avery poked.

'No. It's not,' Nora replied, and Avery got the impression that she was finally seeing the real Nora Miller. 'Do you know what a coup this is? Can you even imagine what this will do for my career?'

'What career? You're a university student!' Avery hit back.

'No, what I am is a person with access. Access to the island, to Dennis, who has let his guard down because he's on holiday.'

'Access that *I* gave you,' Avery realised, the sick feeling in her stomach getting worse.

'Yeah, and I'm grateful, Aves. Very. No journalist would *ever* be allowed on this island or would ever have gotten close enough to write what I'm going to write.'

The manic light in Nora's gaze was almost painful to bear.

'I can't believe this,' Avery said, disgusted.

'Oh, don't give me that,' Nora said, eyes narrowing. 'It's not like you're so squeaky clean.'

A flash of alarm cut through Avery. 'You don't get to do that.'

'What?'

'You don't get to use that against me,' she said.

'Use what?' Nora replied, all mock innocence.

And just like that Avery saw it. Saw all the little subtle things that had brought them here. Nora's sudden and intense friendship at college, her interest in Avery's life, her friends, her *access*. And after Nora had found out about Avery cheating... Nothing ever spoken out loud, nothing that Avery could specifically point to, but subtle hints, a word here and there. The same way that Nora had *just* done.

They both knew what Nora had been implying. The threat about her cheating was unspoken, but echoed off the walls of the villa.

Things had been said that couldn't be taken back. She knew it and Nora knew it too.

'Whatever, I'm out of here,' Nora announced.

'Where are you going?' Avery asked.

'Anywhere but here. I think it's best if we let things cool down.'

It was unsettling for Nora to be the one with the cool head.

Nora took her second phone, shoved it along with some clothes into a rucksack and slung it over her shoulder, and without a second glance disappeared into the night, leaving Avery reeling.

Avery collapsed on to the bed, the villa suddenly quiet. She looked at the time. Her parents had probably already left.

Drinks with the Vandenburgs.

She swallowed the urge to cry. She wouldn't feel sorry for herself about this. It wasn't her fault, she hadn't known what Nora was doing.

She just couldn't tell whether Nora had been doing it from the very beginning or just since being invited to the island.

And yes, it very much mattered. Because if it was the latter, then Nora was just opportunistic. But if it was the former, then Nora would have been playing her this whole time. Everything they'd shared, the whole year . . . it would have been some kind of con.

She's always going to want something more from you.

Avery turned on her side and wrapped herself in the blanket. Syd had been right. Nora had been using her this whole time.

What was she going to do? Sick to her stomach, she whimpered. This summer had turned into a nightmare. All except for Leo. Leo . . . He was working tonight, so she couldn't see him now, but she'd try and find him in the morning. Maybe he'd know what to do.

They only had two days left. Maybe Nora would find somewhere else to sleep for both those nights. And when they were back at college?

If Avery *even* went back, that is. Because Nora could, if she wanted to, tell the Dean about her cheating. Shame, hurt, anger and frustration poured into the scalding-hot tears that ran down her face. All she'd wanted to do was make her parents happy. All she'd wanted to do was get through that first year, and now she might lose *everything* because of Nora.

HUGO

'We're going to need your help later,' Mark called as Hugo pushed out of the Big House. Darian had been glaring at him over breakfast. He knew that his dad wanted to haul his ass over the coals for not 'pulling his weight' around the island this year, but he couldn't risk pissing him off.

Darian chafed at being blackmailed as much as Hugo chafed at keeping secrets, but he was the one that had set them on this path. They were locked in a head-to-head, waiting to see who would break first and Hugo wasn't sure it was even worth it any more.

He hadn't seen anyone since the storm lifted. Mark wanted to spend yesterday with him because the day after tomorrow Hugo would be out of here, back to the States, while his dads would stay on the island, ready for the next round of guests.

It was always strange to think that his dads went through this whole thing all over again with a completely different group of people once he'd left the island. They wouldn't stay for the whole time, though. Just enough to meet and greet and then again at the end, to say goodbye. It helped give the island the 'homey' feel that was important, Mark said. *Their special touch.*

Hugo looked back at the Big House, thought about the apartment in New York, his dorms in Boston. He thought of the mother that hadn't been able to keep him and the father who'd never been mentioned, ever.

He'd had three dads. And only one had seemed to love him. And Hugo was keeping a terrible secret from him.

He jumped into the golf cart, selfishly uncaring that his dads would need one to get down to the beach where preparations were underway for the 'anniversary party'. It had come to be like the 'end of holiday' party, but it had started as a celebration of Mark and Darian's wedding anniversary, and the time leading up to it, a holiday with their closest friends. Fireworks, food, drinks, dancing. It had always been something extravagant, spectacular – something they'd looked forward to. But now he just saw it as a farce. As something hypocritical for both him and Darian.

Hugo steered down towards the beach and for the first time he didn't want to see anyone. Not Syd, or Archie or Avery. He just wanted to be on his own.

The staff were still clearing the badly hit section of the beach down by Luna so he figured that no one would be around Tidal. He parked up there and hopped out, a restless, insatiable energy forcing him forward. Nothing about this summer had gone as he'd wanted it to. Avery, the rest of them ... None of it. He'd wanted, *needed* it to be ... better. He'd needed it to make things OK. To let him know that it – keeping Darian's secret – was worth it. Because right now, it felt as if nothing was worth it.

He stalked through the treeline that bordered the manicured lawns and the picture-perfect beach, and—

Stopped.

Avery was down on the beach playing in the surf. Laughing,

the way she used to laugh with *him*. But she wasn't with *him*. She was with *Leo*.

Instinctively, he hung back by the treeline, watching. Waiting. He wanted to be wrong; he wanted to still have a chance.

But he knew better.

Leo scooped her up into his arms, kissed her – *on the mouth* – and threw her into the waves as Avery screamed in delight. The sound echoed around his brain and his ears, taunting him, infuriating him, infecting him with the kind of rage that he couldn't contain.

He didn't remember moving. He wasn't aware of it, until Avery's gaze shifted from Leo to him, her eyes widening in realisation.

'Hugo—'

The saying is 'seeing red'. But it wasn't like that for Hugo. Instead, rage swelled up from deep within, a thick, dark sludge that stuck to everything, infecting, glomming from one cell to another until even his brain was suffocated with it. It blotted out all thought other than the desperate need to lash out, to hurt someone else the way he was hurting.

Because then someone might understand. Someone might be able to help. But he wasn't rational enough to recognise his own thoughts and by the time he reached the surf he was consumed with rage.

He'd spent this whole time thinking that if he could just get Avery back, then everything would return to normal. He could forget Darian's cheating, he could look Mark in the eye again, he could get his life back, get back on the lacrosse team. He could have *that* life.

Avery Finch, on *his* arm.

The prom-king life.

But that was gone. It was never coming back. And as he realised that, he turned on Leo. He didn't see the English kid that he'd been friends with for ten years. He saw Darian. He saw everyone who had laughed at him or doubted him or left him or rejected him. And before he knew it, he had thrown a punch at Leo, right across the jaw.

Leo half fell to the ground, waves crashing at his feet, holding himself up with one hand, the other on his cheek.

Avery was standing in the waves, covering her mouth in shock.

'Leo!'

Leo waved off her concern.

Hugo's hands fisted by his sides, half wanting to hit him again and half wanting to clutch at his own head in agony.

'How dare you?' he all but screamed at Leo.

'You're so far gone and you don't even realise it,' Leo dismissed, hauling himself back up to his feet.

'What do you mean?' Hugo demanded.

'It's screwed up.'

'What is?'

'The way you think about her, man. It's the way you look at her too.'

'You're talking out your ass, Walker,' Hugo snapped, trying to ignore the way that Avery was making her way towards Leo.

'No, I don't think I am,' Leo said, eyes wary but on him. 'You think this was me? You think, because I wanted Avery, I snapped my fingers and she came to me?'

'Yeah, I do!' Hugo yelled, only realising a little too late by the gleam of satisfaction in Leo's golden gaze that he'd fallen right into a trap.

Leo shook his head in disgust. 'It's about *Avery*. It's about what *she* wants. She's not a possession that I can take from you. Or that you can keep. Jesus, when did you get so messed up. You used to be—'

Hugo closed the distance between them, grabbing Leo by the shirt and hauling him up towards him.

'I used to be what?'

'I was going to say a friend, but now I'm not so sure. But you at least used to be decent.'

'Friend? You were never a friend,' Hugo growled out. 'You were always just the help,' he snarled. 'You are nothing. *Nothing.*' He was shaking with a kind of rage that half scared him. He was out of control, beyond anything he'd experienced before. Heightened but dull at the same time. Truly out of body, with no way back. 'I could kill you,' he threatened, the words out of his mouth without thinking. 'On this island, I could kill you and no one would ever know or care. My parents have enough money to make something like that go away.'

Leo laughed. The bastard actually laughed. Leo shoved out of Hugo's hold and caught him with a left hook that came out of nowhere.

Head ringing and half in the sand, Hugo blinked as he tried to call himself back.

. . . can't leave him like that—
Yes . . . can. Let's . . . later—
Leo . . .

Hold on . . .

Hugo blinked again, and finally pushed himself out of the surf that threatened to drown him, turning to lay on his back.

'You've just lost your job, Walker,' Hugo yelled at the sky.

A pair of trainers came dangerously close to his head and Hugo couldn't even find it in himself to care.

'I don't think so, Hugo,' Leo said, crouching down. 'The only person who can fire me is my boss. That's my dad. And he's the best goddamn chef *your* dads have ever had. He knows it. They know it. So, who do you think Mark and Darian would choose, huh? You're just the adopted son.'

Leo's words landed harder than any punch could have. Because he was right. Because to his dads, the staff probably were more important. Nausea welled in his stomach and he turned away so that he didn't have to see Avery with her back to him, arm-in-arm with Leo. Whatever could have been was gone. There was nothing left for Hugo to lose.

CHAPTER SIXTEEN

LEO

Leo fisted his injured hand in his pocket. He didn't regret it. He might live to, but tonight? No. Hugo had deserved it and more.

The main stretch of beach in between the villas on the inward curve of the island had been completely transformed. It shouldn't have been a surprise, especially as it happened every year to celebrate the Vandenburgs' wedding anniversary. But the sight of it was spectacular, even if he'd been part of the team prepping it in the first place.

Dusk painted pastels across the sky behind a stunning marquee made of white and gold silk – nothing so common as canvas for Darian and Mark – that played in the much gentler breeze, now that the tropical storm had passed completely.

Inside, Leo's father had created remarkable inventions finer than anything seen on Instagram. Everything had been carefully designed to suit the white and gold theme of the evening, culminating in an almost aggressively elaborate menu with plate after plate full of every conceivable sea creature and animal part: hearts, cheeks, legs, eyes, tongue. It was a feast that could have graced a palace, yet was here to serve just twelve people.

The waste would be incomprehensible. The ten-tiered cake – white and gold alternating layers, nearly four days in the making – would be left for the grand reveal just ahead of the firework display, which was why it was still back in the kitchen in the staff centre. But in the meantime, staff were carrying little gold square platters laden with canapés that probably equated to his entire summer's pay.

Several firepits were dotted around the beach, allowing for the guests to wander far and wide. They were all there. The Finches – Annalise in gold, Jonathan in white – studiously ignoring each other, while Carol Devereux – also in gold – talked intently to Darian, and Dennis lounged on a seat, legs stretched out, knocking back a glass of champagne, his gaze following Corrine's every move.

Something crawled across Leo's skin.

The man was arrogant, mean. *Violent*.

Leo was debating whether he should say something to Corrine when he noticed Carol held her glass to the side a little, which was his sign to exchange it with a fresh, full one.

'It's just so desperate,' Carol was saying. 'You'd think they'd get the hint. And the *hubris*. As if they could even consider that we didn't already know.'

She was talking about the Finches, he realised as he returned to the shadows, startled by the venom in Carol's voice – though he probably shouldn't be.

He returned to the staff line, everyone dressed head to toe in black that would – when the moon rose – make them as invisible as the guests wanted them to be. They were lined up along the treeline ready to attend to anyone at a moment's notice. But they were just as likely to melt into the background and disappear.

A little further down the beach he watched the dancers who had been brought over from the mainland, set up to perform the Calinda.

He'd looked it up when he'd got home after the first year he'd seen it and had found it strange that the Vandenburgs had chosen Calinda – a form of martial arts as well as a dance with traditional folk music – as background entertainment to celebrate their marriage.

Every time he saw it, he wondered what his dad thought of these men and women, performing for an audience who had more money than sense, honouring their heritage but being paid to do so. Did it feel as wrong to him as it did to Leo?

The fact that he had never spoken about it with his dad served as a reminder that he straddled two cultures. Two lives. Two *parents*.

It had always made him feel a deep yearning for it to be familiar, for it to be known by him, but it never was. The chants, the drumbeats, the clash of men fighting to a rhythm so strong it took hold of his pulse, the beat of his heart. As if he might tumble forward and get lost in the movement of the dance.

Unlike previous years, where he'd been forced to watch from the shadows as he'd not been invited to the party, today he was standing barely metres away from it.

It was probably as close as he would ever get.

Looking away from where the entertainers were setting up, Leo saw Hugo, dressed in a full white linen suit, glaring at him. The flames of the firepit between them cast shadows across his face, hiding the bruise Leo knew would have spread across his cheek by now.

Pulling his gaze away, he found Archie putting an arm around Sydney's shoulder, but she threw him off and knocked back a mouthful from her water bottle. Her gold sequin dress glittered in the natural fire lights along the beach every time she moved. And for the first time that holiday, Leo was pretty sure that she wasn't drinking water. She was glaring at where Avery stood awkwardly with her parents. Things must still be pretty rough between them after their argument the day before.

Avery looked amazing in a white halter neck with flecked gold threads, her hair tumbling down her back. He shook his head, wondering how on earth he'd got lucky enough to be with someone as incredible as her.

On the periphery, Leo saw Nora talking to Corrine. He frowned, remembering that Avery had told him about an argument she'd had with Nora, but she hadn't gone into much detail about it and then Hugo had shown up and ruined the entire afternoon. The girls' conversation was beginning to get heated, drawing disapproving looks from the parents, but Leo doubted Nora cared much. After all, they'd all be going home soon.

Sydney caught his eye and glared at him, clearly as pissed at him as she was with Avery. Archie looked up and shook his glass at him, and he'd probably be horrified to know how similar it was to his mother's gesture only minutes before. And as the sharp slap of stick against stick and hand on drum and chant began to fill the air, Leo walked over a tray with several cocktail options and champagne.

'Darling, where have you *been*?' Archie asked, all mock luvvie, a wide grin on his features despite the tension in the air.

'Working, sweetheart. You should try it some time,' Leo replied in the same tone.

'Why? I don't have to,' Archie answered with a shrug and a laugh that didn't sound funny in the least.

Before he could do anything, Sydney, without a word, grabbed a glass of champagne in one hand and a cocktail in the other, side-stepped around Leo and headed towards Nora as Corrine stalked back off towards the staging area.

'That girl is going to be the death of me,' Archie said under his breath.

'Should we do something?' Leo asked, hesitating.

Archie squinted at them. 'Let's just . . . see what happens.'

Leo felt Sven's hawk-like gaze on him. 'Shit, gotta go. Keep an eye on that, though, will you?'

'Yes, boss,' Archie mocked with a two-fingered salute and took a mouthful of champagne, his eyes not straying from Sydney.

Leo cursed; they were all going to be wrecked before the fireworks started.

Nick Dawson was skirting the edges of the gathering, weaving in between staff and guests, his eyes working hard to ignore Annalise, who flicked anxious looks between him and her husband.

Automatically, Leo searched for Avery, gaze skating over her father in conversation with a bored-looking Dennis, and found her standing beside the firepit at the furthest end of the party, alone. Maybe he should—

'Don't do it, man,' Domingo warned as he came to replace an empty tray of canapés with a fresh one. 'Sven is watching you. Someone blabbed about seeing you take down Vandenburg this afternoon.'

'Crap,' Leo cursed. A part of him had hoped that it would have stayed between him and Hugo, but in hindsight that'd been foolish. His dad would come down on him like a tonne of bricks.

'Who blabbed?'

Domingo pulled a face and shrugged. 'Look, I'm not saying that sometimes they don't deserve it,' he said, flicking a glance at where Dennis was still sprawled across the outdoor chaise, 'but the boss's son? You've got some big, hairy, fat ones, my friend.' He slapped him across the back.

Leo wanted to laugh and cry at the same time. If he'd known that was all it took to earn something more than disdain from Domingo . . . ? No, he *wouldn't* have done it earlier. Hugo had been out of order, and he'd done what he'd had to, but he hadn't enjoyed it.

Domingo left with his tray and Leo grabbed at the neck of a bottle of champagne, the slick condensation making it slip from his fingers and he only just caught it in time, his heart beating and skin prickling. Christ, he was jumpy.

And it wasn't just him. There was a tension in the air, sparking and crackling, as if the path of the storm had cut through paradise and exposed the truth beneath the veneer.

'Oh my god, seriously?' he heard Carol's sharp exclamation

rise above the music and the clash of sticks of the Calinda performance. 'For heaven's sake, Jonathan, just give it a rest.'

AVERY

Avery looked up at the sound of Carol's voice. Frowning, she made her way a little closer. Something in Mrs Devereux's voice had sent shivers down her spine, and Avery's whole body braced for impact.

'We know, OK, Jonathan? We know about the problems your company is having. You think a visit from the FBI goes unnoticed?' she asked, scoffing.

Oh god.

'We *all* know about the investment fraud, and the financial hole you need to plug. So just stop being so *desperate* about it. It's pathetic.' Avery's stomach turned to stone. Carol's voice had drawn everyone's attention. Staff, her friends, even some of the performers. Darian was staring at the floor pretending to ignore the whole thing and she couldn't see her mother anywhere, and her dad . . . *Oh god.* Her dad was *humiliated*.

'We're not investing with you. We're not throwing our money down the drain. So just. Stop. Asking,' Carol said bluntly.

And instead of storming off, Carol dug in and stared her father down. Avery's heart ached as her father looked around at the faces of the people staring at him, finally making eye contact with her.

I'm sorry.

It was as if she'd heard him say it in her mind. As if she could see it in his eyes.

She took a step towards him, but he raised his hand to ward her off – whether to protect her from his social stigma or because he wanted to be alone, she couldn't tell. But one long agonising moment later he turned, shoulders slumped, and walked away.

Everyone was staring. Her cheeks burned under their attention and it was only when she could no longer see her father's figure heading back to the villa that she dropped into the chair beside her.

It was all too much. Her parents, the Devereuxs. She'd known that Carol was mean, but that? That had been vicious and unwarranted. So what if her dad was looking for help covering the hole made by his business partner? So what if he wasn't as smooth as Mark, or Dennis or Darian? These were his friends, weren't they? Or if her mother was . . . where was her mother?

A pair of sandy feet stopped a couple of metres back from the fire. Avery looked up to find Sydney staring down at her. Avery flicked her gaze to the rest of the party, but everyone else had gone back to their conversations.

Oh god, she'd wanted to speak to Sydney after her confrontation with Nora, but not like *this*. She'd wanted to say that she was sorry, that she'd been wrong about Nora. Only she didn't think that now was the right time.

'Not going to run off after Daddy?' Sydney asked in a mean sing-song voice.

'No, I . . .' Avery started and then she realised what was

wrong. Sydney was drunk. Avery's stomach dropped. 'Syd, are you OK?'

'Me?' Sydney asked, taking a mouthful from the bottle of champagne in her hand. 'I'm just dandy. But thanks soooo much for asking, *Aves.*'

Avery swallowed. This was Syd exaggerated. Alcohol had always done that to her, but tonight it seemed especially bad. But as mean as she was being, Avery was still worried about her. Until she saw Sydney look down, gaze snagging on Avery's wrist, and the look in her eye made Avery flinch.

'It's a bit late to be wearing that, isn't it?' Sydney asked, pointing at the friendship bracelet she'd put on that evening in the hope of making it up to Sydney for being so wrong about Nora.

Avery's gut clenched. 'I was hoping it wasn't.'

'Well, it *is*. Because you've been keeping secrets, haven't you?' Sydney said snidely.

Alarm cut through Avery like a knife. What secrets? What did she know? Suddenly feeling sick, Avery was near dizzy.

'What are you talking about, Sydney?' she forced herself to ask.

There was a bitterness in Sydney's gaze that Avery hadn't seen before.

'That would be telling, wouldn't it?' she taunted.

Whatever she had done to Sydney, whatever had passed between them, she didn't deserve this. Avery knew that.

'Things have been really tough this year, Syd. And you—' Avery cut herself off before she could say something crass.

'You *know* where I was.' Sydney glared.

'For three months, yes. But you didn't tell me,' Avery said, hurt pressing on her lungs. 'You didn't reach out to let me know what was going on. Not then, or after.'

'Well, you'd found your little friend by then, hadn't you? And then you had the aud-a-ci-ty to bring her here.'

'Things were complicated, Syd—'

'And I. Don't. Care,' she spat. 'You chose *her*,' Sydney said, betrayal glittering in her eyes. 'Over me, you chose *her*.'

'Syd—'

'You're so self-obsessed. Do you even know that?' Sydney accused. 'It's always about you. Good Little Avery Finch. "I'm so torn, do I like Hugo, or do I like Leo?" God, your problems are *nothing*,' Sydney said, slightly slurring her words. 'They're *nothing*,' she repeated, before sweeping away like a model on a catwalk – only her exaggerated walk was down to alcohol. Archie appeared from the shadows, trying to talk to her, but Sydney pushed him away. She was, and always had been, dangerous like this.

Avery turned back to the flames flickering in the firepit, shivering despite the heat.

She brushed a hand over her bare arms. White and gold, cold and mean. That's what she would associate with those colours now.

Had she been selfish? The thought twisted her gut as she forced herself to look at it from Sydney's perspective. But how could Avery have known what was going on with her? Because if she had, things would have been different. She *knew* that.

From the edge of the treeline, she saw Nora making her way towards her and, *oh god*, she just didn't want or need this right now.

She knew it was wrong to blame her, but if it wasn't for Nora, Avery wouldn't have lied to her oldest friend. If it wasn't for Nora, this whole holiday would have been different. She was the last person Avery wanted to talk to right now.

'Are you OK?' Nora asked, looking as if she had something else that she wanted to say. But wasn't that the way it always was? Nora always playing some kind of game, running her own agenda.

'No, Nora. I'm not OK,' Avery said, finally wanting to stop pretending, to stop being scared about what Nora might do or say. 'This . . .' Avery said with a helpless shrug, 'this isn't what it was supposed to be.'

'Maybe what you wanted it to be was an impossibility.'

'Yeah. Maybe. But it would have been nice to try that out without you messing everything up, Nora.'

'What?' Nora asked.

'*You*. You did this. You did what you *always* do,' Avery accused. 'Act all innocent, while leaving a trail of destruction in your wake. You're like . . .' Avery laughed bitterly. 'You're like that tropical storm.' Avery was on the verge of tears and she didn't want to cry. Not here, not in front of *her*. 'Syd won't talk to me any more. Hugo is a mess. God knows what's up with Archie.'

If Avery saw even a glimpse of hurt in Nora's gaze it was masked far too quickly.

'Here,' Avery said, loosening the friendship bracelet she'd found in Nora's case, along with one of her rings. 'You might as well have this seeing as you keep taking it. It doesn't mean anything any more, thanks to you.'

Avery threw it to her and Nora caught it one-handed.

'There are bigger things going on here, Aves,' she said, her palm closing over the bracelet. 'It's not always about you.'

'Oh, I am most definitely getting *that*,' Avery stressed. 'But for you, it's about Dennis, right? About you making a name for yourself, on some pathetic *My Week With The Rich And Famous* article?'

That's what Nora had used her for, wasn't it?

'It's not that kind of story, Avery. It's bigger than that,' Nora replied, her voice an angry whisper.

'Of course it's big. Dennis Devereux is one of the biggest names in tech. You think people haven't already tried to take him down? People bigger than a university student?' Avery said, lashing out.

Genuine concern flashed in Nora's gaze at Avery's less than quiet accusation.

'I'm sorry, this wasn't . . . I didn't want *this*,' Nora tried. 'But it'll all make sense in the morning, Aves. I promise. I'll tell you everything then,' Nora swore, but for Avery it was too little, too late, and as Nora disappeared towards the path that would take her towards the villas Avery turned her back on her and stared into the fire.

How had everything gone so horribly wrong?

She turned to look to the line of staff waiting to serve at a moment's notice, and searched for Leo – wanting to see him, wanting the steady reassurance he gave her – but she couldn't spot him. Instead, she saw an almost menacing line of black-clothed figures lining the beach, and for a moment she thought they looked like bodyguards, there to stop them from leaving.

She shook off the thought as a flash of gold caught her eye. Sydney was making her way into the centre of the party, arm out, using the champagne bottle to balance her unsteady gait.

'Ladies and gentlemen,' Sydney said, her voice cutting loudly through the noise of the party. 'I'd like to make a toast.' She clambered on to one of the large cushioned chaise-longues that had been brought down to the beach and used the pendent on her necklace to tap against her champagne glass.

For a moment it looked like she might fall, but she righted herself with a laugh, echoed uneasily by the others on the beach.

'Get down,' Carol hissed, making her way towards her daughter, displaying the most pained smile Avery had ever seen.

'No, Mother. I don't think I will. *I* am speaking now,' Sydney announced. 'Where was I? A toast! Several, in fact.'

Avery cast her gaze across the various expressions on the faces of the adults: alarm, anticipation, disgust, open curiosity and slowly disintegrating tolerance.

'First, to my parents,' Sydney said, and Carol's step faltered just a little, eyes narrowing. Avery's attention, like the others', was drawn to her like a moth to a flame. 'Thank you so very, very, *very* much,' she said, sounding anything but, 'for seeing to my well-being earlier this year. The institution you sent me to was a delight. Worked an absolute treat, Mother. Cheers.' She knocked back a mouthful, ignoring her mother's gasp, which, to Avery, sounded more like outrage and indignation rather than shock.

'To my brother, my darling twin. Who didn't lift a finger for me throughout. Good to know where your loyalty lies.' She tapped a hand to her chest. 'Cheers!' Once again, she took a mouthful. Archie's expression was pained and dark, and Avery's gut twisted.

'And to Avery,' Sydney said, turning to find her by the firepit, flames burning her cheeks and fear for what she might be about to say licking across her skin. 'The bestest friend a girl could ever have. Until she's *not*. Hugo might know something about that. And I guess, *now*, Leo will find that out for himself.'

Like a tennis match, Avery felt everyone's eyes flick from Sydney to her, to Hugo, to Leo. And behind them, the dead-eyed, straight-ahead-stare of staff trained not to react felt almost threatening in comparison.

'And lastly, to Mark and Darian Vandenburg. Every year we come to your magical island, to celebrate friendship and love, and the success we've had each year. Your marriage is the cornerstone of what brings us together. It's just a shame, Mr Vandenburg, *Darian*, that you can't keep it in your pants.'

This, of all things, brought complete silence over the guests.

'But having an affair is not really that special, is it?' Sydney continued, looking around for someone. The tension in the air increasing notch by notch. 'No. It takes a *special* man, a loving father, to blackmail your son into keeping your dirty little secret. Still, we would all very much like to wish you a happy anniversary.' Sydney threw back the last of her drink as Carol finally reached up to drag her daughter off the chair.

Shock cut through her. Darian had been having an affair? And Hugo knew? Avery searched the crowd and found him, staring at Sydney as if he could kill her.

'What are you doing?' Sydney half screamed as her mother

tried to pull her from the chair. Sydney tried to bat away Carol's hands, but her mother's grip was immoveable.

'What I have to do,' she said, hauling Sydney away from the party. 'Clearing up this family's mess.'

Avery wasn't sure if anyone else had heard, but she'd been closest to them. Sydney shoved her shoulder into her mother and stalked off into the trees. Dennis came towards Carol, something dark in his eyes that raised the hair on the back of Avery's neck.

As Sydney passed her, Avery turned to go after her, but Sydney thrust out an arm to push her away.

'Oh, just fuck *off*, Avery!'

A slice of hurt unwound within Avery.

Sydney had made it painfully clear. She was done. Their friendship was over.

CHAPTER SEVENTEEN

HUGO

Happy anniversary?

That bitch.

Adrenaline dumped into Hugo's system. His breath locked in his lungs, every muscle turning to stone in the space of a single heartbeat.

He could see his dads in his peripheral vision, both stuck in place, frozen by Sydney's devastating speech. But, despite the distance, he could still make out the flicker of the muscle in Darian's jaw, the line of tension across Mark's back. The way that Darian white-knuckle-gripped his glass and Mark didn't even blink.

But when Darian eventually moved enough to turn his gaze on Hugo, the world whooshed past and pinholed in on the absolute fury and venom that spewed from his entire being. This was their *anniversary*. It was sacrosanct. It always had been.

Hugo had grown up on stories and lessons about how hard they'd had to fight to get married; the bigotry and the hatred they'd had to survive. Of all days for their dirty laundry to be aired, it had to be *here* in front of *these* people?

Frigid shock turned to fear. Heart pounding, blood rushing, the noise of the party, the clashing sticks of the performers, the flickering flames of the pits and the torches too bright and too dangerous. It all came back in one inhale.

He was going to lose them. He was going to lose *everything*.

Hugo stumbled, feeling unsteady, the sand beneath him shifting as he turned away from the party.

He wanted to die.

Genuinely, in that moment, he wanted the ground to consume him whole. He couldn't take it any more. For months, he had been in agony, hating himself, waiting to be found out, waiting to be rejected by Darian, waiting to see that hurt and betrayal in Mark's eyes – and now it was here. Mark managed to gather himself, cast a smile at those around him and walked towards the marquee. Probably the only people who would recognise the stiff walk were his husband and son.

A pit opened in Hugo's gut and the nausea began to rise. Acrid bile burned his throat. He desperately wanted to go after Mark. To tell him that he was sorry. To beg for his forgiveness. His legs began to shake. He *was* so sorry. He'd never been more sorry about anything in his entire life.

His hand fisted; his nails cut crescent moons into his palms.

God, if he could just go back. If he could undo everything that had happened in the last eight minutes, the last eight *months*.

It wasn't even about Avery any more. She'd just been a part of what he thought he'd lost. What, in his fear and desperation, he'd tried to hold on to. The idyllic life Hugo had before he found out that one of his dads would happily throw him to the wolves when forced to choose between the mirage of a perfect marriage and the son he'd adopted.

And beneath all that? The fear that Mark would look at him the way Darian already had. With loathing and disgust. His life had become a horror film, where the people he'd loved had become strangers and everything he thought he knew was wrong.

Darian looked as if he was about to go after Mark when Annalise Finch came out of the treeline adjusting the hem of her dress and tucking her hair behind her ear.

Hugo, surprised he could feel anything, nearly laughed when he saw Nick Dawson following behind her. Annalise looked around in confusion at having drawn everyone's attention, a painful ugly flush creeping up from her chest to her cheeks as she drew to a halt, realising that they had all seen, that they all *knew*.

Mark turned his back on Annalise and Nick while Dennis stared at them, looking as cruelly disdainful as Hugo had ever seen.

Annalise blanched and Hugo's head buzzed.

Who were these people? They couldn't be the same ones that he'd laughed with and grown up with. They couldn't be the same ones that he'd spent New Year's Eve with. Those people were nice. Civilised. Cutting, yes. But this?

'Did someone spike the punch? Archie asked, coming up beside him.

'I don't even . . .' Hugo trailed off, unable to find the words.

'You OK?'

Hugo barked a laugh. 'Not even remotely,' he replied.

'Right. Then let's get out of here. Luna?'

Hugo nodded. 'Yeah. Let's get out of here.'

'I'm gonna make a quick bottle-shop stop, and I'll meet you down there,' he said, with a slap across his back.

'I need to find your sister,' Hugo growled.

'Don't worry about her,' Archie told him before slipping off to grab whatever drink wasn't nailed down or guarded by the staff.

Hugo glared into the night. He wasn't worried. He was pissed.

He turned his back on the party. He needed space. *Now.* He aimed himself away from the beach to where he could take one of the other paths to Luna, unwilling to risk coming into contact with either of his dads right now.

The sky would soon be shot through with the spectacular fireworks designed by award-winning pyro engineers flown in from England. It was usually the time when everyone came together, united by a childlike joy for explosions and colours. But this year? They were all scattered, blown apart like the very fireworks they'd come to see.

The low-hanging moon picked out the white beach before him, shades of blue so dark it was almost black, and slashes of brightness only managing to crawl towards light grey. For the first time in forever, he didn't see paradise.

Up ahead, he saw Avery standing alone, her arms wrapped around herself as if she was cold. He was about to change direction, when Avery turned his way. He bit back a curse, wishing she hadn't. When she caught sight of him, she halted mid-stride, as if she'd been thinking exactly the same thing.

He looked at her now. The girl he'd thought he'd loved. The girl he'd tried to anchor himself to.

He closed the distance between them with slow strides, giving her enough time to walk away or avoid him. But she didn't move. Instead, she waited for him. And a spike of anger flared in his chest. All he'd wanted since arriving here was to talk to her. And she'd avoided him, ignored him. But this wasn't her fault. Not this time. No, it was all Sydney.

No, it wasn't. It was you. Again. The sharp inner critic toyed. *You told Sydney. You kept the secret from Mark. It's all you. Always has been and always will be. The architect of your own shitstorm.*

Mentally he thrashed and railed but it didn't do him any good. He was trying to keep a hold of his anger – of himself – but his nerves and control were frayed by what had just happened.

'Have you seen Syd?' he asked as he reached her.

'No, she stormed off,' Avery said, shaking her head.

'She's lucky. Because if I find her—'

'You'll do what, Hugo?' Avery asked, her tone heavy with exhaustion. 'She's Sydney. She was drunk.'

'Like that's an excuse,' he shot back.

'Maybe with her it is,' Avery said.

'No. It's not. She's always been like that. Doing whatever she wants and getting away with it. Well, not this time,' he warned darkly.

Avery's eyes glistened in the moonlight. Unshed tears, poking and prodding at his conscience. She'd always hated it when he'd got angry.

'Seriously, Avery. She crossed the line.'

'I know. And I'm sorry, I didn't . . .' She looked down. 'I'm sorry I didn't know about your dad. Darian forced you to keep that from Mark?'

Hugo's lips thinned. He couldn't . . . wasn't able to . . . He shook his head, shook off her question. It was easier to hold on to his anger, to focus it on Sydney. It was probably the only thing holding him together.

'Hugo—'

'No. I don't want to hear it. Not now. You've had all holiday to talk to me. And now I'm not in the mood. So take it somewhere else,' he said cruelly. 'Take it to Leo for all I care.' He pushed on past her to the path that would take him away from here. They could all go to hell as far as he was concerned.

AVERY

Avery stood staring after Hugo as he headed away from the party, feeling something break inside her. Their little group was gone. Shattered into different pieces and she knew that they'd never be the same again. It felt as if she'd lost something precious, something connected to joy and childhood.

And there she was again. Proving Sydney right. She'd been so lost in her own problems that she hadn't realised that they'd been struggling too. Hugo with his dads and Sydney with an addiction. Sydney might have shrugged off being put into rehab, but it was clear that things had been far from OK.

Avery shivered. She had left her cardigan back by the party

and she was too far from the firepits to get any warmth. But she didn't want to go back. She didn't want to see the faces of the people there judging her. And Leo. Oh god, had she got him into trouble? Would he be fired? Would his father lose *his* job?

Her hands came to her temples. This had all gone so terribly wrong. It was supposed to be magical. And it had been, for a few hours in the midst of a storm. But this? This was turning into a nightmare.

Carol Devereux emerged from the treeline and Avery did a double take. She'd changed out of the gold dress she'd been wearing earlier into a white pantsuit. She glared at the woman who had humiliated her father.

'Sydney was sick and I was forced to change,' she explained, misunderstanding Avery's attention.

Avery's thoughts switched tack. 'Is she OK?'

'Of course she is,' Carol snapped.

'Is she, because—'

'I don't want her disturbed,' Carol said, cutting Avery off.

Torn, because Sydney had made her feelings very clear, but still concerned about her, Avery wavered, until Carol saw someone over Avery's shoulder. But the look of revulsion that swam across Carol's features was so cold, it shocked her. Mrs Devereux had always been aloof, but tonight she had tapped into a vein of meanness that made Avery shiver.

She turned in time to see Leo greet Carol and get completely ignored. A wave of anger crested over her, but Leo shook his head to stop her from saying something.

He walked straight up to Avery, wrapped his arms around her and just held her.

'What is going on?' Avery asked, her lips against his arm, feeling utterly bewildered. Whatever had happened tonight had caused more damage than the storm.

'I have no idea,' Leo confessed, his words tangling in her hair. 'Did you catch up with Sydney?'

'She didn't want to talk. I'm worried,' she confessed, pulling out of his arms to see his face.

He seemed to give it some thought. 'Don't be,' he then dismissed with a reassuring smile. 'It'd take more than that to knock down Sydney Devereux.'

Avery huffed out a laugh. 'Probably.'

'Definitely.'

Avery nodded, her concern easing a little, choosing to sink instead into Leo's strong embrace.

'So, I guess the news is out,' Leo said after a few minutes.

'Your job. Your dad. Are you going to be OK?' The words rushed out on a single breath and he smiled and pulled her close.

'I don't know. I guess we'll find out in the morning. But there *is* one thing on my side. Sven delights in making my life hell. He might just be happy enough to have an excuse to beat me up that he'll decide to keep me around for the next four weeks.'

'Beat you up?' Avery asked in horror.

'Metaphorically speaking,' Leo said, but she couldn't tell whether he was joking or not.

They both sighed, simultaneously, and then laughed at themselves.

'Can you sit? I need to tell you something,' Leo said.

'Is something wrong?' Avery asked, her stomach reflexively hardening.

'Not between us,' he assured her, but she wasn't sure that she could take much more this evening.

'Do we have to?'

'You don't want to know?' he gently probed.

For a moment she wondered whether she could say no.

She nodded slowly and sat down on the sandbank, her back to the treeline and the endless ocean in front of her. She felt trapped, when all around her was open, and she wondered if she had done that to herself.

'After you went after Sydney, something happened.'

'Oh god, what did Nora do?' Avery asked, leaning her head into her knees. She'd gripped handfuls of sand that slipped easily through her fingers.

Leo squinted at her in the moonlight. He put an arm around her.

'It wasn't Nora.'

'Oh?'

'No, I haven't seen her for ages so I don't know how much of Sydney's speech she caught, if any of it.'

Avery frowned. She'd been about to say that she was sure Nora had caught the whole thing, but actually wasn't sure she could remember her being there.

'It's, uhm, about your mum,' Leo said.

'What— Is she OK?'

Leo bobbed his head. 'I think so. But . . . she came out of the forest. With Nick,' Leo said, looking at the waves on the shore, not meeting her gaze.

'So?'

'*With Nick.*' He stressed the words.

'Nick . . . *With* Nick?' Avery repeated.

A firework exploded right above them, sending a pressure wave down that echoed through her body and made her jump.

'My mom and *Nick*?'

Oh god, Dad.

But he'd already left by then.

'Who saw?' Avery asked, heart pounding.

'Everyone,' Leo said, rubbing a circle on her back.

Nick.

Nausea gripped her stomach and stung her throat. She'd nearly . . . with Nick, at the staff party. They'd kissed. He'd wanted more. He'd . . .

She groaned. Her mother.

Her mother, who always went on about being perfect, caring about what other people saw. Who wanted so desperately to climb social ladders that . . . And she . . .

Crap. Tears pushed against her eyes until one escaped, rolling down her cheek.

She'd known things were bad between her parents. She'd heard the fights and the arguments.

Another firework soared across the sky.

She wasn't under any illusions. But the shame and embarrassment were hot and sticky and bled into everything. And while shards of bright colours fractured like patterns from a kaleidoscope across the night sky, Avery let herself cry. And Leo held her the entire time.

The last of the fireworks filled the sky in a thunderous series of explosions of white and gold that became so overwhelming she almost feared that it would never end.

But when it eventually did, she dried her eyes.

'Can we stay here tonight?' she asked Leo, her hand twisting in his hoodie.

'On the beach?'

Avery nodded. 'I'm not cold,' she said.

'I'd warm you up,' Leo whispered in her ear, sending a shiver down her spine. She tucked herself into his side as they lay back against the sand. The sky now peaceful after the ferocity of the fireworks.

Just like they had done two years before, they chatted for ages. Talking about plans to meet up after the summer – plans that would probably be impacted by whatever happened with Dad's company, and whatever she decided to do about her midterms. Whether she could come clean to the Dean and tell her parents, she didn't know. But she didn't want to think about that, shutting the thought down and turning back into Leo's side.

She was on the brink of a delicious sleep, nestled against Leo's side, warm and protected . . . when the screams started.

And this time they didn't stop.

CHAPTER EIGHTEEN

AVERY

Sharp, jagged lightning strikes landed in her chest and lungs as Avery ran to keep up with Leo. Fear reached out and caught only more fear.

The screams just didn't stop. They went on and on and on, feral in the air, terrifying by themselves, and horrifying in what they might be for.

Sand sucked at her feet, making running something nightmarish. They reached the pathway just as Archie emerged from the shadowy treeline that wrapped around the Devereuxs' villa.

'What's going on?'

'Are you OK?

'Who's screaming?'

The questions were such a jumbled mass in Avery's mind, she wasn't sure whether she'd heard them or said them.

Archie looked up white and wide-eyed. 'Is that Sydney?'

Avery's mind went blank with fear. She completely froze. Until everything came back in a single heartbeat, focus near painful and overstimulated. She gasped for breath as she followed Archie, who'd taken off in the direction of the screams.

They rounded the corner of the pool area. Leo, who was just ahead of her, turned before she could see anything and caught her in his arms, his face white with horror.

'What is it? What's going on?' she demanded, but he was speechless.

She pushed at his chest, knowing that something was very wrong, but he was immoveable.

Sydney.

People lined the poolside, their faces shocked and scared. Her mother looked away while her father stared dull-eyed into the water. One of the staff members from the party – Domingo – was on bent knees, face a grim mask.

In the water Avery could just make out long tendrils of blonde hair. They sank into a pale-red watermark around a body floating face down, white silk dress undulating on the disturbed water.

Sydney!

But when she looked up, there she was on the other side of the pool, hand pressed against her mouth to prevent another scream. Archie had his arms around her.

But if Sydney was OK then . . .

'Oh god, Avery, I'm so sorry,' Leo whispered, holding her to him.

Why was he saying sorry? Who was in the pool? Where was Nora?

Avery looked around at the faces of the people, searching for

Nora. She'd be here any minute. She would, because if she wasn't then that meant . . .

Strong arms anchored her just as her body began to shake.

Her mother's face, sympathy in her gaze. Pity.

Flinching, Avery shook her head in denial as her mind finally caught up. The long tendrils of blonde hair were Nora's. The blood turning the water candy-coloured pink was Nora's. The body, illuminated by the night lights beneath the water was Nora's.

'Oh god.'

Avery sank to her knees, Leo moving with her, his arms still wrapped around her.

Nora was dead?

'Has anyone checked to see if she's . . .?' Leo asked over her head.

Domingo braced himself against the pool's side and reached out over the water for Nora's outstretched hand.

'There's too much blood. She's not . . . She's dead,' Avery's mother said.

Avery felt Leo shake his head, the move rolling through her body.

'Such a terrible accident,' Carol whispered.

Horror punched goosebumps across Avery's skin and she began to tremble in earnest now. Tears fell hot and heavy over her cheeks.

Nora.

'She must have hit her head,' Annalise concluded, staring at a bloodstain on the large steel planter near the pool. 'Had she had much to drink?'

Avery scrubbed the tears from her cheeks, but they just kept coming as she desperately scrabbled for a foothold, for something, anything to make this make sense. Because Nora *hadn't* been drunk. Not the last time she'd seen her.

Darian pushed his way through the small gathering, still wearing the same clothes from the party. 'Fucking hell.'

The expletive from a man usually so contained was like a bomb going off.

'It's obvious that this was an accident,' Dennis announced. 'The stupid girl –' Avery flinched at his callousness, even her mother gasped – 'had too much to drink, stumbled, hit her head and must have fallen into the pool. Simple as that.'

Avery shook her head.

'She was afraid of the water,' Avery whispered. 'She wouldn't have done that.' She looked around her, wondering why no one was saying anything. 'She wouldn't have come close to the pool,' she repeated louder, craning her head to look up at Leo – sympathy shining in his eyes.

But not agreement.

As if the tension around the pool was enough to set her off, Sydney started crying again, the sound a low moan that was working up to something more, something terrible.

'Jesus,' Dennis Devereux said. 'Someone get her out of here,' he ordered, sounding more irritated than concerned.

'She's hysterical,' Carol said.

'I got that,' Dennis dismissed carelessly.

'No, I mean, she's hysterical. She's out of control.'

'Get her out of here then!' Dennis shouted, shocking everyone into silence, even Carol.

Carol walked around to Sydney. 'Come on,' she said, pulling her daughter away from the poolside. 'I don't want you seeing this. It's too much.'

Sydney pulled out of her arms, but was still making a low moaning sound that made Avery feel dizzy.

'Come on. You could have a setback and you don't want that,' Carol said, her voice low, tone insistent. Sydney shook her head, trying to pull out of her mother's arms, but Carol just held on tighter.

For a brief moment, Syd locked eyes with Avery across the water, but her expression was unreadable. And finally her mother and Archie drew her away from the pool.

Avery felt like something was being torn from her. An ally. Someone who knew that this wasn't right. Someone who knew that Nora wouldn't have got drunk and fallen. Someone who knew that Nora shouldn't be dead.

Mark emerged from the pathway closest to the staff centre.

'The police are on their way,' Mark explained, turning to Darian. Whatever personal issues they might have had between the party and now were put to rest for the moment as they stood side by side and took control of the situation.

'Why do we need the police?' Dennis asked.

'Because a girl died, Dennis!' Annalise exclaimed, as if finally having been pushed over the edge by his callousness.

He glared at her, but said nothing, his gaze dropping disdainfully to the pool. Avery clenched her jaw, unable to do the same. If she kept her gaze away from it, away from *her*, she might still be able to believe that this was all a horrible misunderstanding. That any minute now Nora would come running down the path and shout 'Gotcha!' at the top of her lungs and they'd all yell at her but eventually laugh because that was – anything was – better than . . . than . . .

'Sven?' Darian asked Domingo, who was still kneeling by the pool, staring at Nora's body.

Domingo swallowed, gathering himself before answering, 'On his way.'

'I'm here, I'm here,' the older blond man said, approaching the pool with a jog.

'We need staff to escort everyone back to their villas,' Mark said to him.

Avery shifted, pulling herself to her feet, Leo moving with her. It drew Sven and Darian's attention briefly, but Avery didn't care and neither did Leo because his arms stayed there.

'Cameras?' Darian asked Sven. They were trying to be quiet, but their voices carried above the breeze rippling the water, swaying Nora's body in the pool.

Sven shook his head. 'Out after the storm. They were due to be fixed tomorrow.'

Mark went to stand beside Domingo, gently leading him away from the poolside.

'Such a terrible accident,' Mark said sadly, looking at the pool.

Denial roared through Avery. She didn't know where it came from, but she just didn't believe that this could have been an accident.

It'll all make sense in the morning, Avery. I promise. I'll tell you everything then. Nora's last words echoed in her ears.

Avery had been too angry, too upset to pay attention to her then, but now?

This wasn't right. Something wasn't right.

Staff members started to cajole Dennis into returning to his villa, and her parents tried to get her to leave, but Avery refused. She wouldn't leave Nora alone. Not like that. Not with these people. She just couldn't do that to her.

Sven approached Leo. 'You should be back at the staff centre with the others.'

The warning was clear. Even to Avery's ears. She looked up at him, pleading for him to stay.

Leo hadn't taken his eyes off Sven. 'I'm not going anywhere,' he declared.

'That's your decision,' Sven stated tonelessly as if washing his hands of him, and returned to Mark and Darian's side.

It seemed like an eternity later when in the distance the blue and red flashing lights from the police boats cut across the water. Avery barely noticed the commotion they made as they came up to the poolside where she had sat in a strange vigil over Nora's body. Two in uniform, one in overalls and one man in a suit. Mark and Darian went to head them off at the top of the pool, while everyone else was ushered away from the poolside.

'Is this really necessary?' she heard Darian ask the man in the suit.

'I appreciate your concern, Mr Vandenburg, however we take any death on one of the islands, private or otherwise, very seriously,' the man replied.

'Look, I don't want you yanking our chain just because—'

'Oh, I assure you, Mr Vandenburg,' the detective interrupted, 'you will be treated *exactly* as we would any other person.'

One of the men in the overalls extended a long pole into the water, trying to reach the body.

'You don't need to see this,' Leo said, trying to pull Avery away.

'I can't . . . I can't leave her alone. Not like this,' she said, her voice breaking as her heart fractured.

Her dad put a hand on her arm. 'I'll stay.'

She looked up at her father, so thankful to see the understanding she desperately needed.

'It's OK,' Jonathan insisted. 'Go.'

Avery finally let Leo tug her gently away from the poolside, unwilling to look away, knowing that this would be the last time she saw her friend and hating that it would be like this. Nora had been nothing but life and energy; difficult and complex, absolutely. But she had been her *friend*.

'Where was Hugo?' Avery asked absently as he pulled her into his side.

'I don't know,' Leo said, his voice holding an echo of the same sense of concern she felt.

LEO

'One last thing,' the detective said, raising his voice enough to stop Leo in his tracks. 'No one is to leave the island until further notice.'

The tension rippled out in circles around the poolside. Leo

could practically feel the adults straining against the sudden leash.

'Well, now, that *is* unnecessary,' Darian said, Dennis coming to stand with him, to add his considerable force to their side.

'I am not saying anything nefarious happened here, Mr Vandenburg, Mr Devereux, but no one would want to be left open to accusations of mishandling such a delicate situation. Most especially not you or your guests.'

Whether it was because the detective was genuinely doing his job, or because the man had finally been given an opportunity to stick it to the obscenely rich owners of an island that once belonged to people who could now barely afford the roof over their heads, Leo couldn't tell. But there was no denying the glint of satisfaction in the eyes of a man who had been pushed around for many years and now could finally push back.

'This is ridiculous,' Dennis spat.

'It's also impossible,' Carol said, approaching the group of men from the pathway that led from Solar with a woman by her side.

'Who's that?' Avery asked, clutching the cuff of Leo's hoodie tightly beneath her fingers, her eyes wide as she took in the drama.

'The island's doctor,' Leo explained, watching the conversation intently.

'Sydney's very sick. I've had to give her a sedative,' Leo heard the woman explain.

'We might have needed to talk to her,' the detective pointed out, less angry than mildly irritated. 'She was the one who found the body.'

'She was in no state for it. I want to take her back to the

mainland, on the helicopter if possible. I'm gravely concerned about her condition,' the doctor returned.

'Which is?'

Leo and Avery's gazes met in the darkness.

'Prior to sedation? Hysterical. Possibly a psychotic break. We'll know more when she's assessed in the morning and I wouldn't like to say more until then.'

The detective seemed to consider whether to argue and then shrugged. 'It's not my helicopter.'

'Darian?' Carol asked.

'Of course, Carol. You take whatever you need.'

'OK, but she goes under medical supervision. You and your husband will remain behind.'

If he'd expected Carol to fight that, he was wrong and his eyes tracked Carol as she slipped away to make the arrangements.

With one last devastating look at where Nora lay face down in the pool, Leo turned his back on it all, taking Avery with him. He wanted to get her out of here, to protect her. As shivers wracked her body, he felt raw and helpless in the face of her grief and shock. But he would be there for her for however long she needed him.

Sven's stare was heavy on his back as they slipped away to the Finches' villa. He'd broken the rules tonight. But if neither Sven nor his father could understand why, then that was their problem. Avery needed him and she was more important.

They were passing under the cliff that reached down from the Big House when the hair lifting on the back of Leo's neck made him look up. Hugo watched from the end of the manicured lawn that sat above the curved bay, meeting Leo's gaze with such silent fury it left him momentarily shocked.

But one blink and he was gone.

Avery murmured something, calling his attention back to her and Hugo was immediately forgotten, Leo struggling and failing to hear her words.

He bent his head to hers and asked, 'What was that?'

'She didn't fall,' Avery said.

Leo bit his lip. It had looked like an accident, but he understood her concern. Nora had been very careful about steering as clear as possible from the water.

'She didn't fall,' Avery said again, but when her words were swallowed up by a sob he pulled her into his arms and carried her back to her parents' villa. Holding her to his chest as she let her grief free, his heart broke for her.

He took the small path towards the front of the villa and opened the door with his staff key card, putting Avery down only once they had crossed the threshold. He followed her into the villa, absently taking in the dark teak interior and warm cream tones of the expansive open-plan living area, and caught up with Avery at the end of a hallway, standing in the doorway to a suite.

The suite she had shared with Nora.

He bit back a curse and came to stand behind her, relaxing infinitesimally when she leaned back against his chest.

'Do you want me to go in and get some clothes for you?' he asked, not imagining for a second that she'd want to spend another night there.

He waited and eventually she shook her head.

'But will you come with me?'

'Of course,' he said, taking her hand when she held it out to him.

One half of the room was neat and tidy, and the other half looked as if a bomb had gone off. Leo didn't need to ask to know that Avery's side was the neat side.

Avery let go of his hand as she skirted the chaos of messy clothes, shoes and towels as if it were a pit of writhing snakes, and slipped into the bathroom.

While Avery grabbed what she needed, Leo heard the front door open and close. He peered into the hallway to see her parents, heads together, whispering. Annalise looked up, caught him watching, glared and turned her back, *dismissing* him, all in the space of a heartbeat.

Leo tempered down an instinctive spike of anger at such a blatant insult and turned his attention back to Avery. She was all that mattered.

She came out of the bathroom wiping her face and stared at the mess of clothes on the floor in the corner, frowning.

'What is it?' Leo asked.

'Her phone.'

'What?'

'Nora's phone,' Avery repeated. 'It wasn't in the pool. She never went anywhere without it.'

Avery pulled out her mobile, keyed in her pin and clicked on Nora's number, the ring tone audible in the quiet of the villa.

'What are you doing?' Annalise asked, coming into the room.

'I'm trying to find Nora's phone,' she explained.

'Why?'

'So I can call her mother.'

Annalise opened and closed her mouth.

'What?' Avery demanded angrily, as if wanting a fight.

Tension coiled in Leo's gut.

'I don't ... I don't think that is a good idea,' Annalise hedged.

Leo blinked and Avery let out a gasp of disbelief.

'You don't think that her mother has a right to know?' Avery asked.

'No, that's not what I said. I just don't think that we have all the information yet.'

'All the information? What more does she need? Her daughter is dead, Mum!'

Leo's gaze, flicking between the two, saw Annalise Finch blanch at her daughter's statement.

'It's not that simple,' she said. 'At this point, there could be ... We could be ...'

'There could be legal implications,' Jonathan Finch said, coming to stand behind his wife.

'Oh god. Really? You're worried about getting *sued*?' The horror in Avery's voice was sharp and bloodied. 'Nora's dead, and you're worried about getting sued?'

Both Annalise and Jonathan looked at Leo, as if he was somehow to blame for their daughter's outburst.

Avery turned to him then too, her eyes hot and angry and devastated by betrayal, pleading with him to get her out of there. That was all he needed.

'Grab your stuff,' Leo said, his voice low. Oh, he was under no illusions that her parents had heard, but it was clear he'd spoken only to her.

Avery grabbed her bag and handfuls of clothes as Leo turned back to her parents. As Annalise tried to talk to Avery but got nowhere, Jonathan's gaze was hard on his. Leo gave an equally hard gaze back.

'I'm here for Avery, nothing else,' Leo told her father. 'I just want her to be OK.'

Something glinted in the dark-brown eyes that he'd passed down to his daughter, and eventually he stepped aside, letting Leo and Avery pass, hand-in-hand, on their way out of the villa.

Wordlessly, they took the pathway towards Tidal, Leo flinching against the cool bite of the air against his bare arms.

'What happened to her phone?' Leo asked.

'I don't know. It's gone,' she said, turning into his chest and beginning to cry.

CHAPTER NINETEEN

HUGO

Hugo stared up at the ceiling. He blinked, heart pounding as his alarm went off, screaming at him that it was 9.30 a.m.

He slammed out his hand to shut it off. *Why couldn't he remember?*

There was a significant chunk of time from the night before that he had no recollection of.

Hugo fisted his hand and stuffed it into his mouth, suffocating the scream he couldn't hold back any longer. His head was sore from the abuse he'd done to it last night with all the vodka he'd shared with Archie on the beach after turning his back on his dads. After they'd heard what Sydney had told *everyone*.

Vodka. *That's* why he couldn't remember. He'd clearly drunk so much he'd blacked out.

The next thing he remembered, he was standing on the cliff at the bottom of the Big House's manicured lawn, looking down at the pool. Seeing the police hauling Nora's body out of the pool, dripping with water and blood, hair a tangled mess. And then Leo walking Avery back to her villa.

Hugo's mind circled back to Nora.

It had been an accident. It *had* to have been an accident.

But then he turned on his side and came face-to-face with what was scaring him so much.

The white T-shirt on the floor, beside his jeans from last night.

The white T-shirt with blood on it.

Shit. *Shit!*

The first thing he'd done when he'd woken up and seen it was check himself for cuts or scrapes. But there wasn't a mark on him. And while there were huge gaps in his memory, he *knew* the only blood he'd seen yesterday was pooling into the water around Nora's dead body.

Had he been so out of it, he'd done something unimaginable? Unforgiveable?

He'd hated Nora, that much was clear, but could he have done *that*?

Acidic, angry fear crept up his throat and he launched out of bed, just making it to the bathroom in time to throw up. More alcohol than food disappeared down the sink drain, and after washing it away with water he turned off the tap and sank to the floor, back against the vanity.

Shit. Shit. *Shit!*

Once he knew his stomach wasn't going to revolt on him again, he shoved himself into the shower, scrubbing at his skin as if he could wash off the night before. But it couldn't stop his thoughts.

Why did he have a T-shirt covered in blood?

He switched the water from hot to frigid and bore the pain of the ice-cold shards against his skin, until the shivering became too much. Hugo got out of the shower, dried himself off and reached for a fresh pair of jeans and a new polo.

But all the time he was conscious only of one thing: the T-shirt.

He clenched his jaw. He couldn't stay here. He didn't know where he'd go, he just knew that he had to get *out*.

He crept from his room and slipped down the stairs. His dads were arguing again. Hugo swallowed and as he reached the bottom of the staircase he caught the tail end of the conversation.

'The State Department have notified the ambassador, who will be here tomorrow. Sven should be the one to pick him up.'

Hugo sank back against the wall, knowing that it was sick to feel relieved that they were talking about death instead of kicking him out of the house.

'I don't see why we should—'

'It happened in *our* resort, Darian. We can't just do *nothing*,' Mark snapped.

'We've done enough,' Darian replied with a level of exasperation that was near tipping point. 'We called the police, didn't we? It's not our fault that little twit had to go and get drunk and fall into a bloody pool when no one was watching.'

'The ambassador will act as an intermediary between us, the police and Mrs Miller.'

'Well, that's something at least.'

The sound of the telephone ringing cut off whatever Mark was about to say.

'Hello?' Mark answered the phone. 'Yes? How can I help you?'

'Who is it?' Darian hissed, clearly hating to be out of the loop.

Hugo crept closer to the wide double doors between him and the sitting room.

'What do you mean?' Mark asked.

'Who is—'

'Shut up,' snapped Mark, pulling both Hugo and Darian up short. Mark *never* snapped. Never even raised his voice.

'Right. OK,' Mark said in clipped tones. 'Well, we'll need to think about that. I'll call you back,' he added before hanging up.

Hugo peered through the gap between the door and the frame. He saw Mark sink on to the chaise, dazed.

'What's going on?' Darian demanded.

Mark shook his head. 'That was the police commissioner. The autopsy came back.'

'That was quick.'

'That's what we paid for,' Mark said tonelessly.

'And?'

'There was no water in her lungs.'

'What? She drowned, didn't she?'

Hugo's heart stopped beating.

'No. She died *before* she went into the water.'

'So? What does that have to do with anything?' Darian demanded. 'She fell *after* she hit her head.'

'She'd have had water in her lungs if she was disorientated and fell into the pool after hitting her head. No water in her lungs means that the hit to the back of her head was what killed her. And she couldn't have pushed *herself* into the pool after she was dead,' Mark explained. 'Meaning that her death wasn't—'

'An accident. *Shit!*' Darian shouted in fury.

The image of a white T-shirt covered in blood filled Hugo's mind, the buzzing in his ears hitting a high-pitched scream.

Nora *had* been murdered.

Punching out of what felt like a two-minute free dive, adrenaline dumping into his veins, Hugo began to shake. He thrust a hand out to the wall to keep himself upright when everything in him wanted to fold in on itself as if he was being sucked backwards into a black hole.

Could he have done this?

Oh shit. Oh shit.

'That little bitch,' Darian growled. 'Getting herself killed on our resort. How much will it cost us to make this go away?' he asked, barely stopping to take a breath between being told about a murder and deciding to cover it up.

'Five hundred thousand. American,' Mark replied, shocking Hugo perhaps the most. He'd have expected Mark to ask what Dorian was talking about. To object. To explain that they had to tell the truth. But he hadn't. Not only was Mark not surprised by Darian's question, he'd had an answer ready.

Five hundred thousand dollars. That was how much it cost to cover up a murder.

'They *deliberately* held this back until they knew the ambassador was on her way,' Darian spat. 'It's blackmail.'

'Likely,' admitted Mark.

And if they found out it was *his* fault? That they were being blackmailed? That *he'd* done this . . . That he'd *killed* someone?

Hugo didn't stop to think twice. He rushed out of the villa only half aware of his dads calling out his name. He launched himself down the steps and on to the pathway that led away from the Big House.

Guilt, anger and shame twisted in his gut like he'd been on a three-day bender. Yes, he'd hated Nora. But not enough to kill her. *Surely* not. The vicious thought that he could have been capable of such a thing caused bile – sharp, acidic and hot – to coat the back of his tongue and he dropped to his knees on the grass and retched.

Was this what his birth parents had seen in him? Evil? Was that why they gave him away? Was that what Darian and Mark would see? Would *do*?

He coughed and hacked, his throat burning and his stomach churning, over and over again until all he could do was pray that it stopped enough for him to take a breath. After what felt like an eternity, his stomach eased, his breathing slowing. His heart still pounded like a freight train, but he was able to move. Able to stumble forward and keep going. Away from the Big House. Away from his dads.

He walked aimlessly, without a destination in mind . . . until he did. Until he realised where he was.

Hugo came to a stop under the piercing sun of a bright-blue sky, on a morning that should have been paradise, beside a pool where only hours before Nora Miller's body had been found.

The area was taped off, the yellow plastic fluttering in the wind seeming more celebratory than warning. He stared at the water rippling beneath the gentle breeze as if it could give him answers. As if it could tell him what happened.

Approaching footsteps should have startled him, but in a

strange way he'd expected them. Because he wasn't the only person who had been drawn here, almost against their will.

Avery and Leo arrived together, from the path that came from Tidal. And for the first time ever, Hugo didn't even care that Avery was wrapped in Leo's arms. This time it wasn't jealousy or anger he felt. It was loss. Avery had been someone he could talk to, to confide in. He'd trusted her. And right when he needed her most, when he wanted to tell her about the fears that were piling in, filling him up and threatening to burst at the seams, she was the last person he could go to.

Archie arrived from the opposite direction, coming from his parents' villa, his gaze skating over them and landing on the pool, lips thinned, jaw clenching, muscles pulsing.

Hugo wasn't sure whether he wanted to speak to him or not. Was he ready to find out what had happened last night? Archie would know, wouldn't he?

'I can't believe this happened,' Avery said, staring at the middle of the pool.

The silence was as loud as a scream. Hugo held his breath.

'Was it *really* just a horrible accident?' Avery asked. 'She didn't even like being *near* the pool.'

Hugo looked from her to Leo, who said nothing but met his eyes.

Cold sweat broke out across his skin.

There was no water in her lungs.

AVERY

The silence that met her statement made Avery want to howl. They *all* knew that Nora had hated the water. And now they were pretending like that didn't matter.

Her body ached from the tension that had gripped her in a vice ever since last night. After her argument with her parents, she and Leo had gone back to Tidal. He'd run her a shower and when she'd stood there staring at it, he'd slowly and patiently stripped off her clothes, then his own, and got in with her. He'd not tried anything on. Just let the hot water wash her, warm her, and then he'd wrapped her in a towel and got into bed with her and held her until dawn. And throughout it all, he'd not said a single word, not pushed her or rushed her. And even if he had, she wasn't sure what she would have said.

'Of course it was an accident,' Archie snapped, biting his thumb. 'Why would anyone want to kill her anyway. She was—'

Archie bit off his words, but his sentence hung in the air between them all.

'What was she, Archie?' Avery yelled across the pool. 'Nothing? No one? Not worth killing?'

'Dude, I didn't mean it like that and you know it,' he said, his tone defensive rather than ashamed.

She shook her head, not quite knowing what to believe any more. She barely recognised the affable, easy-going guy he'd been only yesterday. Instead, he was now pale-skinned and hollow-eyed. And she knew that it wasn't for Nora.

No. None of them had even *liked* her.

The thought pushed tears to her eyes and thickened her throat so much she had to swallow just to breathe. She looked across the pool at Hugo, but he was staring at the water as if not even aware of the conversation going on around him. How did he get so far away from her? How did they all get so far away from each other?

Even Leo didn't really understand. It wasn't as if he'd liked Nora either.

'I'm just . . . I'm just worried about Syd, that's all,' Archie insisted.

A spike of guilt plunged deep as she realised she hadn't given Sydney a single thought last night or this morning. 'Is there any news?' she asked.

Archie shook his head. 'Dad went over this morning to see how she's doing.'

'I thought no one was supposed to leave the island,' Leo said, his tone pointed.

Archie just shrugged. 'He'll be back this afternoon,' he said sulkily.

Avery felt frustration ripple through Leo's body. She could imagine how he saw it. One rule for them, another for him. Things that she'd not even noticed before this holiday now looked strange, mean, *unjust*.

It was like the storm had come through, leaving the island relatively unscathed but decimating *them*. The group. Her friends. And she knew without question that things would never be the same again.

It'll all make sense in the morning, Aves. I promise.

But it didn't. And Nora's last words to her now just seemed like some cruel joke.

Leo's arms tightened and flexed around her before he hung his head into the curve of her neck. 'I'm going to have to go. Dad's been messaging. Says he needs to see me.'

She knew it was childish and silly, but she didn't want him to leave her. She didn't feel safe without him, but she nodded her understanding, knowing that her voice would give her away if she spoke.

'I wish I could take you with me, but that would only make things worse,' he whispered for her ears only.

She turned in his embrace, not caring what Archie or Hugo saw or thought, and Leo pressed a kiss to the top of her head.

'Are you going to be OK?' he asked.

'Yes,' she said, hoping he didn't hear the tremble in her voice.

'Really, because I could—'

'No,' she said, cutting him off, not wanting him to get into more trouble with his dad. 'It's OK. Go, I'll be fine,' she promised, and watched him walk off to the staff centre, trying to ignore the awkward silence that settled between the rest of them.

Archie kicked a pebble on the ground and when it landed in the pool, each of them flinched. He shook his head and rubbed the back of his neck.

'I've gotta get back,' he said, barely stopping for a breath before he turned back down the path towards his parents' villa.

That left just her and Hugo.

He bit his lip, and when his eyes met hers, what she saw there made her heart ache.

Anguish, confusion, hurt, desperation.

'Hugo—'

'I have to go,' he said, cutting her off, and leaving her alone beside the place where her best friend had died.

Unable to bear being there any more, she turned randomly down a path, paradoxically seeking the solitude she resented. She wanted to wrap it around her so thick that it would make her numb. So that she couldn't feel all the things crowding at her, wanting to come in. Grief. Loss. Fear. Anger. Resentment.

Her friends didn't understand. Couldn't, when she couldn't even understand it herself.

Couldn't understand how awful she was for being angry at Nora for doing this. For leaving her. For, oh god, making everything about *her*.

Dammit, Avery thought as she wiped furiously at the tears that were in free fall. How could Nora have done this to her? How could she have left her when the last words they'd shared had been hurtful and *hateful*. Guilt and misery took chunks out of Avery as she cried for the friend she would miss desperately.

When she next looked up, she saw the tree stump where she'd waited for Nora the night of the staff party they'd crashed. When Nora had been the happy, teasing, fun, easy-going carefree *her*. Before everything had got so complicated.

Avery wanted to scream, to shout, to yell – but somehow nothing came out. It tore at her insides, desperate to escape, but still she kept it in. Heartsore and miserable, Avery collapsed against the tree stump, with the forest to her left and the beach in front of her; a mocking slice of a paradise so beautiful it hurt to look at it.

Nothing about Nora had ever been easy. There was always something simmering, something being calculated; there was always a sharp edge waiting to be discovered, waiting to cut. Here, where no one could see, or hear, Avery could admit that.

'You could be such a bitch,' she whispered, laughing at herself sadly.

I know, babes. But you loved me anyways.

'Yeah. I did.'

And it was true. She hadn't known Nora for the same amount of time as the others. But Nora saw things that they hadn't. About Avery. About life, and Avery had liked that. Wanted that in her life. Oh god, she was going to miss her so, so much, she realised as the future that she'd thought she would have spun away with Nora in it.

Jagged sobs wracked her body and she didn't fight it. Not this time. She knew they needed to come out. Lanced like some poisonous infection, they scratched her throat and left her chest raw. It was loud and messy and, somewhere in the back of her mind, she thought that Nora would have approved.

Eventually they subsided enough for Avery to pull herself together. Eyes puffy and swollen, she probably looked an absolute state but, somehow, she felt better. Aside from Leo, she didn't care about the rest of them on the island. Not any more. She'd get through this, get home and figure things out. This wasn't—

Her phone beeped and she reached for it thinking it might be Leo.

But the incoming message wasn't from him.

Her hands shook as she saw the name on the screen.

Nora.

Confusion spun her mind out to a thousand different places as she opened up the messaging app to see the voice note icon.

Her hands shook as she tried to click on it, but her finger slipped on the screen and an alert popped up.

Do you wish to delete this?

No!

Panic nearly made her drop the phone, but desperation made her hit play before she could second-guess it.

'Hey, Aves, now this is we-ird.'

Avery hit pause, barely able to hear Nora's voice over the heartbeat pounding in her ears. She had to calm down. Get herself together. Brace herself for whatever was coming.

She hit play again.

'And, actually, it's not like you'll ever hear this anyways. It's a "just in case", really. I hope to god you're *not* actually hearing it because that would mean –' Nora's laugh was staticky in the phone's speaker '– well, that would mean that these bastards really *will* commit murder to keep their secrets.' There was a pause. 'Maybe it's not so funny after all,' Nora said, her tone sobering. Another pause, before she started to speak again. 'Yeah. So, this is timed. Pre-recorded. It's about an hour before the anniversary party for the Vandenburgs. And I've nearly got everything I need. I just . . .' A deep breath. An awkward laugh. 'OK, Aves, here it is. If anything happens to me, then you need to find my phone. The other one, that you found before. I've stashed it somewhere safe. It's where I'll keep all my secrets. You know where it is. You'll think you won't, and you'll get pissed off with me – *and* with yourself – 'cos you do that, Aves.

A little too much. You should cut yourself some slack, you know? Anyways. Find the phone. And when you do, the PIN is easy. You're the only one who'd know it,' Nora said, laughing.

The sound of it turned her heart and her stomach at the same time.

'Find the phone, Aves. And don't trust anyone. They're all bastards here,' she said, somewhat bitterly. 'Ha. Paradise, indeed. Whatevs. Loves ya, Aves. Even if I *have* been a royal bitch this holiday. I do. Really.' Her tone was determined. 'Then again, I'll be deleting this in a few hours, so you'll probably never know that.'

The voice note cut out midway through Nora's laugh. The sound disturbing; violently truncated.

Avery stared at the phone. And then she replayed the voice note over and over again until she knew every word, every nuance. Confusion cleared, replaced by anxiety and frustration.

If anything happens to me.

It had happened. Nora was dead.

Murdered.

Oh god, Avery thought, her fingers pressing against her lips. *What had Nora done?*

You'll know where it is.

But she didn't. She didn't know where Nora's phone was at all.

CHAPTER TWENTY

LEO

Leo stared at his father, trying – for what felt like the hundredth time this trip – to find some kind of connection, some kind of familial bond. But he was half convinced that the man glaring at him from the other side of the desk felt absolutely no interest in him beyond what he felt for the rest of his staff.

'You are making a big mistake, son.'

Leo fisted his hands behind his back and raised his gaze to a point just above his father's head and braced himself. In the small office behind the island's central kitchen, his father was only just getting started.

And Leo was just about getting done.

After leaving the poolside, he'd stopped by his room, grabbed a quick shower and a change of clothes and came here. With only one intention. To get this over as quickly as possible so that he could get back to Avery.

'This job? The kinds of opportunities these people offer? You will *never* see anything like it again,' his father said.

Leo's jaw was beginning to ache and he was seriously at risk of losing a tooth. His father didn't get it. He was talking about Leo's job, when a girl had just died. And not just some stranger. A girl he'd known. Avery's best friend. He might not have liked her all that much, but he knew her name. He knew the sound of her laugh. His father just couldn't understand the emotional impact of it.

And just like that, he realised that all this time his father had missed the entire point of Leo's visits to this island. As if the puzzle pieces finally slotted together, Leo was struck with startling clarity: *this job* was all it had ever been for his father. That's all he thought he was giving to his son.

A job. An opportunity.

His heart gave an aching twist. For years he'd been looking to his father for some kind of connection. His mother had given him almost everything, but the one thing she couldn't give him was a connection to his Caribbean heritage. That was his dad's responsibility, and one he seemed wholly uninterested in taking on. Leo had come here, year after year, hoping for something more. Hoping to learn about himself, about his father, about the kind of man he should be.

But all he'd learned, Leo realised now, was what *not* to be.

This job for him? The money? Yeah, he'd hoped to use it to pay off some of his student debt. To lighten the load his mother felt was her *sole* responsibility. A load he knew was too heavy for her.

But he didn't want the money enough to lose his conscience. And as for a connection to his heritage, to his family, *he* could approach his aunties and cousins himself if he wanted to. He didn't need his father's permission; Leo saw that now.

'How you act reflects on me,' Mitchel Walker said, unaware of the direction of Leo's thoughts.

'Oh,' Leo finally said, his tone seeped in scorn. 'So this is about *you*. Not me.'

Fury flashed in his father's eyes.

'You got a mouth on you,' Mitchel Walker warned.

'Well, I guess you know who to blame for that,' Leo replied, no longer scared of losing what he'd never had.

His father launched out of his chair, sending it screeching back against the wall.

The anger and violence pulsing in the air felt dangerous. Or was that just because of what had happened to Nora? He didn't know any more.

'You have no respect!' his father shouted, his finger bullet-pointing his accusation.

'That's bullshit. *Sir*,' Leo added, for extra insolence. He was done. Pandering to the overzealous hierarchy in this place. Pandering to the false respect accorded to men with louder voices and meaner fists. Nothing was worth selling his soul for. And that's what it felt like, playing along here. As if he were cutting off pieces of himself and putting them up for auction.

'I'm warning you. Get it together, or pack up your shit, Leo, and get off this island.'

That one threat had the power to cut through his anger. The warning that would remove him from Avery when she needed him the most.

It had him holding back the words that would have got him fired.

As if sensing this, his father pressed on.

'You will be on shift tonight at the Big House. Drinks reception.'

'What?' Leo asked, unsure as to whether he was more shocked that the Vandenburgs were planning to have drinks after Nora had been found dead on their island, or that *he* was to be there serving them. 'Why?'

'Not my idea, that's for sure,' Mitchel Walker said. 'Personally, I don't think they like you messing around with their friend's little girl.'

And this was their way of putting him back in his box.

Punishment. Everything in him railed against it.

His father's gaze had already returned to the paperwork on the table, his son already dismissed.

Leo's jaw flexed under the pressure of gritted teeth. Toeing the line was the only way he could stay on the island and be there for Avery. He couldn't leave her now. Not like this.

'OK.'

'OK what?'

'OK, I'll do it.'

'You will be on your best behaviour – especially around the Vandenburgs – and you will *not* be seen with any of their children. Do you hear me?'

'Yes, sir,' Leo bit out. His father had been specific, and so would Leo. He had absolutely no intention of being *seen* with Avery. But the first place he was going, when he left here, was to her.

His father was glaring at him as if he knew. 'Get out.'

Leo didn't need to be asked twice.

He stalked from the small office, purposefully slamming the door behind him and ignoring Domingo's grinning face, having clearly heard the argument from outside.

'Don't start,' Leo said before Dom could even begin what was sure to be a level of piss-taking he didn't have time for.

'Big. Hairy. Fat ones.'

Leo couldn't help but bark out a laugh. A laugh he desperately needed after the last twelve hours.

'Have you seen—' Leo tried.

'Nope. Not seen nothing or no one,' Domingo said, his hands raised either in surrender or *I'm not touching that with a bargepole*, before disappearing into Mitchel Walker's office.

It didn't matter, Leo would find her.

But an hour later, all he'd got was sweaty and frustrated. Avery wasn't answering her phone and he'd looked everywhere. He'd already been to her villa and received a curt 'no' from her mother.

He'd swung by the pool, and the main beaches as well as the private one at Tidal, hoping she might have gone back there. But she wasn't there, or in the villa. He was probably worried for no reason, but anxiety pricked his skin like seawater in sandfly bites.

The only place left that he could think of was the spa, but he couldn't even begin to imagine that Avery would be pampering herself so soon after Nora's death. Despite that, he approached the wooden structure that, to him, looked like a cross between a Buddhist temple and what he imagined a New York yoga studio to be like. Built with a walkway that bisected the building beneath the large thatched roof, the view cut straight between the two wings, straight down towards the private beach.

Thankful there was no one on reception, he poked his head

into treatment rooms and studio spaces carefully, but the entire place was empty. If Avery wasn't here, there were only a couple of places left to look, but he very much doubted she was in the forest, or near one of the jagged cliffs at either end of the island.

He walked down the corridor that cut the spa in half, the subtle scents of eucalyptus and patchouli in the air reminding him of his mother's incense sticks. He stepped out on to the dark wood deck at the back, which offered a view of the sweeping curve of the bay and several of the large bed-sized sunloungers, looking somewhat bereft without their linen drapes.

Where could she be?

He was about to give up when he heard a quiet curse and the sound of something behind him.

He turned and quietly stepped to the side of the spa that brushed up against the edges of the thick treeline. Rows of sleek wooden lockers pressed up against the spa next to a smooth marble bench, the area clearly for guests to leave their things before treatments.

And down on the floor, scrabbling to pick something up, was Avery.

'What are you doing?' he asked.

AVERY

Avery stifled the scream that tore up her throat, trying to get out, even as she recognised Leo's voice. With one hand pressed against her racing heart, the other arm cradling Nora's phone to her chest, she let the shiver loose over her skin.

'You nearly gave me a heart attack,' she said, glaring at him.

'Sorry,' Leo said, his hands raised in surrender as if only then realising how scared she'd been.

'No, it's . . . Oh god. It's . . . I don't even know . . .'

She was terrified. She'd thought she'd known what Nora had been up to. She thought Nora had just been doing a puff piece about the rich and famous. Yes, it would have been disastrous, but it would only have been a scathing diatribe about how obtuse and awful they all were. Which wouldn't have been enough to kill her over, would it?

'You found her phone?'

'Yes,' Avery said and then, 'No. It's not her phone . . . It's her *second* phone.'

'Why does she have two phones?' Leo asked as if it were the weirdest thing in the world.

Avery stared at him, her mind spiralling, making it hard to focus on what he was saying.

'Avery, what's wrong?' Leo asked, concern etched into his features. He pulled her into his arms and she let him wrap her in his strong embrace. She wanted that strength. Needed it.

'I think . . . I think something terrible happened,' she whispered to him. 'I think . . . I think Nora was murdered.'

His arms flexed around her and she braced herself to hear him tell her that she was being silly, that she was imagining things . . . But he didn't.

'OK,' he said simply. 'OK,' he said again, as if quickly thinking things through and making decisions. 'Let's get out of here first, and then you can tell me why.'

Avery nodded her agreement and let Leo lead her away from the lockers where she'd found Nora's phone.

It had taken her a while to figure it out. Avery had gone straight from the tree stump back to the villa and searched the room, her bag – the entire place – from top to bottom. She'd even searched her own things, in case Nora had slipped it in there. And then she *had* got pissed off with herself. Nora had been right about that, which had only made Avery more miserable. She'd listened to the voice note again and again until her head spun.

I've stashed it somewhere safe. It's where I'll keep all my secrets. You know where it is.

It wasn't until about the thirtieth listen that Avery realised what had been bugging her about it. The choice of words.

It's where I'll keep all my secrets.

But they were on the island. Nora didn't keep her secrets here. She hated that it had taken her so long to realise. Avery had thought back over their entire holiday, where they'd been, what they'd done, who Nora might have trusted – and eventually she remembered.

Marta, with the clever fingers. Nora had said that she would give her all her secrets.

And that's when she remembered the lockers.

The lockers where Leo had found her.

She thought she'd have to try every locker, one by one with a multitude of codes, until she saw one locker with a crudely carved 'A ♡ N' in the corner. She'd pressed a finger to the damaged wood, affectionately thinking that *of course* Nora had put A first and not the other way round.

After that, the code had been easy – Nora's birthday – and

Avery had got that on the first try. But the PIN on the phone? That was a different matter entirely.

Avery followed Leo out on to the sun-drenched beach, the afternoon painfully bright and stark in comparison to the dark, tree-covered lockers. Squinting, she raised her hand to shade her eyes, and looked over her shoulder. Paranoia bit at her ankles. What if someone had been *watching*, waiting for her to find this? What if they were being followed right now?

And what if this was all just paranoia and some kind of twisted joke that Nora didn't get a chance to finish.

Avery's head hurt and exhaustion hit her like a wall. She hadn't slept in over twenty-four hours. Maybe she wasn't thinking straight.

Leo took her free hand in his and led her away from the spa, past the beach and the marina, and cut down behind the pool and the tennis courts towards Tidal. Everything looked different today. Before she'd seen beauty, luxury, fun ... *paradise*. But now? The beach looked cruelly stark, isolated and painfully hot with sand that would burn bare feet and cliffs that would cut and slice into flesh. Birds that could be eaten by crabs and secrets that were dark enough to kill. She stifled the sob that rose in her chest and forced herself into a small jog to keep up with the furious pace Leo was setting.

Relief broke through the tension when she caught sight of the villa, instinctively feeling like it was a safe space, and followed Leo down to the door as he opened it with his key card. She felt his concerned gaze on her as she walked towards the kitchen and put Nora's phone on the countertop as if it were an unexploded bomb.

'OK. What's going on?' Leo asked patiently, eyeing the small mobile.

Avery let it all come tumbling out.

She told him about the argument she and Nora had had, when Avery had first seen her second phone. The article that Nora was planning to write about Dennis. She played him the voice note Nora had pre-recorded and sent to her. And she told him about finding the phone after tracking it down to the spa.

'And you think that someone was willing to kill her over an article?' Leo asked, his scepticism coming to the forefront of his tone.

'No,' Avery said helplessly. 'That's just it. I *don't* think anyone would,' she replied truthfully, as confused as Leo. 'Honestly? They could just throw some money at whoever Nora had planned to publish the article and make it go away. And even if she'd intended to put it out herself, so what? Dennis Devereux flashing the cash and being a bit of a dick. It's hardly headline news.'

Leo leaned back against the countertop, his brow furrowed.

'So, what's on the phone then?'

'I don't know. I can't figure out the PIN,' Avery said, spinning away in frustration.

'And you tried the same number as the locker PIN?'

'Yeah. I didn't think Nora would have been *that* stupid, but yes, I tried.'

Leo rubbed the back of his neck in frustration.

'Play the voice note again?' he asked.

Avery put her phone beside Nora's and hit play on the voice note.

You're the only one who'd know the PIN.

'Why you?' he asked, staring at her as if she should have figured it out by now.

'Because we are – we *were* – friends? I don't know.' She shrugged, impatience, grief and frustration crashing together in waves.

'Clearly she thought something might happen and was covering her bases.'

'Yes, I got that,' Avery snapped, feeling helpless and hating it.

Leo cocked his head to one side, his gaze softening. 'I'm just trying to help.'

'Oh god, Leo, I know. I'm sorry,' she said sincerely, going to him then, wrapping herself in the strong solid heat of him. Leaning on him in a way she'd never been able to do with Hugo, or anyone else. 'It's just that . . . I need to figure this out. If Nora was murdered . . . If this isn't just some stupid, terrible joke, then this phone might be the only evidence of . . .'

She bit off the words before she could finish them, still unwilling to believe that someone on the island could have murdered her friend.

'I've tried to think of important numbers. Her birthday, our dorm-room number. The last four digits on her phone number. The day we met, the day I asked if she wanted to come here to the island. None of them work.'

Leo placed his chin on her head, the weight comfortable as she lost him to his thoughts. His chest expanded with a sigh, pressing against her body. Pushing her out and pulling her back in again.

'But . . . those are all things about you *both*. Or her. That's not what the message said,' Leo explained. '"*You're* the only one who'd know the PIN" is what Nora said. So it's about you. *Avery.*'

'No,' Avery replied, catching his train of thought, realisation casting goosebumps across her skin. 'Not Avery. *Aves.*'

She crossed back over to the kitchen counter and picked up Nora's phone. She pressed the screen, the keypad lit up, and with shaking fingers she entered the number.

2837

AVES.

'Oh shit, we're in,' Leo said, locking his shocked eyes with Avery's.

She stared at the phone, suddenly not sure she wanted to know. Not sure she wanted to delve into it, but also knowing that she couldn't not. This might have got her friend killed. She owed it to Nora to find out what the hell was going on.

Biting her lip, Avery picked up the phone and swept her finger across the screen. There were only two apps on it: the voice recorder and the icon for cloud storage.

Remembering the file she'd seen uploaded when she first found the phone the night before the party, and not quite ready to hear more of Nora's voice yet, she clicked on the cloud app. It opened to a single folder.

DEVEREUX

She cast a gaze at Leo, who nodded and opened the folder. On display were JPEG icons and documents with different numbers and dates, all bearing the Deveureux family name.

She clicked on the first JPEG and when it loaded she dropped the phone.

It landed on the counter with a clatter.

'Jesus, Avery, what—'

Leo flinched, violently, catching sight of the phone's screen, cursing low but loud.

Bruised thighs. Haunted eyes. Red angry handprints on pale skin. And one bandage around a jagged cut caused by a fall on the island.

'That's Corrine,' he said, horror and disgust unspooling in his voice.

'Why is she . . .?' Avery's brain struggled to make sense of what she was seeing. Corrine was in her underwear, staring straight at the camera. 'Did Dennis do that to her?' she asked Leo, whose eyes refused to meet hers.

'I . . . Yeah, I think he could have.'

'And Nora took photos . . .?'

'As proof,' Leo concluded. 'Evidence.'

Avery swallowed, returning to the phone and, staying well clear of the JPEGs, clicked on a voice note.

Arrogant. Rich. Entitled.

Nora's words were violent angry bullets tearing out of the small speaker on the phone.

He thinks he can get away with it. But he's wrong. He can't.

The voice note clicked off, leaving an echo of shock and anger ringing in the silent room. Avery hesitated for just a second before clicking on another voice note.

I tracked down Corrine after she came back to the island. I'd only wanted to see if she'd seen something or got any useable info on Dennis. But I never imagined . . . I didn't know. I didn't . . .

The recording cut off. Avery clicked on the next one, not wanting to hear any more but unable to stop.

Corrine let me take photos and I helped her as much as I could. Convinced her to put all her clothes into a bag and keep them. Evidence. She might need it one day. And, of course, I might too. This was . . . I mean, I knew it was a possibility. But seeing it . . . She was so scared.

A thumping on the door to the villa made both Avery and Leo jump.

'Who knows we're here?' Leo demanded.

'I don't know,' Avery replied, shaking her head.

She reached for Nora's phone and put it in her back pocket, while Leo tried to peer through the window. He shook his head, and the thumping sounded again.

Stalking towards the door, Leo pulled it partially open, as if ready to jam it shut again, but then he allowed it to swing fully open.

'Hugo? What are you doing here?' Leo demanded.

'I need to talk to Avery.'

'How did you know where we were?' Leo asked suspiciously.

'I saw you,' Hugo said bitterly, before seeming to regret his tone.

Before Leo could answer, Hugo called around him. 'Avery?'

She pulled out of the shadows of the corridor and came to stand behind Leo. The moment she saw him she knew that something was terribly wrong.

'What happened? What's wrong?' The words spilled out of her mouth.

'I think . . . I think Nora was murdered. And I think I did it.'

CHAPTER TWENTY-ONE

HUGO

The look on Avery and Leo's faces wasn't at all what Hugo had expected.

'Why?' Avery asked.

'*Why?*' Hugo repeated, utterly confused by their reactions. 'I tell you I think I murdered Nora and you ask me *why*? As in why did I *do* it? Or why do I *think* that?'

Leo pulled Hugo into the villa, marching him down into the open-plan kitchen and living area.

'Why do you think Nora was murdered?' Leo said, taking over from Avery.

Hugo turned to Avery, not wanting to talk about this in front of Leo, but she just shrugged and Leo glared at him long enough to let him know he wasn't leaving.

'I overheard my dads talking,' he confessed, suddenly unable to meet Avery's eye. Not after what he should have told her earlier, by the pool. 'The post-mortem results came back and showed that there was no water in her lungs, so . . .'

'She was dead before she went into the pool,' Leo finished,

shaking his head. But the expression on his face was not surprise. It was as if he'd already known.

'She really *was* murdered,' Avery said, as if they were having an entirely different conversation to the one Hugo was trying to have.

'Wait, you knew?' he asked, confused.

'The pool was a cover-up,' Leo continued as if he'd not spoken. 'Nora was murdered somewhere else.' And then, finally, Leo turned on him. 'But why do you think *you* did it?' Leo asked.

Nausea welled in Hugo's gut, overriding his dislike at the way Leo was controlling the conversation, if you could call this a conversation.

But he'd made his decision. He'd come here looking for help, and Avery was the only person he trusted – even if she was involved with Leo – and he was going to stick to it. He couldn't carry on the way he'd been. Enough with the secrets and lies; they were making him ill. If he'd done something, he was going to step up and take the blame. But if he hadn't . . . he just didn't know any more.

'I was completely out of it last night. After I spoke to you,' Hugo said to Avery, 'Archie and I went to the beach and got wrecked. I can't remember, like, *anything*. Apart from Nora being dragged out of the pool. And then there was blood all over my T-shirt when I woke up.'

'Whose blood?' Leo demanded, putting himself in between him and Avery.

'I don't know. It's not mine. I don't have a scratch on me. But I don't . . .' Hugo could feel hot wet heat press against the backs of his eyes. He fisted his hands. 'I need your help,' he said, no longer above pleading. He couldn't carry on like this. It was awful.

'A T-shirt?' Avery asked, a frown marring her features as she peered at him from behind Leo's shoulder.

Hugo nodded. 'I saw it this morning. In my bag. It's got blood and . . . *Shit.*' He was going to be sick again.

'You weren't wearing a T-shirt last night,' Avery said. 'You'd *never* wear a T-shirt to your dads' anniversary. They wouldn't let you,' she said.

Hugo swallowed.

What? No, he . . .

Avery was right. He'd been wearing a vest beneath the shirt he'd put on that evening, not a T-shirt.

'Then whose damn T-shirt is it?' Hugo yelled.

'Don't look at me,' Leo said, raising his hands in surrender.

Hugo collapsed on to the sofa, breathing hard. Relief pouring through him, his body near trembling with it. He cursed, hand pressed against his chest.

'Do you have it?' Leo asked.

'What?'

'The T-shirt.'

'No! What, you think I'd just be carrying around a bloody T-shirt with me?'

'What did it look like?'

'A white T-shirt. With a bloodstain on it,' Hugo deadpanned.

'Branding? A label? Anything that could tell us who it belonged to,' Leo pressed.

'Yeah, OK, CSI. My bad. I missed that when I was *freaking*

out thinking I'd killed Nora!' he shouted, the words rolling together in his anger.

'Hugo, are you—'

'No, Avery,' he said, cutting off her question. 'I'm *not* OK. I thought I'd . . . *killed* Nora. I mean, I know I didn't like her, but I've been so angry and . . . I thought something must have happened.' He swallowed bitter bile, stinging his throat. 'And then when I heard my dads talking about the autopsy . . .'

Avery slowly took a seat beside him, taking her phone out of her back pocket, and put her arm around him awkwardly. And he didn't even care. Christ, he was just so thankful that—

'What the hell is that?' he asked, catching sight of the screen of the phone that displayed an image of a woman, naked, bruised and staring at the camera. He tried to crawl backwards on the sofa, desperate to escape the look in her eyes, but the cushions stopped him.

Leo scrabbled to pick up the phone, but the image was seared into his brain. The cry of a bird soaring past startled him and he felt an ice-cold sweat break out at his neck.

'It's nothing,' Avery tried to say, but it was too late.

'Nothing? Are you for real right now, Avery? What is going on?' Hugo demanded, turning to glare at Leo.

Hugo watched the silent play of a conversation pass between them as Avery glared at Leo until Leo finally turned back to him.

'Dennis Devereux sexually assaulted Corrine. When they were on the mainland,' Leo said.

Hugo swallowed the protest on his lips. Everything in him wanted to deny it, but in the last eight months his entire world had been stripped bare. People he thought would never do things like cheat, lie, betray ... they had proved him wrong. Why would Dennis Devereux be any different?

Hugo cursed. 'But what does Nora's death have to do with that?' he asked.

Avery looked away, her thumb tapping on her thigh. 'She was writing an exposé on Dennis and stumbled on to this, I think. We don't know. Maybe she confronted him and something went wrong,' she said with a shrug.

'You think Dennis killed Nora,' Hugo repeated, trying to bring the pieces all together.

'I mean, I know she pissed off a lot of people,' Leo said. 'Sorry,' he added to Avery, 'but she did. Only, Dennis is the person with the biggest motive. The most to lose. And if he found out about the article ...'

'Yeah, but what I don't understand is that if Nora and Corrine had proof, why didn't they just go to the police?' Avery asked, looking between him and Leo.

Please, C, I've only got one shot at this. We've only got one shot.

The conversation Hugo had overheard the day of the storm came to the surface of his mind.

Enough. I told you already. I don't want to do this.

Oh god, he'd heard Nora and Corrine arguing about confronting Dennis.

'Actually, I think,' Hugo said before swallowing, 'I think Corrine didn't want to.'

'What?' Avery asked.

'I heard them arguing the day of the storm. Corrine didn't want to do it, confront Dennis.'

Leo was scrolling on the phone, looking through the voice notes. 'The day of the storm?' he asked.

'Yeah,' Hugo confirmed. 'I think Dennis was offering Corrine money and she wanted to take it,' he explained.

'Hold on, this might be something. It's from that day,' Leo said, placing the phone on the coffee table in front of them and hitting play on a voice note.

Corrine's out. She's going to take the bastard's money. Unless I can find something that actually ties him to her, some kind of proof. Or something that would convince Corrine to change her mind. Without her I have nothing. And this whole thing just goes away, swept under the carpet. Like all the other times. Because this was most definitely not the first time for him.

Hearing Nora's voice – so angry, so *alive* – cut little jagged tears into the air in the room. Goosebumps ran over his skin and a shiver tripped down his spine.

'She got desperate and went looking for proof,' Avery realised.

'And Dennis killed her,' Leo concluded.

Hugo shook his head. 'What do we do?'

'We?' Leo demanded pointedly.

'Yeah, OK, I've been a dick,' Hugo admitted. 'But this is serious. And what about Archie and Syd? He's their father.'

'I'd want to know,' Leo said firmly.

'Would you?' Hugo asked, knowing that that kind of conviction had been sorely tested for him personally. 'Really? That your father was capable of . . . *that*. And that if it got out, it would ruin your *entire* life. Everything you knew, everything you *had*? Everything that was your life?'

Leo dropped his gaze after a beat.

'Syd's in no state to hear this and we can't tell Archie,' Avery said decisively. 'Not until we have proof of what Dennis did to Nora.'

'Yeah,' Hugo said, thinking things through. 'And then what? You think once we find proof that Dennis will sit here and wait patiently for the police to turn up and arrest him?'

'He'll run,' Leo said.

Hugo nodded. 'Of course he'll run. The moment he realises the truth is out, he'll be on that helicopter on the way to Equatorial Guinea.'

Avery sank into the sofa beside Hugo.

'We need Corrine,' Leo said quietly.

'We can't use those pictures without her permission. Even Nora wasn't going to do that. It's ... a *violation*,' Avery stressed.

'And if she didn't want to speak *before* Nora was murdered, she's not gonna want to talk *now*,' Hugo bit out.

'I don't know. I saw her that night by the pool. She was terrified, yes, but she was also horrified.'

'The police wouldn't be able to ignore us if Corrine was with us.'

They all agreed.

'So, you're going to speak to Corrine?' Hugo asked Avery, surprised when she started to shake her head.

'I think it should be you,' Avery said to him.

'Me?' Hugo replied, as shocked as Leo appeared to be.

'I'm not sure that's a good idea,' Leo said, his eyebrows in his hair.

'I agree?' Hugo said, not ever having thought he'd agree with Leo ever again.

'You're the only one here who could offer her something that I, Leo, and even Nora couldn't. Your name. It's just as big, if not bigger than Dennis's. It could protect her. And I think she needs that right now.'

Hugo's heart pulsed. He wasn't sure how long he'd have the Vandenburg name – if his dads would decide to disown him after Sydney's speech, or what his future with them would even look like. But if it was the last thing he did with his name, then Hugo could live with that.

Swallowing and nodding, he agreed. 'I'll find Corrine. Speak to her. Try to convince her to come to the police with me.'

'If that doesn't work?' Leo asked, his gaze steady.

'I'll go alone and we'll finally see just how much power the Vandenburg name really wields.'

'And while you do that . . .?' Avery said.

'We need to find physical evidence of what happened to Nora,' Leo continued. 'Because if she was dead before she went in the pool, then she was killed somewhere else. And what's the bet that it happened at the Devereuxs' villa? And if Dennis murdered Nora, there *will* be evidence,' Leo reminded them.

'Like a bloody T-shirt?' Hugo asked.

'Yeah, but how did *you* get it?' Leo asked.

Hugo couldn't answer that. He shook his head and instead asked, 'So, what? You want to go and sneak around their villa?'

'Yes,' Avery said. 'If he killed Nora, I want to find the proof and make him pay.'

Both Hugo and Leo looked down at Avery and one nodded after the other. But then he glared up at Leo.

'If anything happens to her, I swear—'

'Back off, macho man. She'll be fine with me,' Leo replied just as angrily, squaring off against Hugo.

'Stop it,' Avery said, slapping her palms on their chests and pushing them apart. 'We don't have time for this. Can you get off the island?' she asked him.

Hugo nodded, pulling the keyring from his pocket. 'Dad's boat.'

Avery nodded, and Leo rolled his eyes.

It hurt, seeing them together, but it wasn't the same as it had been before. Maybe Sydney's speech had forced the secrets out. And in doing so, it had given them less power. Less . . . darkness.

'We're going to do this, right?' Avery insisted. 'We're going to make sure he pays.'

'And what if your dads want to pay them to make it go away?' Leo asked.

'They won't be able to. Not this time,' Hugo said with fierce determination.

AVERY

Leo left the room to call Corrine to ask if it was OK for Hugo to come and talk to her. No one wanted to retraumatise her after all she'd been through, so Avery suggested Leo call her first. Hugo turning up out of the blue would have probably terrified her.

It left her and Hugo together, alone, and for the first time in a while things felt ... different. Better, maybe? She couldn't imagine what he must have been through, not just in the last few hours, but in the last few weeks and months with his dads. She hadn't known and she felt bad about that.

'Are you OK?' she asked hesitantly. It had been easy for her to forget how close they'd been. To brush it under the difficult emotions caused by their break-up. But they *had* been close. She had always cared about him. Loved him in a way, just not the way that a relationship needed.

Hugo looked at the floor. 'I don't know any more, Avery. Things have been so messed up. What happened with Darian made me question things I'd never even thought of.' Avery felt the sadness roll off him. 'Everything started to spin out of control and I—' He swallowed and looked at the ground, hiding his eyes, his shame. 'I behaved like a complete bastard. I got it into my head that that if I got you back, everything would be OK. Like it was when we were together.'

'Was it, though?' Avery asked gently. 'Was it that good?' Because now that she knew what it was like to be with Leo, now that she understood how it *could* be, she knew that there had been nothing even remotely like that between them.

'Aves, I'm not sure this is the time,' Hugo said, trying to skirt the issue.

'I'm not sure there will ever be a good time,' Avery replied. 'But I want you to know that I'm so sorry,' she said.

'Me too.'

'About—'

'Yeah, I'm going to need a little more time for *that*,' he said, cutting her off before she could mention Leo. 'But I get it. Really, I do.' He nodded his head as if punctuating his words when Leo returned to the room.

'She's waiting for you,' he said, speaking about Corrine.

'How did she sound?' Hugo asked.

'Scared, but angry.'

'I can work with that,' Hugo replied, getting up from the sofa. 'OK.' He nodded at them both and, not really needing to say anything more, made his way out of Tidal.

Avery leaned backwards against Leo's chest watching Hugo leave, his arms coming around her, holding her to him, and she inhaled slowly.

'I don't like it,' Leo said into the silence.

Avery didn't have to ask. She knew he was railing against the decision they'd all made, the one that meant he needed to be at the Vandenburgs' that evening to work the drinks reception, while she searched the Devereuxs' villa.

'Someone needs to be there to keep an eye on them. And my family has not been invited,' Avery pointed out.

She didn't have the mental energy to worry about how her parents would feel at being sidelined. Because of her. Because of Nora. Maybe even just because of her parents. The fractures in the group that had been friends since their university days had been showing for a while now. Just like they had between Avery, Hugo, Syd, Archie and Leo.

'I can't even believe they're actually *having* drinks.' Disgust painted Leo's words. One she felt herself.

'But it *does* mean that their villa will be empty for that entire time,' she pointed out. 'And you can let me know if anyone leaves. It should give me enough time to search the villa properly *and* to get out.'

'I. Don't. Like it,' he said again.

She turned in his arms, looking up at the face she knew so well. She cupped his jaw, ease in her heart, knowing that it was right – that *he* was right for her.

Forever, her heart whispered hopefully.

Rising up towards him, she pressed a kiss to his lips, which were in a firm thin line. He gazed at her, trying to hold on to his anger as she peppered kisses over his jaw, his lips, until she felt him sigh in exasperation. The next time she veered close to his mouth, he captured hers with a kiss.

When she came up for air, there was wicked joy shining in the depths of his eyes.

'Is this how you plan to get out of all our arguments?' he asked, a tease in his tone.

'It depends. Did it work?' she asked back, a smile curving her lips.

It was hardly appropriate given everything that was going on, but Avery wanted to cling to this moment, the unexpected gift of what they'd found together.

He opened his mouth to speak when her phone vibrated with a message from Hugo.

Corrine's in. We're heading to the boat.

Avery and Leo rushed out towards the marina.

They reached the lookout in time to see Hugo manoeuvring the boat out of the small bay, Corrine huddled beside him in a blanket. He was already passing the tips of the island's crescent end when Mark came running down from the Big House. Hugo was too far out to even yell at, let alone stop. But the hairs on her neck raised when Mark glared in their direction.

It was done. The plan was in motion. There was no going back now.

Twenty minutes later, Avery tapped her thumb on her thigh, wishing she'd had time to get back to her villa to change. But Leo had been due at the Vandenburgs' and she needed to find some kind of evidence before Hugo, Corrine and the police returned or . . . or Dennis might just get away with murder.

She was still only wearing her denim cut-offs and a T-shirt. And even though the air was thick with humidity, it felt clammy against her skin. Waiting for Leo's text – confirmation that the Devereuxs' villa was clear – she picked over one of the final voice notes Nora had left.

> *God knows how long he's been doing this for. His cover-up is too slick, too assured. How many people have lied for him, and more? I can't believe it stops at this. He has too much money and too many connections. People who will be invested in keeping this quiet.*

There had been a pause.

> *How far does this corruption go?*

Avery's pulse skittered in her throat. Nora had been right. A lot of people were invested in Dennis's ongoing success. People like the Vandenburgs. People like her parents. They'd all done business with each other.

Her mobile chimed, the noise shrill and startling in the night air. She grabbed it from her pocket and turned the sound off, looking around to make sure she hadn't been heard; her heart pounding in her chest.

They're all here. Be quick.

Leo's message cut through her thoughts.

She had to go, and she had to go *now*.

Avery jogged up to the entrance of Solar, scanning the area for any staff members that might be coming or going. Leo had told her that the Devereuxs had dismissed any on-site staff presence following Sydney's breakdown, but Avery couldn't run the risk of being seen.

She waved the key card Leo had given her over the scanner and the large, heavy door clicked open.

Solar was completely different to the villa she and her parents were staying in. Where Coastal was dark mahogany and shades of cream with textures soft and comforting, Solar was near aggressive in its luxury. She'd been here a few times over the years, but it still stopped her momentarily in her tracks. Cool grey marble, gold fixtures, sharp edges. Everything looked *hard*. Cold. *Mean*.

And extremely clean.

She was about to step on to the smooth, sleek flooring when she realised that her shoes were covered in sand and grit. She toed them off and picked them up before stepping over the threshold.

The door opened immediately on to an expansive living area. A sunken seating area on her left faced an imposing open fireplace, and a raised area on her right was furnished with a lavish dining table that matched the marble flooring and marble seats.

In front of her were floor-to-ceiling windows that stretched across the entire length of the enormous room, through which she could see the villa's wings that thrusted forward on the left and right sides of the building towards a white-sanded beach that cut a pale line between the villa and the sea, startlingly bright against all the pale, cool colours of the villa.

Consciously or not, the villa replicated the horseshoe curve of the island, but no matter how expensive or luxurious, the villa's stark contrast with the life of the island outside, the power of nature, just left her feeling cold.

Feeling . . . *dead*.

Nora had been here, she was sure of it. The night of the firework party. Looking for what Avery was looking for now. Evidence. A shiver cut across her skin. Nora had seen what Avery was seeing. Had she felt excited, or scared? Had she been so desperate to get her name in the papers, to make something of herself that she had confronted Dennis herself?

She shook off the tremor that tripped down her spine and forced herself over to the sunken seating area. Here the floor had been carefully carpeted in white, seamlessly flowing from the marble flooring that was matched by the coffee table.

The sparseness of it all was so different to the clutter she was used to at her villa; her mother's magazines, the crime books her father loved to read, the clothes Nora had left draped around the living area. But here there was nothing. Stripped bare. It was almost antiseptically clean. And then she realised why she'd thought that.

Bleach. She could smell bleach.

Putting her shoes down carefully, she circled the coffee table, staring at it and noticing an imprint of where it had been moved from, gouged deep into the carpet. She ran her finger along the sharp edge of the circumference, following the curve around to the other side and—

Ouch.

She yanked her finger back. The pad of her finger had been scratched by a chip in the surface. She stared at it, looking closer, rearing back when the smell of bleach became almost overpowering.

With shaking hands, she reached for the base of the coffee table and, straining, shifted the huge, heavy thing over to the left. She let it drop with relief, turned back and gasped.

There on the carpet was a blood-red crescent, startling against a sea of white.

She stared at it for what felt like an age.

Here. Nora had been killed *here*.

Avery swallowed, reached for her phone to take a picture of it, when she saw that she had three messages and a missed call.

Oh god, she'd had it on silent.

She swiped to read the messages, just as the *beep beep beep* of the front-door keypad sounded.

Someone had come home.

CHAPTER TWENTY-TWO

AVERY

Adrenaline sliced through Avery's chest, making her skin prickle and shrink.

Shit!

She didn't know what to do. The front door to the villa opened directly on to this room. She'd be seen immediately. Leaping around the coffee table, she grabbed her shoes and launched up the steps to the landing, her feet slipping out from under her as she hit the marble floor and nearly fell.

Twisting painfully to her side, she thrust her hand out just in time to catch herself, and scrabbled back upright to slip behind the door to the left wing of the villa just as she heard the front door swing open.

But she was still too exposed. She couldn't be found here. She couldn't. Dennis had already killed one person. Would he kill her too?

Mind made up, she retreated into the dark shadows of the villa's master suite, looking for a way out. She hurried down the hallway towards the bedroom, pulse pounding, throat thick and muscles burning, even though she'd run less than twenty metres.

There, on the other side of the bed was a glass window. If she could just get it—

'Avery? What are you doing here?'

The voice made Avery turn in shock. And then relief had her nearly sagging to the floor.

It wasn't Dennis. It wasn't Carol.

'Archie,' she said, pressing her hand against her chest and bending over, sucking huge lungfuls of air into her body. She nearly laughed in relief. 'Oh god, Archie,' she said, shaking her head, not quite registering the look in his eyes as he watched her step away from the window. 'What are you doing here?' she asked, breathless.

'What am *I* doing here?' he asked, bemused. 'In my own villa? I came to charge my phone,' he said, waving it in his hand. 'What are *you* doing here?'

'Oh, I'm sorry. I can explain.'

'Really?' The curtly delivered word was the first indication that something wasn't quite right.

Her phone vibrated in her hand, the incoming message from Leo.

Are you out?

It was listed above the earlier messages she hadn't seen because her phone had been on silent. Messages she could now see.

Get out. Archie on way. Something's wrong.

She frowned at her phone and looked back up at Archie, her stomach dropping before her mind could catch up with what her gut was trying to tell her.

'What are you *doing* here, Avery?' Archie asked, pressing, serious. The expression in his gaze one that she'd never seen before from the light-hearted, easy-going guy she knew.

'I ... I wanted to leave something for Sydney,' she said, remembering the lie she'd come up with earlier. 'I wasn't sure if we were going to be leaving before she came back.'

Archie barked out a laugh that sounded more like a scoff.

'Come back? You think she's going to come back? *Here?*' Archie spat.

'Is something wrong?'

'No, why would anything be wrong?' he asked, and she couldn't read his tone. Sarcasm? Sincerity? She couldn't tell any more.

Get out. Get out.

She took a step back and his gaze narrowed on the movement, one hand fisted by his side, gripping something tight.

'What was it?' Archie asked.

'Mmm?' Avery said, her gaze taking in his white T-shirt as she tried to figure out what he was playing with in his hand.

'For Sydney? What did you bring her?' he said again.

'I ...'

Archie rolled his hand and she finally saw what was wound between his fingers.

No. It wasn't possible.

'I ...' She was distracted by the last time she'd seen it. 'Archie, why do you have my friendship bracelet?' she asked, her mind simply refusing to make sense of everything her body was beginning to react to.

Adrenaline. Flight. Fight.

Run.

But her bare feet were stuck on the marble floor, her phone and shoes pressed to her chest.

'This?' Archie looked at the threaded bracelet in his hands as if seeing it for the first time. 'It's Sydney's.'

'No, it's not,' Avery replied, having caught sight of the blue lettering on the cubes.

'Yes it—' His own laughter cut his words in half, the sound terrifying and chilling. He looked at the bracelet in his hands, and then back up at her. 'Really? Is it? How funny,' Archie said.

All she saw was a yawning blankness in his gaze. It wasn't her friend standing there, not the boy she'd known for ten years. It was a stranger.

A murderer.

Run.

This time she listened.

She yanked open the sliding window using all her weight, and launched herself out on to the deck, losing precious moments trying to close it behind her. She jumped off the deck on to the pathway, her bare feet grounding into the rough surface, causing her to cry out. But she couldn't stop to put on her shoes. Not yet. She needed to put some distance between her and Archie.

Archie.

He had killed Nora? But why?

She veered off the path between the treeline and the beach. She'd get nowhere on the sand, but she might have a chance to lose him amongst the trees.

She hurled herself deeper and deeper into the forest. Fronds lashed out at her face, scratching and cutting her exposed skin.

She rolled on a torn branch and twisted her ankle, falling to the ground on her knees and hands.

Agony whipped around her ankle like a flame and she shoved a fist into her mouth to prevent herself from screaming. With her pulse and breath so loud in her ears, she couldn't hear him. And she *had* to be able to hear him coming.

She needed to think. She couldn't just run.

She locked an inhale in her lungs and tried to listen to the sounds around her.

In the not-far-enough-away distance, she heard Archie call her name.

'A-very. A-very.' The sound was a taunting sing-song, making her want to cry.

Shoes. She needed to put on her shoes.

She'd lost her phone somewhere between here and back at the villa and she certainly wasn't going to go look for it. Scratches criss-crossed her arms that were beginning to fill with thin lines of blood, her body shook and her breath was jagged in her lungs again as the need for oxygen – for life – surpassed everything.

'If you'd just left it all alone, none of this would be happening, Av-er-y,' Archie called in a voice that sent terror straight into her veins.

How had she missed it? How had they all missed it? Whatever this evil was that consumed him.

'So,' he said, from a little closer, 'this is all *your* fault, really.'

She could see him now, about twenty feet away, her eyes locked on him as she tried to put her foot into the shoe. Her ankle screamed in protest, but she couldn't stop. Archie turned back and forth, trying to find her. And when he took a step in the other direction, she just *ran*.

She had to get back to Leo. Or her parents. She had to find *someone*.

'You can run, Little Finch. But it's not going to help you,' Archie said, with that frostbitten laugh. 'You don't even know where you're going, do you?'

That taunt struck home, pulling her up short. She took a second to look around – not hearing Archie's footsteps any more.

He was hunting her. Stalking her. He was the one in control.

No. She *wasn't* helpless. She *wasn't* weak like everyone thought.

'You should've heard the way Nora talked about you,' Archie said, from somewhere *much* closer than she'd expected.

She pressed a hand over her mouth, her other hand fisting the earth in the ground by her feet. She tucked herself into a tiny hollow at the base of the tree behind her, making herself as small as humanly possible.

Her entire body protested with the near primal instinct to flee.

But Archie was so close now. She just had to wait. He'd pass her and then she could run.

And everything would be all right.

'It's not that she's a bitch, it's just that she's sooooo boring.' Archie's pitch-perfect mimicry of Nora cut deeper than the lashing from the forest. 'And *pathetic*,' he said, before switching back to his own voice. 'Avery Finch!' he exclaimed so loud it startled her. 'Cheating on her exams. Who knew! You dark horse,' he said with a kind of horrific pride. 'Did you know she told us that? That she was willing to sell you out to get closer to *us*. Closer to *Dad*?'

The betrayal cut deep and she thrust her white-knuckled fingers into the forest floor; earth, roots and leaves crunching under her palm. Wet heat pressed against the backs of her eyes, causing a single tear to drop down over her cheek. She shoved it away with a mud-covered palm and steeled herself.

Footsteps passed right behind the tree she was tucked into. Her ankle throbbed and adrenaline shoved needles into her skin. Something skittered over her leg and, shivering, she brushed it off.

Suddenly a howl rang out, almost inhuman in its fury, the switch from taunting to terrifying so extreme.

'Why?' Archie demanded. 'Why are you making me do this, Avery?'

She wanted to look, wanted to see him, but she couldn't move. If he found her . . .

'If you'd just let it go, we'd all be sitting having dinner together. But your little Nancy Drew act has screwed that up. And it was such a shame too. Sydney really liked you.' His voice was getting further away as he passed her, through the trees back towards the beach.

She counted to fifteen. Launching up from her hidden nook, she swallowed the pain and—

Yanked back by a fist in her hair, she screamed out loud, crashing against Archie's chest as he swung her around and viciously backhanded her across the face.

She collapsed to the floor. Her ears rang, her vision blurred, shock numbed her for a blessed few seconds before pain exploded across her jaw and cheek. Her hand instinctively went to her face. She couldn't feel anything but agony. Blood bloomed on her tongue and she coughed when the metallic taste slid down her throat, sending a violent amount of hurt through her head. She tried to push herself up, but her arms were shaking too much and she collapsed back down to the forest floor.

'. . . your fault . . . die . . . everything round here?'

Archie's incoherent rant pierced through the high-pitched whine in her ears.

Her heartbeat was frantic and she knew that she was going to die if she didn't do something.

'Why?' she asked, but it came out as more of a cough again.

'What was that, Little Finch?'

She swallowed the instinctive recoil from his tone. 'Why did you kill her?' she said again, pushing herself up from the forest floor, desperate to buy herself some time. Leo would come. She knew it. He'd come for her. All she had to do was keep Archie talking.

Archie cocked his head to one side, looking at her as if she were an insect.

'She was in our villa. Going through our stuff. Desperate because she couldn't get that staff girl to turn on Dad.'

'Corrine? You knew about Corrine?'

'Of course I did. Dad was never capable of being discreet,' he said, disgusted, as if *that* was his father's failing.

'He raped her, Archie!' Avery cried, still capable of being appalled by his callousness.

'If she was so traumatised, why didn't she go to the police, huh?'

Avery could only stare in horror as Archie blamed Corrine, as he blamed Nora – even *her* – for everything.

'But Nora wouldn't drop it. "You don't know what he's done",' he said, mimicking Nora again. 'The audacity! As if she knew Dad better!' Archie barked out a genuinely mystified laugh.

Avery swallowed. 'She realised. Didn't she, Archie? That you knew?'

He shrugged. 'She fought a lot harder than you did,' he said with a wicked glint in his eye. 'Didn't help her, though.'

Her gut twisted in horror. The crescent sliver of blood on the carpet. There must have been so much more. The remembered smell of bleach filled her nose.

'The white T-shirt,' she said, staring at Archie, who was wearing one just like Hugo had described. 'It was yours.'

Archie laughed. 'Hugo was so out of it. He was passed out on the beach so hard, I went and came back and he didn't even notice.'

'Why bother?' she asked, breathless.

'Always safe to have a back-up. No way the Vandenburgs would let Hugo go down for murder if they thought it was him. They'd have covered it up without question.'

The devastating truth, irrefutable, crashed through her. Her gaze locked with his as she reached across the forest floor, inch by inch, to the large thick branch just out of reach.

'Don't look at me like that,' he said irritably, as if her opinion of him mattered somehow. 'I did what I had to do. And now you, Avery Finch, are what I have to do.'

He closed the distance between them and she waited, every part of her body tensed as she let him get closer and closer and—

She grabbed for the branch and launched up to strike him across the head with it. It landed with a sick thud, Archie stumbling to his knees. It wasn't what she'd wanted, but it was enough. She set off, sprinting through the forest, Archie following not long after.

She scrabbled through heavy undergrowth that was beginning to thin out, but instead of emerging on to the beach, to her horror she found herself at the jagged rocky cliff. She'd been running in the wrong direction.

She was as far away from help as possible, with Archie behind her and danger in front of her.

But she had no choice. She had to keep going.

The ground beneath her changed from the soft forest floor to the dark, sharp-edged rock, rising high into the night sky. She'd never been up here before, it was off-limits, but Archie's sing-song voice taunted her from behind.

'A-ver-y,' he admonished. 'You're doing all my work for me, Little Finch. You're going to get yourself killed.'

Despite his words, she could hear him struggling as much as she was – his breath heaving, his feet scrabbling for purchase. She slipped and landed hard, a flinty edge slicing into the fleshy part of her palm. Blood flowed quickly, dripping from her fingertips, making her hands slip even more.

She thought she saw a flash of yellow and turned. Was someone coming? She started to make her way across, rather than up, even though it took her closer towards Archie.

There it was again, a figure in yellow, picked up by the moonlight.

She was now desperate, her body reaching the limit of what it was capable of.

She slipped down the side of the cliff, covering more ground recklessly, rocks slashing at her calves and thighs, just as the figure emerged from the treeline.

'Carol!' she screamed, not caring about Archie any more. 'Carol. Help!'

Carol held her arms open, a look of grave concern on her face. 'Avery, what's wrong?' she asked as Avery hurled herself into the older woman's arms.

Thank god, thank god.

'It's Archie, I . . . I'm so sorry,' Avery tried to say between gasps of breath.

'What for, Avery? What's wrong?' Carol asked, concern in her voice.

Oh god, how could she explain?

'Hi, Mom,' Archie said almost gleefully.

'I've told you not to call me that,' Carol said sharply, and Archie looked shamefaced.

'Sorry, Mother,' Archie replied.

Avery's pulse raged in her ears. 'We have to go,' she whispered up to Carol. 'We have to get away.'

'Oh, sweetie.' Carol looked down at Avery in her arms, almost apologetically. 'I'm afraid not,' she said, twisting Avery around so that she faced Archie and tightening her grip.

'Mrs Devereux, you're hurting me,' Avery whimpered.

'Well, that's what happens when you're foolish enough to

poke your nose where it's not wanted,' Carol said with a ferocity that cut Avery like a knife. 'You were supposed to make this look like an accident,' she said to Archie. 'What's taking you so long?'

'It's fine. I just need a few minutes,' Archie said, scratching the side of his head with the opposite arm. 'Poor Little Avery Finch. So overcome with guilt that the friend she'd brought with her had died, anxious about her father's looming bankruptcy and some distinctly poor life choices recently, that she felt compelled to end her own life,' Archie concluded to Avery's horror.

'Fine,' Mrs Devereux said. 'But make it quick. I have to get back before they notice I'm gone.'

Carol pushed her into Archie, who grabbed her before she could even try to twist free. 'And, Archie, don't screw this up. I'm fed up having to clear up after you all. Do you hear me?'

Her voice was glacial.

'Yes, Mother,' Archie said, chastised.

Avery's breath caught in her throat as Archie hauled her backwards over the sharp rocks. She was just able to make out Carol disappear towards the villa before Archie struck her with the back of his hand, knocking her to her knees. Her head ringing, she was unable to feel the cut and bite of the sharp stone or the blood trickling down her bare legs.

They drew closer to the sharp cliff face, the dark sea thrashing against the rocks, white peaks bright in the moonlight. It swirled and churned violently, threateningly, furiously.

Anger, whipped up like the sea, tore through her.

She didn't want to die.

Some ancient, primal knowing bled one final burst of fight through her entire body and this time it was Avery who howled like an animal, screaming like a banshee, bearing her entire weight down on the arms that held her, and bit into Archie's forearm.

The move pulled Archie off balance and he slipped. She used the moment to try and pull out of his hold, but he was like steel wrapped around her. Something desperate and violent emerged from deep within. She wanted to live.

She clawed and bit and pushed and kicked, stumbling and falling to one knee, but, pushing herself back up, she struck him again and again.

There was almost nothing left for her to give; she was pure animal, pure instinct. She grabbed whatever bit of Archie she could get hold of and thrashed it against the sharp jagged rock beneath them. She screamed and for a moment her gaze locked with Archie's and she thought she saw fear.

Just as she went to smash his head against the sharp rocks, two arms reached for her from behind and she thought it was Carol back to finish the job. Screaming she lashed out, unable to take it any more.

But nothing dislodged the hold.

'It's OK. It's OK. Avery, it's me. It's Leo. It's me, Leo. You're safe now. You're safe.'

His words took a long time to penetrate. Even seeing him wasn't enough to call back the terror that had taken over her. The instinct to fight. To survive. When she trembled, Leo placed a blanket around her, not letting her go, and she was thankful. He was anchoring her in place. Over his shoulder, she saw Sven restraining a barely conscious Archie, while others stood and watched on in horror.

'Hugo's on his way,' Leo said in quiet tones as if he were talking to a child. But she wasn't a child. And she wasn't weak. She just couldn't quite find the words to tell him that yet.

'Dennis?' she asked, her voice raw, ripped to shreds from her screams, her teeth chattering.

'Dennis managed to get out on a helicopter, but he won't get far,' Leo assured her, as she fought to control her rage. 'You're OK, you're safe,' Leo insisted, as finally his words began to penetrate and tears welled up from somewhere deep and endless.

Her breath shuddered in her lungs as a circle of staff members surrounded them.

She looked out at the dark line across the horizon and could just make out a string of boats making their way to Mokani, blue and red lights flashing.

Hugo was coming.

The police were coming.

It was over.

She was safe.

CHAPTER TWENTY-THREE

LEO

Leo legged it the moment he'd realised that Archie had left the Vandenburgs' drinks reception. Fear had gripped his chest in a vice, squeezing the breath from his lungs, making him dizzy.

He'd arrived at Solar with a sense of creeping horror, as he'd realised what had been bugging him about the T-shirt that Hugo had found in his bag. It *couldn't* have been Dennis's. The man never wore anything but a button-up. He'd pounded on the door to the villa, but there had been no sounds from within. Going round the outside, he'd seen a jagged path of freshly broken leaves in the forest behind the villa.

He'd followed the trail until he'd seen Carol, looking as if it were the most natural thing in the world for her to be taking a stroll in the dense forest, having left the drinks at the Vandenburgs without a word. Instinctively giving her a wide berth, he'd been about to turn towards the beach when he'd heard the first of Avery's screams tearing through the night, coming from the direction of the jagged cliff.

By the time he'd burst through the dense foliage at the base of the steep outcrop, the eerie light of a low-hanging moon had picked out the shocking scene in minute detail.

He'd watched in horror as Archie had viciously backhanded Avery across the face, but by the time he'd reached the rocks, Avery had somehow grappled with Archie enough to be on top of him. Wildly, she'd torn at Archie, laying into him over and over again, stopping only when Leo had pulled her back.

He hadn't cared a single second for Archie. His only thought had been for her. That she might hurt herself, or go too far. And he'd held her tight, as Sven caught up with him, having seen him rush out of the Big House.

It had taken him the merest moment to figure out what was going on. And Leo saw it. The hesitation, the assessment: that Archie was more valuable than Avery. That Sven should be protecting Archie. But then others arrived – the Vandenburgs, Domingo – drawn by the commotion, and the situation was no longer in Sven's control.

'I'm so sorry,' Leo whispered to Avery now, his cheek against hers, not sure he was ever going to calm down. 'I'm so sorry I didn't get here in time.'

'We didn't know. We couldn't have known,' Avery whispered as if still disbelieving what had happened and, finally, whatever adrenaline had been holding her upright left her body. Just as she began to collapse, Leo picked her up and went to sit on a flat rockface with her in his lap.

She tried to speak again, but her voice was gravel, damaged by the screams of terror he'd heard as he'd fought his way to get to her. Just the sound of her voice sent rage to boiling point beneath the surface of his skin.

They both looked over to where Sven stood, holding a shotgun trained on Archie, and his dad, who had arrived a few minutes ago, faced off against a much smaller, furious-looking Carol.

'How did you know?' Avery asked, her voice for him but her eyes on Archie, refusing to move as if worried that he might somehow break free and come for her again.

She swept a hand over his forearm as if trying to soothe him and his guilt at not being there for her. It wasn't an accusation, but curiosity.

In quiet tones, as other people began to gather – more staff members and Nick Dawson – he told her how he'd been working the bar tonight and hating every minute of it. How he'd been relieved that Archie had been too distracted to mock him, and that Carol and Dennis had been snapping and waspish. How once he knew the truth, it was almost impossible to believe that he'd not seen the true extent of corruption and depravity before.

It had taken everything in him to maintain civility. And he'd only done it in order to protect Avery while she searched the Devereuxs' villa. He told her about the phone call that Darian had taken and how he'd snuck out to try to listen in. It had been the police, checking up on Hugo's accusation. Leo told Avery how furious Darian had been, and how he'd only just made it back to the veranda in time, before Darian could catch him. But that was why he hadn't immediately noticed that Archie had disappeared. And that it was only when Carol had disappeared too that he'd realised something was going on.

By the time he'd finished explaining what had happened, the rest of the staff had arrived. They'd come with torches and golf carts, with full beams pointed at the cliff, illuminating it in some eerie light that made him think of horror films.

It was as if the entire population of the island had gathered in one spot, all the usually invisible, unseen hands that worked this resort, come to bear witness. They wouldn't let this be swept under the carpet. Not this time.

He looked around at the shocked, angry faces of the people left on the island, wondering if any of them would ever feel the same way about Mokani as they had done before.

It had been a place of luxury, paradise, safety, indulgence.

Now he didn't even know what it was.

Avery continued to rub his forearm, and Leo knew it was more than that. It was connection, reassurance. They were here, they were alive and they were together.

'And Hugo?' Avery asked.

Leo nodded towards the treeline where Hugo was leading a much bigger group of police officers than had come the night they'd found Nora's body, making their way towards them.

'He's here.'

Avery didn't make a move to go to him, but Leo felt her relief in seeing that he'd returned with the police.

Together they watched Hugo take in the scene. Eyes wide, he looked at Archie, Carol and then Avery.

Leo tensed, seeing the anger in Hugo's gaze, but when their eyes met he realised it wasn't anger at Leo but with himself, with Archie – with the entire situation.

Hugo's face was grim as he made his way over. He stared back and forth between Avery and Archie, eyes wide as he tried to absorb everything. 'What happened here?'

It took Avery a couple of goes at clearing her throat before she found her voice.

'Nora had gone to the Devereuxs' villa the night of the fireworks party looking for something to take down Dennis after Corrine decided not to go to the police. Archie caught her snooping around and realised what was going on. He knew,' she said bitterly. 'About Dennis and what he'd done to Corrine. Archie knew and he didn't care. They fought in the living area and Nora fell, hitting her head.' Leo felt the tension tighten across Avery's body. 'He panicked, knew that she couldn't be found there and had to move her. He must have thought he could get away with making it look like she was drunk, fell, hit her head and toppled into the pool.'

Her words were clipped, short, as if speaking hurt.

'He moved the body? On his own?' Hugo asked.

'With Carol, I think,' Avery explained. 'She told Archie to get rid of me. Up on the cliff.' This time tension filled Leo's body, his hands flexing around her. 'Said it would look like a suicide, due to my guilt over Nora's *accident*.'

'And the T-shirt?' Hugo asked, realising that it could only have been Archie who'd planted that on him.

Avery nodded, and Hugo looked away. They all needed time to process everything that had happened. They'd been so sure that it had been Dennis, never once imagining that their friend, the boy they'd grown up with over the last ten years, would have been capable of something like this.

'The lengths people will go to for what they want – to *keep* what they want, what they *have* . . . It can be surprising sometimes.'

Coming from Hugo, it felt like an acknowledgement and an

apology rolled into one. The look in his eyes when Leo returned his gaze confirmed it.

'I guess we don't really know until we're faced with it ourselves,' Leo said, an extended olive branch.

Hugo nodded and it was an understanding between the two of them. One that Leo hadn't realised he'd badly needed.

Leo ran his hand down the length of Avery's hair, whispering soothing sounds as the island's doctor came to check her over. Avery refused to move from Leo's lap, even when the doctor tried to inspect the nasty jagged cut deep into her palm.

Just then, Avery's parents arrived, looking frantic and worried. Annalise Finch stopped in her tracks at the sight of Sven and Michael corralling Carol and Archie, but her father – having searched the crowd and found Avery – rushed over to them.

And that's when Avery's tears started to fall. Tears that turned into shakes that wracked her body so hard that the doctor demanded that she be taken away from the cliff and put her into one of the golf carts with her mother.

Leo was expecting Mr Finch to tell him that he'd done enough but, instead, Avery's father nodded towards the other golf cart and drove them back to their villa, keeping the golf cart ahead of him in the vehicle's beams the entire time, as if he couldn't bear the idea that his daughter would be out of his sight, even for a second.

'Do you need to let your father know where you are?' Jonathan Finch asked as they pulled up to Coastal.

Leo thought of his dad. The warning he'd given him. The fact that he was just as bad as the rest of them, clinging to the hierarchy with a white-knuckled grip because the alternative was worse. The alternative was realising that he was part of the system that had held him down his entire life.

'No. I'm where I need to be.'

Jonathan nodded and gestured for him to follow the doctor and Mrs Finch, leading Avery into the villa.

HUGO

Hugo reluctantly headed back to where his dads were standing with Sven when Leo and the Finches left for their villa. Avoiding Darian, avoiding *everything*, wasn't an option any more.

Mark looked haunted and Hugo wanted nothing more than to go to him, needing reassurance, needing the safety only a parent could offer. But he just wasn't sure that he'd get that. Not after everything. Not after keeping Darian's secret, and then going behind their backs to the police with Corrine.

Sven was herding staff back to the bunk house, taking with them the little beams of light that had lit up the cliff like a Christmas tree. After the rush of activity, the thinning numbers made Hugo feel more isolated and shocked by the evening's events.

And then Mark came up and drew him into a hug. A part of Hugo held back, terrified to lean on him, in case he would take it away when no one was looking. But the events of the night had been too extreme and he sank into his father's embrace, wanting to cry like the little child he wasn't any more.

'It's going to be OK,' Mark whispered into his ear.

'Is it?' Hugo asked. 'Is it really?' He couldn't even dare to hope any more.

Mark drew back to meet his gaze intently. 'We are going to get through this. I love you. Nothing that's happened changes that. Nothing that could *ever* happen will change that, do you understand?'

Wet heat pressed against Hugo's eyes. It was all he'd wanted to hear for the last eight months. Eight months of agony and pain and doubt and hurt and shock and anger.

Darian came over and put his hand on Mark's shoulder, but Mark shook him off.

'We'll talk at the house,' Mark informed him curtly.

'I know but—'

'We'll talk at the house,' Mark repeated, his voice utterly devoid of emotion.

Hugo followed Mark towards one of the golf carts, and a staff member drove the three of them in stony silence back to the Big House that didn't feel like a home any more. As they got out of the cart Hugo wondered whether he was imagining the dynamics shifting subtly. Mark leading the way, Hugo numb with shock and Darian following, seeming angrily sulky now.

The door clicked closed behind them and Hugo cringed, bracing for a future he couldn't even imagine. This had been his greatest fear for so long, but after everything that happened tonight – convinced that he'd find Avery hurt, or worse, dead – Hugo was done. If she had survived that, he could survive this.

If Mark turned on Hugo, deciding to side with Darian, or if Darian decided to take his anger out on Hugo, he would survive.

'Mark—'

'No,' Mark cut in. *'I'm* talking now.'

Hugo stilled. He'd never heard his dad talk in that tone, let alone interrupt Darian.

'In the blue room,' Mark ordered.

Darian looked like he wanted to argue, distinctly uncomfortable with Mark's authority, but he went anyway. Hugo thought Mark's eyes softened when they landed on his. Wishful thinking? He didn't know any more.

Hugo followed Mark into the room and sat on the corner of the large sofa, while Darian stood by the fireplace. The tension in the room made Hugo feel nauseous and he prayed he could get through the conversation without being sick.

Mark chose to stand opposite Darian at the other end of the carpet. It looked like a play that Hugo didn't want to watch, but couldn't tear his eyes away from.

'I love you, Darian,' Mark announced with conviction. And Hugo's stomach dropped as Darian's shoulders lowered a little. 'I've always loved you,' Mark said. 'From the moment we met, my life was bright and passionate and all the things that my family had refused to let me be or have.'

Darian went to close the distance between them, but Mark held up a hand to stop him, leaving Darian wrong-footed.

'I was never under any illusions about who you are. People tried to warn me, but it didn't matter. Because I loved you. And I accepted you for who you were, wholly and truly. I accepted the bad with the good, because the good was so much *more*.'

Darian seemed to hesitate. Hugo's breath caught in his lungs, wondering where this was going.

'I accepted a long time ago that you would hurt me,' Mark

said, nodding. 'I accepted that it wasn't intentional. You didn't do it on purpose. It was simply a part of who you are. I don't know about all of them, but I know about *enough* of them. And I have done from the very beginning.'

Shock tore through Hugo, not once considering that there might have been more, or the possibility that Mark had known about them. Fear and hope metamorphosed into electric currents unspooling across Hugo's skin as he and Darian hung on to Mark's every word.

'And like I said, that was OK. Because I love you and that will never stop,' Mark said, breaking Hugo's heart. Mark had made his choice. Hugo had lost—

'But you hurt my son.' Mark's tone vibrated with possessive determination. It didn't even sound like Mark any more. It sent shivers over Hugo's skin. 'You,' Mark said, as he closed the distance between him and Darian. '*You*,' he repeated with a level of fury that Hugo had never seen before, 'Hurt. My. Son.'

He hadn't raised his voice, but it felt like it. A cry that none of them would ever forget.

'You will leave this house. This island. You will vacate the property in New York.'

'Mark—'

'You will leave all of our jointly owned properties until Hugo and I are ready to talk, *if* we are ever ready to talk. I don't care that you betrayed me, Darian. But you betrayed *him*. And until I am absolutely, one hundred per cent sure that he neither fears you, is hurt by you or is threatened by you in any way – in *any way*,' Mark stressed, 'you are no longer part of this family.'

'Mark—' Darian tried again.

'Don't test me,' Mark warned, his fury colder than ice.

Darian stepped back, his gaze never wavering from Mark until he seemed to finally remember that Hugo was there, was part of this. Hugo didn't know whether to be hurt or relieved, but when Darian looked at him, for just a moment, he thought he'd seen shame. But then he blinked, and it was gone.

He took a breath. 'Hugo. I am truly sorry. There are no excuses. I . . . I'm sorry and I love you and I—'

'You no longer have the right to say that,' Mark interrupted. 'Love doesn't do what you did. Now get out,' Mark announced.

Darian, for the first time in Hugo's life, bit his tongue, nodded and did exactly what he was told to do.

Mark turned to Hugo and held his arms open. And Hugo went to him, tears wetting his eyes, his heart hurting and healing at the same time.

They stayed like that for a long time.

Until, finally, Mark decided that they needed something sweet. Heading to the kitchen, Mark retrieved the ice cream from the walk-in freezer.

'Right,' Mark said, handing him a spoon. 'Plans.'

This was how Mark regained control. Making plans. Hugo knew Mark needed this. Hell, *he* probably needed this.

'College. Do you want to go back?' Mark asked.

Hugo bit his lip. He did. But he didn't want to leave Mark.

'Whatever it is, whatever you think or want, you need to be able to tell me, and I need to be able to listen. I meant what I said, Hugo. You are my son. You come first. Whatever you need.'

And finally, Hugo started to tell Mark what he wanted.

They made plans for him to return to college. Mark would find an apartment nearby. Hugo would begin therapy; Mark would have some sessions with him. They didn't mention Darian's name once. And as for Christmas and New Year, Hugo admitted that he didn't want to be anywhere that could be mistaken for their home. He wanted a fresh start. He wanted to go to Switzerland again. The trip to his family's ski resort with Avery had been awkward and stilted. He needed something fun to look forward to.

'New Year's Eve in Switzerland,' Mark said. 'I think we can make that happen.'

CHAPTER TWENTY-FOUR

AVERY

Avery sunk deeper into Leo's hoodie. She'd made him give it to her; demanded it in a silly possessive way that he'd seemed to like rather than loathe. It smelled of him and she couldn't, wouldn't, let it go.

The police had come to talk to her shortly after the doctor had assessed her and cleaned and wrapped her cuts. They'd taken Nora's second phone. Avery hadn't told them that she'd forwarded all the voice notes to her own phone and account. She was sure they'd have tech people who would notice what she'd done and let them know, but she didn't care. It hadn't been about Dennis, or what he'd done. It had been about Nora. Keeping a piece of her.

Not all the voice notes had been about Dennis, and not all of them had exactly been nice. But they'd been complex, funny, hard and determined Nora Miller. And Avery wanted to remember her the way she was.

The police informed her that they'd found Nora's main phone in Archie's room, presuming he had plans to get rid of it later.

They took her statement in front of her parents and Leo, the cool, efficient questions bringing out details that horrified her family.

Before they left she'd asked about Nora's mother and was told that the State Department was handling everything. Her parents asked the police to let them know about any costs that needed covering. It had eased something in Avery, her gratitude slowly unwinding the tension between them from their previous argument.

Soon after that, Leo had left to go and get the remainder of his things on the island. Her parents had agreed to let him come back to America with them. There was still over a month and a half before college started and, Leo, having planned to spend the entire time working on the island, now found himself with a lot of time to spare.

She'd thought her parents would say no, would absolutely baulk at the idea of letting him come with them, but they'd not even batted an eye.

That might change following the conversation that she was about to have with them now, though, she thought. Sitting across from them at the large table, she held the scalding-hot mug of herbal tea in hands that just wouldn't get warm, no matter what she did. She swallowed, her throat still sore from the night before, and almost laughed.

How wild to feel so scared of a conversation with her parents after nearly being killed by one of her closest friends. And then that laugh turned horribly close to tears and she had to shake herself out of it.

'I need to tell you guys something,' she said, unable to meet their eyes. 'I am . . . failing my course.'

'*That's* what you wanted to tell us?' her mother asked with a surprised laugh.

'No. Yes. Partly,' she said, stumbling over her words. 'But it's *because* I'm failing my course that I did something stupid.'

Her father looked at her with a serious gaze.

'I cheated on my midterms.' She pressed on before they could say anything. 'It was stupid, and I'm so sorry, and I regret it so much. I've regretted it from the moment I did it.'

'Avery,' her mother admonished. 'Why didn't you say anything? Why didn't you come to us?'

'Because it was so important to you, Mum. It was so important that I be the perfect daughter.' Avery tried to keep her voice level, but it was hard. 'You were so determined that I'd go to university and become this amazing businesswoman and take over Dad's company.'

Wide-eyed, Annalise looked to her husband, as if for help or support.

'If this is because the business is in trouble—' her father hedged.

'No, it's not that. It's just . . . genuinely not what I want to do,' she admitted finally.

'Oh for god's sake, Avery, we all have to do things we don't want to do sometimes. How else are we supposed to get ahead in this life?'

'Annalise,' her father snapped.

Annalise bit her tongue, but Avery could see that she was finding it difficult.

'Look, it's a lot. It's *all* been a lot. But I want to tell the dean. I want to come clean about cheating. I'll take whatever punishment he deems fit and whether or not I continue on there . . . well, I guess that's up to him.'

'Do you have to? I—'

'Stop.' Avery glared at her mother from across the table. 'Perhaps not everyone in this family is OK with cheating,' she said pointedly. Her mum blanched and her dad looked away.

'I want to tell the dean,' she said again, determined. 'I want to take a year off and I want to reapply for a degree that *I* want to do.'

'And what's that?' her father asked.

Avery bit her lip. 'I don't know yet,' she lied. She wasn't quite ready to share the renewed dream she had of becoming a veterinarian. It was so small and precious she couldn't expose it to her parents just yet. But before that, before she did, she needed some time to face up to the mistakes that she'd made and give herself the space to make the right decisions in the future. 'But it won't be business, Dad,' she said gently, knowing how much of a dream it had been for her to follow in his footsteps.

Her father laughed, a little sadly. 'There might not be anything to take over anyway,' he said, shrugging, having failed utterly to get the backing from either the Devereuxs or the Vandenburgs in order to plug the hole made by his business partner's theft.

She left her parents to finish *that* conversation and returned to the room that she'd shared with Nora. The room she'd avoided again last night, instead remaining with Leo on the large leather sofa in the living area of her parents' villa, dozing on and off until the police had come.

She'd tried to ask them about Dennis, but all they'd said was that they were unable to talk about an ongoing investigation, and she just about resisted the urge to remind them that they wouldn't *have* an investigation if it wasn't for her.

Just.

But they *were* investigating him and that was enough for now. Just as they'd left, the police had warned them that a few journalists had already picked up on the story, and were heading this way. It had spurred her parents into action. They had enough time, at least, to get out and get back home.

Avery went to the bathroom and retrieved her toiletries. She threw them into her suitcase, zipped it up and hauled it to the door to the bedroom, before turning one last time to look out of the large sliding windows.

The deck, the hot tub, the horizon line . . . Avery saw them differently now. She rubbed at her forearms, a shiver working its way across her skin making the scratches and the stitches itch under the bandages on her arms and palm.

She had refused to go to the mainland. She didn't need X-rays, nothing was broken. Her mother had fought her hard on it, but eventually her father had stepped in and her mother had backed down.

'Avery, are you ready?' her mother called down the hallway.

So ready, Nora's voice whispered in her mind, and Avery smiled sadly.

'Yes, Mum,' Avery replied.

Godforsaken, Nora had called the island, and Avery was left to wonder if her friend had always known the deep-rooted rot at the heart of this paradise.

Leo appeared in the doorway, his bag slung over his shoulder. 'Come on,' he said, angling his head towards the door.

Avery went to lift her own bag, but he shooed her away and reached for the handle. She leaned into him, her arm slipping around his waist, and together they left the villa.

Their luggage was taken down to the marina in one golf cart, with Avery, Leo and her parents in another. In previous years all the guests would have left the island together. A grand farewell, with staff and cocktails and goody bags with gifts that would make your eyes water.

But not this year.

Carol and Archie had been taken away by the police the night of the ... *attack*, Avery forced herself to acknowledge. She hadn't seen Darian since then either – Hugo had simply said that he'd gone.

Only a handful of staff now remained on the island. Leo had explained that the Vandenburgs had cancelled all future planned trips to the island and paid off the entire workforce, *plus* a bonus that practically doubled their salaries tied very securely to the NDAs they'd all already signed.

Leo hadn't liked the wall of silence that was threatening to descend over the events on the island but, between them, all the evidence Nora had gathered and Corrine now agreeing to testify, there was enough information for the truth to come out – even though they could already see the beginnings of some very powerful people who seemed particularly interested in maintaining Dennis's reputation for their own interests.

As Avery took one last look at the cliff where she had nearly lost her life, Mark and Hugo arrived on another golf cart to see them off.

Hugo came over to her and Leo and she was relieved to see he looked about a million times lighter than he had done the whole trip.

'You doing OK?' Avery asked him.

'Yeah, I am,' he said, pulling her into a hug. It was different to how Leo made her feel, but Hugo was still familiar. He was a friend. He'd been there when they'd needed him. It was enough.

'You?' he asked, and she nodded.

She *was* going to be OK. She knew that now.

Hugo released her and bobbed his head at Leo, his acceptance of them together meaning more than Avery could say.

'How's Mark?' she asked.

'Good. He's going to come and stay in Boston with me for a while. Until we can get things settled a bit more.'

Avery nodded, knowing how much that would mean to Hugo.

Looking over to where Mark stood with her mother, she noticed an awkwardness between them that hadn't been there before. Something that had irrevocably damaged their friendship as they tried to say goodbye. It wasn't as if they could do what they usually did: say that they'd had a *wonderful* time and that they just *had* to do it again next year.

She watched her mother say something that caused Mark to frown and tense and Avery picked up their words on the breeze.

'I don't know what you—'

'It would have been a shame, that's all,' Annalise interrupted him. 'If Nora's death had been ruled as an accident.'

Avery's senses went on alert. She glanced at Hugo, whose attention had also been caught by the conversation. He turned to look at her and Avery shrugged helplessly, never imagining that her mother would use the information Avery had shared when she and Leo had tried to explain what had happened.

Her mum, trying to blackmail Mark Vandenburg?

'Archie would have gotten away with it. Perhaps to continue to do even more damage. And Dennis? Well, we still don't know what's going to happen there.' Annalise patted the hair being teased by the wind back into place. 'I suppose his most trusted supporters may consider themselves at risk for investigation. In this instance, it's perhaps lucky that we,' she said, looking to her husband down by the boat, 'already have open lines of communication with the FBI.' She finished with a shrug that belied the severity of the threat implied.

The tension spiralling between the two adults bled out into the air tinted with salt and aggression.

'Avery,' her father called, beckoning them down to the jetty where the boat waited to take them back to the mainland.

Avery turned to look at Hugo, unease filling her stomach.

'That's a "them" problem. No more secrets, right?' Hugo offered eventually and Avery smiled, thankful that whatever her mother was trying to do would not impact the new fragile relationship between her and Hugo.

'Right,' she said in agreement. 'See you soon?' she asked as they hugged one last time.

'Yes,' Hugo said, and although there was no trace of a lie in his tone, Avery wasn't sure that they *would* be seeing each other soon. If again. So, she held on to him a little longer and a little harder, feeling him do the same.

'Look after yourself,' he whispered in her ear.

'You too,' she replied, before she and Leo went to join her father where he was waiting at the end of the jetty.

Mark nodded to Jonathan, but remained grim-lipped until Annalise was nearly at the boat.

'Annalise.' Mark's words halted her. 'Get in touch,' he said, almost begrudgingly. 'About the shortfall. I'll see what I can do.'

Avery could almost feel the relief pouring over her dad in waves, and noticed a small glint of satisfaction in her mother's eyes. But it was Mark she was drawn to, realising that it was the first time that Mark had spoken for himself with an 'I' and not on behalf of him and Darian with 'we'. And as Mark caught her gaze, he seemed to realise the same thing.

She offered him a small smile, a sympathetic one, both having been changed irrevocably by the events that happened on Mokani Island.

'I'll do that,' Annalise said, putting her arm around Avery's shoulders and guiding her and Leo towards the boat.

'Do you know what? I think everything's going to be just fine,' she said to Avery and Leo, utterly oblivious as to what the last twelve days had cost everyone else. 'We should come back next year,' she announced, before she disappeared to the back of the boat, missing her husband's fury, his daughter's horror and Leo's confusion. Jonathan went after her, leaving Leo and Avery by the bow.

'I don't . . .' Leo tried, clearly unable to find the words.

'There's nothing to say to that. Nothing,' Avery decided.

She smiled at him as he grinned at her, and it turned into a laugh that spiralled outward into something uncontrollable. Leo laughed with her, and soon they were both gasping for breath.

Tears ran down their cheeks, their throats aching with laughter so hard that their hands had to clutch the rails to keep themselves upright as the boat backed away from an island that should have been paradise, but was anything but. And Avery didn't care what she looked like. What people thought. She just cared that she felt so much better than she had before.

Finally, the laughter died down and Avery and Leo were left leaning into the rail, the sea breeze fresh on their faces, holding back the grief, hurt, pain and tension of the last few weeks.

'I want to get a tattoo,' Avery confessed, eyes closed, her face turned into the sun.

Leo waited, as if sensing there was more.

'A butterfly. Like the one Nora had on her ankle,' Avery explained.

'To remember her?' Leo asked tentatively. They hadn't properly spoken about Nora, or how Avery felt.

'Yeah, but also to remind myself,' Avery nodded, opening her eyes. 'I spent too long being wary and jealous of her, rather than enjoying her.' She felt Leo's gaze, full of questions. 'She was so free and careless. Too much sometimes,' she said, and then smiled, Leo's response a quiet rumble on the wind. 'OK, a *lot* of the time,' Avery conceded. 'But she was *irrepressible*. I've spent so long tying myself in knots trying to be things for other people: my parents, Hugo. The perfect daughter and student, the perfect girlfriend. And it made me do things that I should never have done.' She swallowed. 'I should never have dated Hugo. I love him but only like a friend. And cheating on my midterms? I'm not that person,' she said, holding the long strands of her dark hair back from the wind.

'I think a tattoo would be cool,' Leo said as he pulled her into a hug. 'But I think it should be something that represents *you* not Nora.'

Avery heard what he was trying to say. And maybe he was right. A fresh start and a new beginning. She wiped at her cheeks, drying the tracks left behind by tears from talking about Nora and turned back to face the horizon line where soon the mainland would appear.

'I keep thinking about Sydney,' Leo said. 'What must she be going through.' He shook his head. 'Her brother and mother are murderers, her father is an abuser at the very least. She has no one left.'

'She has *us*,' Avery said determinedly. 'We'll be there for whatever she needs,' she promised, knowing that they were bound irrevocably by what had happened on the island.

For a while they watched the swell of the speedboat fan out into the water, white on a jewel-toned sea.

'It feels weird to go back to college like none of this happened,' Leo said, tucking her into his side.

'I don't think I'm going to go back, at least not yet,' Avery confessed. Leo knew about her determination to tell the dean about the cheating, but she hadn't told anyone about the idea that had begun to take root.

'Yeah?' Leo asked with a smile. No judgement. Just curiosity.

'Yeah,' she said, gaining confidence, gaining conviction. 'I think I'm going to take a year off. Travel around Europe.'

Maybe Italy, France or Spain. Maybe you could come with me, she thought.

'What about your folks?' he asked, nodding over his shoulder to where they sat arguing behind the pilot.

'I think that if they stay together, and they probably will now they've found the money to plug the financial hole in the business, then they're going to have enough on their hands to worry about than me doing a bit of travelling,' she said, her eyes drawn back to the island that was getting smaller and smaller in the distance.

'I mean,' Leo said, shifting from foot to foot, 'I know the UK isn't part of the EU any more, but it is still part of Europe—'

She cut his tease off with a harmless slap to his arm and her mouth found his in a kiss. '*Of course* I'm coming to England. To you,' she said, her gaze growing serious, the weight of her feelings for him filling her and making her happy.

'Good. Because I'm not planning on letting you go, Avery Finch.'

And she loved that was how he saw her. Avery Finch. Not Good Little Avery Finch. Just her. And it was all she had ever wanted.

She might only just be finding out what she was going to do next, and where she might go, but whatever and wherever it was, she would – like Nora – do it under her own steam, following her own dreams. And that, Avery decided, would be more than enough.

EPILOGUE

The moon hung low in a sky blanketed by stars as far as the eye could see. The night was so clear, that the moon's face was near startling in its brightness. The breeze coming off the sea was warm, despite the hour of the night.

A groan cut through the stillness in the room, before a burst of colour shot into the sky and exploded in shards of candy-pink light.

Sounds from the party on the beach further down covered the noise of Nora's gasp.

'Please,' she tried, begging for help. Her head pounded, her thoughts dizzy and incoherent. Her gaze remained on the white ceiling above her.

She needed to get up, she needed to get away.

But she wasn't sure why and from whom.

She reached to the back of her head where it hurt, and stopped when it sent a slice of pain through her body. She pulled her hand back – it was covered in blood. Her blood.

'I think I need . . .' Nora's voice, groggy and broken to her own ears, trailed off.

'What?'

'Help.'

'I'm afraid it's a bit late for that.'

Nora frowned. Why was it too late? Why did her head hurt so much? Where was Avery?

'Stop moving around so much. You're getting blood all over the carpet,' came the stern command.

'Sorry,' she replied automatically.

Her head rolled to one side, seeing through the window a crescent shore framed with palm trees, the moon spreading silver on all it touched, an explosion of white and gold like a dandelion blown in the wind – but none of it enough to match the natural beauty of the island.

She wished . . . She wished it had been different. But it truly was paradise, she thought taking her last breath.

The *beep, beep, beep* of the villa's door cut through the silence, but nothing masked the shocked gasp that filled the room.

'What did you do?'

Archie's question broke Sydney's concentration. She looked up irritated and indignant at her brother's apparent horror and she glared at him in the dark.

'I did what I had to do,' she said, looking down at Nora's body. She was nothing more than an irritation too, now. A snag to be tidied before anyone could see.

'Why?' Archie said, coming closer as if unable to help himself. 'Jesus. What happened?'

Sydney scoffed. 'She came sniffing around, trying to dig up dirt on Dad.'

Archie stared at her, his expression unreadable and it pissed her off. Their mother had always spoiled him. Let him get away with doing absolutely nothing for this family.

'Here,' she said, tossing the friendship bracelet she'd retrieved from Nora into Archie's waiting hand, not wanting anything to tie her to the dead body. 'Get rid of that later.'

'Later?'

'Yes, later,' Sydney snapped, pulling up Nora from the floor to inspect the pool of blood she'd have to clear up. 'Well don't just stand there. Give me a hand,' she told Archie.

They'd take her to the pool. Make it look like an accident.

Archie gingerly grabbed hold of Nora's legs, his hand slipping in some of the pooled blood causing him to drop her awkwardly, getting a spatter of blood on his T-shirt.

He cursed and picked her back up.

'What are we going to do?'

Whatever they had to.

P. C. ROSCOE

has sold cheese in Borough Market, scrubbed pans in a canteen, poured more pints of beer than is strictly necessary, processed invoices for a multinational, researched TV scripts, and edited romance. But her favourite job, by far, is writing, where she gets to immerse herself in tension-filled, high-stakes stories. She grew up in London and recently moved to a cottage in Norfolk where she splits her time between writing, cooking disasters and half-finished DIY projects, and she honestly couldn't be happier.

COMING SOON